GAME FOR LOVE

Bad Boys of Football 3

This book is a work of fiction and any resemblance to persons, living or dead, or places, events or locales is purely coincidental. The characters are productions of the author's imagination and used fictitiously.

Chapter One

"All I've ever wanted for you is true love, Cole. And family. The family you should have had all along. But most of all, I wish I could leave this earth knowing someone special is looking after you."

Eugenia Taylor's hand was small and cold in Cole Taylor's large palm. The pale, fragile woman lying in the hospital bed was so much more than just his grandmother. She'd been his mother and father too, after his parents had died when he was five.

He couldn't believe she was dying. Refused to believe it, even after a long and painful talk with her doctor.

Stage four melanoma. There was nothing they could do.

Damn it. Cole gently stroked the soft skin on the back of his grandmother's hand. *There had to be something.* He'd spent the past ten years as a middle linebacker for the San Francisco Outlaws fighting like hell for his team, taking any and every hit that came his way. Now, he wanted to fight for his grandmother, wanted to take the hits dragging her under, wanted to protect her the way she'd always protected him. He would have traded places with his grandmother in a heartbeat.

Wanting to comfort her, he said, "Don't worry about me,

Grandma. I can look after myself."

"You're a good boy, Cole. You've always been a good boy, even though I know you're no saint."

Jesus, if his grandmother knew what he did with the groupies when he was on the road with the team...

"I've been waiting for you to finish sowing your wild oats. I've been waiting for you to find a woman who will give your life true meaning." She shook her head. "Promise me you'll find her, honey. Promise me you'll find her soon."

The lump in his throat was so big he could barely swallow past it. Without thinking it through, without even really knowing what he was about to declare, he said, "I've already found her, Grandma."

His grandmother's face lit up and for a moment she actually looked like she used to. Before she got sick. If only he'd had more time to deal with his grandmother's illness—if only she'd been to the doctor before last week.

If only he'd spent more time with his grandmother and less time with whatever woman he'd been screwing, then maybe he would have seen the signs earlier. Back when there was still something the doctors could do to cure her.

"Oh honey, that's wonderful. Why didn't you tell me about her before now?"

Oh crap. He should back out now, admit that he was kidding, say that he was freaking out about losing her and had told the lie because he didn't want her to be disappointed in him.

Instead, channeling the last chick flick he'd been forced to sit through, he said, "She wanted to take it slow, even though she knows how much I love her."

He waited for his grandmother to call his bluff. She'd always seen through him. There was no way she wouldn't see through him now.

"Bring her here, Cole. I want to meet the woman who has stolen my baby's heart."

Cole lied when he needed to, but not to his grandmother. Never to her. All he'd wanted was to make her feel better. Clearly, she wanted a wife and children for him so badly that she was willing to believe anything at this point.

Now what could he say? He sure as hell wasn't going to bring one of the women he'd slept with recently to meet his grandmother. Not when none of them qualified as "nice" girls.

Still, somehow the words, "Tomorrow, Grandma. I'll bring her tomorrow," came out of his mouth, if only because he knew how happy they would make her.

She couldn't stop beaming at him. "I can't wait." She closed her eyes and relaxed back against the pillows.

Forcing himself to get up before she realized that he hadn't given her a name or any other pertinent information about "the woman he loved," Cole leaned over to give her a kiss on the cheek, then walked out into the hospital corridor.

Somehow, somewhere, he needed to find a nice girl. Stat.

Where the hell was a guy like him going to find a nice girl in Las Vegas?

* * *

"Jeannie's wedding was such a tear-jerker, wasn't it?"

Anna Davis smiled at her Aunt Lena. "It was beautiful. They're obviously very much in love."

How was it that her cheeks actually hurt? Sure, all weekend she'd been smiling, but she'd been through this three times already, having planned all four of her sisters' weddings in the past two years.

"You know, dear, we all thought you'd be the first to get married. Do you remember how you used to dress up as a bride when you were a little girl?"

It wasn't easy to keep smiling while she was gritting her teeth, but somehow Anna managed it. "You know how little girls are. They love to play dress-up."

As a first-grade teacher, Anna was reminded of this every day. There was nothing children liked more than using their imaginations. At what point were they taught to stop doing that?

But Aunt Lena was shaking her head. "Actually, if I remember correctly, your sisters never played dress-up. They were too busy with sports and winning academic prizes. You were the only one focused on wearing white and walking down an aisle. How strange that you're the only one still waiting for your Prince Charming."

"Maybe I should grab the nearest available guy and pop into one of those quickie wedding parlors."

Anna didn't know who was more shocked by her response—

her aunt or herself.

Finally, her aunt said, "Oh Anna, you would never do something like that."

Anna was about to agree, when she suddenly realized what was behind her aunt's—completely true—statement.

She doesn't think I have any guts.

Taking a glass of champagne off the tray of a circulating waiter, Anna shrugged. "You never know. There is something about weddings, after all. And this is Las Vegas. Anything can happen here."

But she got small satisfaction out of walking away from her aunt's open mouth. Because at the end of the day, Anna was still not only the only Davis girl who hadn't dressed in white and said "I do," she was also the only one without someone to love.

* * *

"Cole! Right here. Looking good, man. You crushed the Jaguars last Sunday."

Cole looked up into the paps' flashbulbs. What kind of crazy was he, looking in the Wynn Las Vegas hotel and casino for a nice girl? But he'd just wasted an entire day looking in the places he'd assumed she'd be—the library, an animal shelter, even a knitting store, for fuck's sake—and had come up empty.

The chicks in the library wouldn't let him talk long enough to try to ask them out.

The animal shelter had been full of nauseatingly happy couples and kids. Not to mention the fact that one of the mutts had taken a strange—and overpowering—liking to him. The shelter manager had shoved fifteen pounds of squirming, licking, sniffing black and brown fur into his arms. Cole didn't do pets—too much responsibility, knowing something would be waiting for him every day at home, depending on him. Still, those big brown eyes had almost done their job on him and he'd barely gotten out of the building mutt-free.

Strangely, the knitting shop was where he'd felt the most comfortable. His grandmother had always been knitting something during her breaks at the casino when he was a kid and the clickety-clack of her needles was the backdrop to his childhood. Which was why he hadn't had it in him to pick a girl up in the yarn store. It would have felt like he was betraying his grandmother...even though he was already a lying son of a bitch.

Daylight had come and gone and Cole wasn't any closer to bringing his "true love" to his grandmother's hospital room than he had been that morning.

He'd gone up to his suite at the Wynn to wash away the stink of failure. He was good at two things: football and one-night stands with women who didn't expect anything more. Not "true love."

If anyone was a magnet for huge tits in low-cut tops and skirts so short they should be illegal, it was Cole. Not that he'd ever thought to complain about that, of course. Not until now.

Not until his grandmother had told him her dying wish.

A wish that he was going to grant, even if it killed him.

Getting out of the shower, Cole wrapped a towel around his waist and walked to the floor-to-ceiling windows of his wraparound suite. Looking out at the flat stretch of casinos, he didn't see flashing lights and tourists walking the strip. He saw home.

His grandmother had been one of the greatest poker dealers on the circuit. He'd learned so much from her. How to deal straight—and crooked. How to work hard. And most of all, how to stick with something.

Giving up had never been an option. Not for her, not even after her son and daughter-in-law died in a private plane crash, leaving her with a five-year-old who had more energy than sense. And not for Cole.

Sure, he was athletic, but his grandmother was the reason he'd made it into the pros, when it would have been easier to quit and get a "real" job at least a hundred times.

He dropped his towel to the floor and yanked open the closet. It was time to stop crying like a baby over his day. He was going to get dressed and find himself a good girl, damn it.

If there was someone looking down on him from up above—and Cole had more reasons than most people to think that there was, after some of the pileups he'd walked away from on the field—he was pretty damn sure that He was laughing right now, saying to anyone who would listen, "Do you believe that dick wad actually thinks he's going to find a good girl to bring to his grandmother in the next eight hours? I've saved his ass too many times before. This time, I think I'll let him fry."

But Cole didn't care. He'd made a promise to his grandmother, and by God he was going to keep it.

* * *

Anna stuck out in the night club like a sore thumb.

And she had only herself to blame.

After Jeannie and Dave had left for their honeymoon, Anna's three remaining sisters and spouses decided they weren't ready for the party to end.

"You've been so busy that you probably want to go back to your room and soak in the tub, don't you?" Jane said when they told her their plans to go out dancing at the Wynn Las Vegas.

Her sister was right. She was dying to kick off her shoes and veg out in front of some brainless TV. But, again, Anna was struck by the inadvertent subtext of her sister's sentence: *We all know how boring you are. The whirlpool tub is going to be the highlight of your day, isn't it?*

For the second time in one day, Anna bristled at what her family thought about her. Evidently she was not only gutless, but boring, too.

And here all this time, she'd thought she was perfectly normal.

Nice.

But as she looked at her sisters and brothers-in-law happily paired off all around her while she stood solo, Anna made a split-second decision. "Actually, I'm in the mood to dance."

Six sets of eyebrows went up. Finally, her oldest sister, Jill, said, "But you didn't even dance at Jeannie's reception."

Of course she hadn't. She didn't dance. Ever. But the pity in her siblings' eyes cracked something inside Anna's chest wide open.

She was sick and tired of always standing on the sidelines, watching everyone else have fun. Especially when all it had ever gotten her was the prospect of a quiet night in her hotel room.

Alone.

"You know we'd love to spend more time with you," Joanne said with gentle understanding in her eyes, "but we understand if you're tired."

"I was saving my energy for tonight," she'd told her stupefied siblings as she'd swept out of the reception hall, her head held high, her shoulders thrown back in what she hoped was a confident, ready-to-have-lots-of-fun way.

She'd show her family. Not only was she going to dance, but she was going to find the most dangerously sexy man in the room to be her partner.

Oh yes, she'd have them all gaping at her as she did the bump and grind—or whatever it was called—with a hot hunk.

The only thing was, she thought as she all but gulped down another glass of Chardonnay the cute bartender at the Tryst nightclub in Wynn Las Vegas had handed her, it was one thing to make a silent vow in the heat of the moment ... and it was another entirely to actually make good on it.

Thirty minutes after her reckless declaration at Jeannie's reception, Anna had to admit that she was way beyond her comfort zone. She wasn't used to such loud music, or being around half-naked people who all seemed to like being smashed against each other like sweaty, drunk sardines.

What had made her think she could come to a casino nightclub and not just fit in, but own it?

The only things she owned were pink bunny slippers and a library card that had been used so many times the numbers were almost all smudged off.

Glad that her sisters and their husbands were all too busy dancing—or too drunk—to notice her slinking out of the nightclub with her tail between her legs, Anna was about to put her empty glass down on the bar when a low, rough voice said, "I noticed your glass was empty. I hope champagne is okay."

Anna looked up into the darkest eyes she'd ever seen as a heat that had nothing to do with the crowd infused her, head to toe.

She'd vowed to look for *sinfully dangerous*.

Looked like she'd found him.

Chapter Two

As the small brunette took the glass from his hand, her fingertips barely brushing against his knuckles, Cole was surprised to feel his cock immediately growing thick. Hard.

He'd always had a strong sex drive, strong enough that if he didn't get his rocks off at least a couple of times a week, he'd hit too hard during practice from sheer sexual frustration. He'd gotten the call from his grandmother right after Sunday's game and had headed straight to Vegas. Usually within a couple of hours of landing in his old hometown, Cole had at least one woman under him. This time, though, he'd gone without. The only thing that had mattered was taking care of his grandmother.

And fulfilling her dying wish.

"I love champagne. Thank you."

Cole stared down at the woman, who was holding the glass in a death grip. Jesus, was her hand actually trembling? If he wasn't careful, the first available good girl he'd seen all day would run and he'd have to go to his grandmother's room alone in the morning.

Okay. First he needed to stop breathing in the woman's sweetly scented hair, something he'd never, ever noticed on anyone. Second, he needed to think past the heavy throbbing in his cock for three seconds. Long enough to figure out what to say or do to make her feel safe with him.

The problem was, he'd never been with a girl like this. Didn't know the first thing about making a nice girl feel safe and comfortable.

Not when he'd spend the past fifteen years perfecting wicked.

Finally, he decided on, "I couldn't help but notice you from across the room."

And it was true; she'd been the only square peg in a room full of round holes. Hell, she might as well have been wearing a halo for all the innocence pouring off her. Now that he was close, he realized she even smelled innocent, like fresh strawberries in a sunny field, or some shit like that.

At first, he'd been too busy congratulating himself on his reverse psychology of finding a sweet girl in a club to think about how this was actually going to go down. But now that she was staring up at him like a doe caught in the middle of a busy freeway—and he was as hard as he'd ever been without touching more than her fingertips—he realized this was going to be a first for him: He was going to have to work for it.

Or else risk losing the one woman he needed.

"*You* noticed *me?*" Champagne sloshed out of her glass and splashed across her chest as she gestured at herself in clear surprise.

Cole looked down—even further down that he was already looking just to see her eyes—and realized she had a pretty good body. Maybe even great. It was hard to tell with the pink, shiny dress she had on, but from his vantage point her cleavage was pretty awesome. Awesome enough that his cock was begging to come out and play.

"You have beautiful eyes," he began, but then, figuring she might buy his lie if he pulled his gaze back up to her face, he forced himself to stop ogling her tits and actually did look into her eyes.

Cole was stopped cold by eyelashes so long that when she blinked, the curling tips brushed against the tops of her cheekbones. Her eye color was unlike any he'd ever seen, a combination of blue and green that had him thinking of cool mountain lakes and perfect summer days.

She blinked, smiled, and the way her eyes lit up stopped his breath for a second.

"No, not beautiful," he said, almost to himself. "Stunning."

Her eyes got even bigger, along with her smile—and his cock. "They are?"

He moved closer, those big eyes of her acting like a magnet on him. A lock of her hair fell in front of one of them and he reached out to slide it to the side, his fingertip barely grazing her skin.

He felt her tremble beneath his touch, even as something shook inside him.

What the hell was going on here?

He'd come looking for a good girl. Not another one-night stand.

But he couldn't think straight anymore. Not when all he wanted was this woman beneath him, naked and panting, her blue-green eyes flashing with ecstasy as she came in his arms. Not when all he could think of was relieving the heaviness in his groin with the woman who had put it there.

Stop drooling and woo her, asshole.

"Dance with me."

He had her hand in his and was halfway to the dance floor, borderline desperate thoughts of pressing his thick erection against her belly riding him with every step, when he felt her tug at his arm.

It was a surprisingly strong tug for such a little thing.

"I don't even know your name."

She hadn't said anything to him about football yet, so he'd already guessed that she was one of the few people who weren't fans, thank God. A chick looking for fame would only complicate things further. Still, he didn't want to risk anything by giving her his full name, just in case she recognized it from the papers and got ideas.

"Cole."

She cocked her head to one side, managing to look cute and sexy at the same time, and his erection pressed hard enough into his zipper he wouldn't be surprised if it marked his skin.

"You know," she said, "I think I could have guessed that. You look like a Cole."

"And you look like an angel."

Her lips turned up in another smile and knocked the wind out of him. Again. He'd already thought she was pretty. But when she smiled, she was breathtaking.

"Almost." Her smile trembled and she looked shy again. "My name is Anna."

He couldn't wait another second to touch her, to know whether her curves felt as soft as they looked, and tugged her closer, pulling her as close to him as they could get in a public bar with their clothes on.

Lord, but he wanted to get even closer. No clothes between them, no other music than the sound of her passion as he made her come with his hands. His mouth. His cock. Jesus, he could feel the pre-come rushing already. Just from holding her.

"Dance with me, Anna."

Her name was soft on his tongue, just as soft as he knew her skin would be when he finally got her clothes off.

She didn't push him away, but she did shake her head and bite her lip before saying, "I don't really dance."

He had to laugh at that, appreciating the flash of irritation in her eyes at his response. "Are you saying I'm going to be your first?"

His question hung in the air between them, heavy and pulsing with double meanings. Jesus, he'd never been with a virgin in his life. Never wanted to be. Not when he appreciated a woman's experience so that it was wasn't up to him to do all the work. But the things he wanted to do to this woman—right fucking here, right fucking now—were crazy.

Batshit crazy.

Her flush—and lowered eyes—answered his question. "No. Of course you're not my first."

"Are we still talking dancing, Anna?"

Her gaze shot up to meet his again and she opened her mouth, but no words came out. She looked so cute, standing there trying to figure out how to respond to his very forward question. He knew he wasn't being fair, playing with her like this, but it was so much fun.

He was having fun.

Cole Taylor didn't have fun. He was all business, all about crushing the competition. Sure, he partied as much as the next rich, single, pro-football player, and of course he took the best-looking women in the world to bed, but it wasn't so much about having a good time as it was about taking his due.

And yet, standing in the middle of a Las Vegas nightclub with a woman whose name he'd only just learned—but whom he wanted more than any woman he'd ever met—Cole felt completely off his game.

The truth was, he was tired. It had been a long, frustrating day looking for a nice girl to take to his grandmother.

His dying grandmother.

"Cole? Are you okay?"

He blinked and looked into Anna's clearly concerned ocean eyes, felt something soft and warm on his forearm and realized she'd reached out to touch him.

Women looked at him in lots of ways—with dollar signs in their eyes, with lust, with anxiety when he was about to dump them—but never with concern.

Never like they actually cared about him.

"My grandmother is sick."

Shit, where had those words come from?

She moved even closer, put her other hand on him. "I'm so

sorry."

He worked to swallow past the lump in his throat. "I am, too."

Together they stood like that for several moments, her comfort flushing through his veins, heading straight for his heart.

"Are you sure you'd still like to dance? Maybe we could find a quieter place and we could talk instead."

She was right. He didn't want to dance. But he didn't want to talk, either.

He wanted to kiss her.

He put his hands on her face, brushing his thumb against her lower lip. She went completely still, not blinking or even breathing as he lowered his face to hers. He didn't want to scare her and tried to go slow, even though all he wanted was to shove her against the nearest wall and wrap her legs around his waist as he sank into her wet heat.

Her breath was a sweet puff of heat against his mouth as he moved in to kiss her, her lips as red and tempting as plump berries in summertime. Cole liked kissing, always had, happy to spend plenty of time at first base even when most guys were already going for the home run. It was a bonus that kissing made chicks hotter, hornier.

But holy hell, no kiss had ever been like this. No kiss could have prepared him for Anna. Her mouth was soft and so damn sweet, he lost track of his plans—forgot all about taking it slow and not scaring her. He had to taste her, had to run his tongue along the seam between her lips, from the center then out to first one corner and then the next. Hunger like he'd never known took him over, made him forget everything but the promise of pleasure.

A groan escaped as she opened up for him, her tongue tentatively finding his, a small stroke of sweetness that had him burning up head to toe. His hands slid up into her hair—so damn soft, he couldn't believe it—and his fingers tightened on her, pulling her closer.

She whimpered her pleasure into his mouth, the soft press of her curves against his hard muscles driving him crazy. His erection throbbed against her belly as he deepened their kiss, no longer able to be gentle, to worry about boundaries.

And then, suddenly, everything turned and she was the one kissing him.

Devouring him.

Her arms moved around his torso, her hands and fingertips all but scratching at him. Her tongue battled with his, her lips sucking at him, her teeth nipping and feasting on his mouth.

His kitten had turned into a lioness.

The club, the music, the overpowering scents of booze and sweat and perfume, all fell away as they made out in the middle of it all. She was heat and curves and pure sex in his arms and he knew if they'd been alone he'd be a heartbeat away from sinking into her, from taking everything she offered and giving her everything she demanded.

Something flashed in the back of his head, something he was supposed to remember, something he was supposed to do, but he couldn't follow it, not when he was utterly, hopelessly lost in Anna.

Sweet Anna.

Finally, she pulled away from him, gasping, her tongue coming out to lick at her swollen lips as if she were still trying to taste him.

"I've never done anything this crazy."

Her words trembled with confusion—and so much desire—that his mouth found hers again a moment later and she was so sweet he knew it would kill him when he finally had to stop tasting.

Instinctively, Cole knew it wasn't the champagne that made her taste like sugar. The sweetness was all her.

Grandma would love her.

The thought came at him blindside. He'd almost forgotten why he was here in the first place, why he'd picked her out of the crowd.

He didn't know anything about Anna other than how good her body felt against his, how right her kisses were, how much he liked her scent, how hard she made him—and how perfectly she embodied the "nice girl" he was sure his grandmother wanted to see with him.

He hadn't thought beyond finding someone to play the role he needed her to play, but now that he had, he was surprised to find guilt dogging his heels. He didn't know Anna well enough to not want to hurt her.

And yet...his gut twisted at the thought of what he needed to do.

And he did need to do it.

Because he owed his grandmother everything.

It was that vision—of his grandmother, pale and frail in her hospital bed—that had him leaning into Anna, brushing her earlobe with his lips.

"Let's do something really crazy, Anna."

She shivered as his lips made contact with her lobe. Even though he knew he needed to be holding focus, that his goal was the most important thing here, not how much he wanted pretty Anna, he had to pull her earlobe between his teeth and nip at it.

So perfectly, incredibly responsive to his every touch, Anna arched into him, her full, hard-tipped breasts practically searing him through her dress and his shirt, another whimper of need, of desire sounding from her lips.

"So sweet," Cole murmured against her soft skin as he ran his mouth down her neck, his tongue dipping into the hollow of her shoulder bone. Her breasts, full with arousal, pressed up and out toward his mouth from the neckline of her pink dress. He was half a breath away from unzipping her dress right then and there so that he could swirl her nipples against his tongue, when the crash of a glass at the bar pulled him back into the here and now.

Her eyes were cloudy with desire, only partially focusing as she said, "What could be crazier than this?"

Jesus, he'd completely forgotten about his question, about where he was going with it. Again.

How was one tiny woman—a woman who wasn't even his type, for fuck's sake—turning his brain, and body, completely inside out?

Needing space, needing air to get his brain to function again, he made himself move back an inch from her curves, from her warmth. But all that did was make it easier for him to look at her. She was so pretty—and so damn pure despite the way she'd been kissing him like a wildcat in heat—that his stomach twisted even as he said, "What's the craziest thing you can think of doing with me tonight?"

The club was dark, but not dark enough that he could miss the flush across her cheeks, or the way the heated vee between her thighs shifted closer to his rock-hard erection in an dance as old as time.

The smile curved his lips before he realized it. "Don't worry, baby, we're definitely going to be doing that, regardless of your answer."

She licked her lips. Her sweet, plump, cherry-red lips. "I don't —" She shook her head, her shoulder-length brown hair moving across her shoulders. "I wasn't going to say—"

"You do," he countered, "and you were." Dropping his lips back down over hers, he said, "But since that's a given, what other kind of crazy have you got for me?"

Her fingertips tightened on his shoulders. "You and me doing ...

it's a given?"

"Yup."

"But we just met."

"Lucky us."

He was glad to hear a surprised little giggle escape her lips, but then, too soon, she was back to her arguments."I don't do things like this."

"I know you don't."

She frowned and, without thinking, he reached up to brush away the lines between her eyes. He wanted to see her smile, not frown.

"How?"

Her soft skin against his fingertips had him losing his train of thought. Hell, how could he possibly think without any blood left in his brain? Not even close to knowing what she was asking, all he could do was echo, "How what?"

"How do you know I don't do things like this?"

"I just do."

Her full lips pressed together. *Shit, that wasn't the right answer.*

"Because I look boring."

"Hell, no." A little bit of spark came back into her eyes, enough to tell him that he was heading in the right direction again. Thank God. "You've been anything but boring."

She cocked her pretty head to one side, the hair brushing against her shoulder blades, making him wonder what it would feel like brushing over his dick as she blew him, sixty-nine position.

"But you're surprised by that, aren't you?"

Jesus, he thought as he corralled his brain back to the conversation, what was this? Twenty-fucking-questions?

A lie lay on his tongue, whatever she wanted to hear, but what came out instead was, "A little, yeah."

"I knew it." Her victorious expression disappeared as quickly as it came. "Tell me why you're so surprised."

The first words that came into his head were, "You were wearing a halo."

He nearly groaned at the stupidity of blurting that out when he saw her outraged expression.

"A halo?" She actually reached up to the top of her head, as if she needed to make sure that she did not, in fact, have a halo hanging over her soft brown curls.

"No," he said, trying to backpedal as fast as he could, "not a halo. You definitely weren't wearing one of those."

He needed to change the subject, get them back to ... Hell, what had they been talking about?

"Then what?"

Shit, he wasn't thinking fast enough. Could barely get his brain to function when he could still scent her arousal, when he was still ridiculously hard and throbbing behind his zipper.

"It's just that you just looked so innoc—"

Her eyes narrowed as she waited for him to finish and he decided it was smarter just to shut up. Whatever he said about her looking pure or innocent was just going to piss her off. He knew that now. He didn't know why, just that it did.

Just as he didn't know how the hell one tiny little woman was throwing him more off his game than a field full of three-hundred-pound guys all coming at him with everything they had.

Her nostrils flared and he couldn't believe even that looked cute on her. Jesus, he had it bad for this one. In under an hour she practically had him spouting poetry.

And shooting in his pants from just looking at her.

"I'm sick to death of everyone thinking they know exactly who I am! I'm sick of everyone assuming all I want to do is smile and organize things while they go off and have their big romantic sunsets together! I'm sick to death of never, ever doing something so crazy that I get to regret it in the morning while secretly having loved every second of it! For all people know, I could be bringing guys like you home every Friday night and trading you in for a new guy on Saturday!"

Her hands had fisted on his chest now and he was sure she didn't realize it, but she'd been hitting him to emphasize each of her points, one thump at the end of each sentence like an exclamation point.

Still, the picture of her throwing him over for another guy not twenty-four hours later had him growling with a sudden spurt of jealousy. "Have you done that?"

The low rumble of his question seemed to snap her out of her momentary fury.

"Seriously? Are you asking me that for real?"

His hands came around her shoulders, jealousy burning hotter than it ever had. If she said yes, he'd hunt down every one of those guys and break their necks with his bare hands.

"Have. You. Done. That?"

He'd seen enough game tapes to know that he had one of the meanest glares in football, but instead of being cowed by the four snarled words, Anna's answering smile was the brightest one yet, so stunning that he almost felt blinded by her beauty, by that light that surrounded her.

"No," she said, still smiling. "I haven't." She went to her tippy toes and tilted her face up to his to press a soft, short kiss to his mouth. "But thank you for thinking that I could have if I'd wanted to."

On the verge of dragging her by the hair up to his room and tying her to his bed for the rest of the night, he growled, "Hell, baby, you could have any guy here in ten seconds flat."

But he only wanted her to want him.

"That's the nicest thing anyone has ever said to me."

Not even trying to understand her—no question about it, women were one huge, endless mystery—Cole pulled his focus in tight again. "If you want to be crazy for once, I can help you. What do you say, Anna? Should we be crazy together?"

"You mean crazier than—" She actually looked both ways and lowered her voice to a near-whisper. "—sleeping together?"

He chuckled against her mouth, swiping his tongue against her lips for another quick taste. At her indrawn breath he said, "Oh yeah. A whole lot crazier."

A half-dozen expressions moved across her face.

Pleasure.

Excitement.

Curiosity.

Desire.

Doubt.

And then, as if it were single handedly going to lock down the coffin on his plans: Full-on fear.

But then, instead of pulling out of his arms and saying no, she took a deep breath and said, "You're not talking about gambling or karaoke, are you?"

This time when he laughed against her lips—he was proud of her for not running, ridiculously impressed with her for staying in with him as long as she had—he was surprised to feel her tongue slide out across his mouth.

Knowing what she wanted—because he wanted it just as much—he plundered her mouth with his. He wanted to map out every sinfully sweet corner and crevasse, wanted to spend hours kissing her until he knew exactly what made her moan with pleasure.

Finally, he let her up for air and when she looked up at him, panting and aroused and so damn beautiful he could hardly believe it, he was blindsided by the strength of what he felt for a woman he'd just met.

Not just pride, but something more. Something even bigger, something he'd never felt before, something he'd never wanted to feel.

Shit. This wasn't in the plans.

His grandmother. He had to remember that he was only doing this for his grandmother. He had to remember that the only reason he'd looked for a girl like Anna wasn't because he was actually looking for someone to love, but because he just needed it to look that way for a little while.

His throat tightened again at the thought of losing his grandmother. At how quickly his life with her could come to an end.

"Marry me, Anna."

She stumbled back from him in her surprise—shit, he was right there with her, as shocked as she was at the words that had come out of his mouth—and he had to move fast to catch her before she was knocked over by the couple dancing in front of him.

She stiffened as he pulled her back against him, no longer the soft, pliable woman he'd held until then. He hated to see that frown where there'd been nothing but helpless desire before.

"Oh my God." She looked like she was trying to catch her breath. "Did you just ask me to marry you?"

But even as she asked, he could see her growing stronger. Steadier.

For the second time since he'd seen her innocence shining out at him like a beacon from across the room, Cole was struck and surprised by her strength. She wasn't stuttering now, she wasn't panting with passion. Instead, she suddenly reminded him of his tenth-grade Calculus teacher, a woman who hadn't cared that he was going to make millions in the pros, unlike most of his other teachers. She'd been hellbent on teaching him math and he'd had to excel, or else. Thanks to her, he'd easily been able to take his earnings and multiply them in the stock market.

He'd never much cared if his women were strong, just as long as they were willing when he was ready to go—which they always were. So then, why did he find that surprising hint of strength, of backbone, so sexy in this one?

"I need you, Anna."

And he did need her, desperately, only this wasn't just about his grandmother anymore.

He needed her for himself, too.

The realization that his need for her had somehow gone way beyond physical, not only had his gut twisting, but his chest clenching too.

"Please, Anna. Take this chance to be crazy and marry me."

She blinked once, twice, three times in clear surprise at his plea, her beautifully long eyelashes fluttering against her cheekbones. He had to press a kiss to each eyelid.

"Marrying you is more than crazy, Cole. It's certifiably insane."

God, he loved hearing his name on her lips. A sudden vision came at him of her lying beneath him on his bed, her eyes shining with pleasure as she cried out his name.

She was right. Getting married was insane, for so many reasons. He hadn't told his grandmother he was married, or even engaged. He'd just said that he'd found love. So then, why did it seem so crucially important that Anna agree to marry him?

Insane didn't even come close.

"I don't get it. Why would you want to marry me?" She looked up at him, her lack of comprehension clear in her beautiful eyes.

Would her eyes ever not take his breath away?

But instead of crafting an answer that would convince her to marry him—something other than the inexplicable *Because I think I could fall in love with you* that kept ringing through his brain—he found himself telling her the only other thing in his head.

"Your eyes are like the ocean, Anna. So beautiful I could stare into them forever."

She looked stunned and pleased in equal measure, but then, suddenly, she was looking away from him and saying, "Oh no."

Following her gaze, all he saw were people dancing and drinking, the same as they had all night.

"What's wrong?"

"My sisters. They look worried."

She had sisters? And they were here, in this bar, right now?

A moment later she was cradled in his arms again and he wasn't sure if he had pulled her closer—instinctively claiming her—or if she was the one hiding out against his chest.

"Shoot. They're coming over here."

He felt his heartbeat kick up, knew he was about to lose her, that she was about to disappear from his life as quickly as she'd come into it, but then her hands moved to his, her slender fingers strong and sure, her blue/green eyes clear and beautiful as she tilted her face up to his.

"Yes, Cole, I'll marry you."

This time he was the one floundering. "You—you will?"

"Yes. I will." She shot another quick glance at the three women advancing on them. "But we need to leave right now or it isn't going to happen."

And the next thing he knew, his innocent angel was pulling him across the dance floor, through the throngs of people, and out through the casino so fast that even the paps didn't have time to catch a shot of them...on the way to their wedding.

Chapter Three

"Welcome to Cupid's Wedding Chapel. How may I help you?"

Anna was more than a little surprised by the question. They were in a Vegas chapel at eleven at night. Was there something other than marriage on the menu?

"We want to get married," she blurted, the words all sliding into one another in her haste to get them said.

Cole shot her a half-surprised, half-amused glance and she sucked in a breath as she took in his beautiful face. Oh God, was she really doing this? Was she really about to marry a man that she didn't know anything about apart from his first name?

She shot a glance at his face, her eyes automatically going to his mouth. No, that wasn't true. She knew how well he kissed. That the merest touch of his lips to hers, the slow slide of his tongue against hers, had her wanting things she hadn't even known were out there for the taking.

Thrill bumps ran up and down her skin as he brushed his thumb across her palm, again and again in a circle that had her practically panting with lust. Truthfully, she still hadn't gotten used to holding his hand. From the moment they'd left the club, down the back street behind the casino to the nearest chapel, he hadn't let go.

Holding his hand shouldn't have been such a big deal—and really, it wasn't. The thing was, Anna loved holding hands. Really, really loved it. Almost more than she liked sex, in fact.

There was just something about being connected to another person like that. Joining with them and not having to let go, not even in public. And it was so deliciously tactile, especially when Cole's hands were so big and warm and slightly hard across the top layer of his skin.

The way he held her hand in his made her feel, well, precious. Cared for. Even though she knew it really didn't mean anything. It was just his way of guiding her down the street, of claiming her in front of the chapel attendant.

And, God help her, she couldn't stop imagining what it would feel like to have those hands of his moving across her bare skin. Her breasts peaked beneath her silk bra, the vee between her thighs growing even warmer.

The chapel attendant cut into her lusty thoughts with, "A wedding! Wonderful. If you'll just come over here to pick out your package, we can get started."

Cole held her still in his arms and another delicious shiver ran through her. She'd always been a firm believer in women taking care of themselves—heck, that's what she had done for the past decade—but she couldn't deny that there was something really seductive about being held firm by strong hands.

Almost helpless against the newly sensual bend of her thoughts, Anna had to wonder just how Cole's strength would play out in the bedroom.

The bedroom he'd promised he was taking her to tonight, married or not.

Cole's response came in that dangerously sexy voice, low and confident. "We'll take the best package you've got."

The wiry, smiling man nodded. "Certainly, sir. And how are you doing tonight, ma'am?"

Anna smiled as brightly as she could around the knot of nerves tightening her stomach muscles.

"Fine, thanks."

"Only fine? On your wedding night?" The man winked at Cole. "Well, we'll have to do our very best to change that, won't we?"

Cole's hand tightened on hers and she quickly said, "Actually, I'm great. Amazing. Phenomenal." She knew she was babbling, but she wasn't sure how to stop now that she was on a roll. "Who wouldn't be thrilled about marrying Cole?"

The wiry man studied Cole for a long moment before nodding. "Yes. He looks like he'll make a wonderful husband."

Anna automatically turned her gaze to Cole. He looked like he couldn't decide whether to yell...or laugh. And yet, even as a vein in his neck throbbed under their combined perusal, Anna found herself silently agreeing with the man helping them to get married.

Cole really did look like he was going to make a wonderful husband.

Why she thought that, she didn't know, especially since she had no data whatsoever to back it up—apart from his kissing prowess, that was—but there was no denying his strength, his rock-steady composure even in a Las Vegas chapel during a spur-of-the-moment wedding.

"We need a ring."

Both Anna and the man behind the counter jumped at Cole's commanding tone.

They needed a ring. A wedding ring.

Deep breaths, that's what she needed. One after the other until the right amount of oxygen returned to her brain.

"Of course, sir." The man reached under the counter and pulled out a velvet box. "Here is our selection."

Cole all but growled his displeasure when they looked inside. "No."

"Sir?"

Cole didn't answer. He simply pulled a cell phone out of his pocket. "James. I need a diamond ring. No less than five." He turned his attention back to her for a brief moment. "What ring size are you?"

She looked down at her ringless hand. "I don't know."

"Excuse me, sir," the chapel attendant said, "but I can guarantee that she's a six." He smiled at her. "I've been doing this for a very long time."

Cole spoke into his phone again. "Six." After a short pause, he said. "No, that's unacceptable. Five minutes ago." He looked up at the sign on the wall. "Cupid's Wedding Chapel, behind the Wynn." He put the phone back in his pocket. "The ring will be here in five minutes. What paperwork do you need us to fill out?"

"Great idea," she chirped. "We should get the paperwork done right away!"

She felt Cole's eyes on her, felt herself flushing as he said, "We need a minute alone."

The man behind the counter nodded quickly. "Of course, sir. I'll just go check on a few things in back."

Cole had a way of focusing all of his attention on her that rattled her brain—and made her panties shockingly damp.

She couldn't believe the way she heated up beneath his gaze. No other man had ever made her feel this way, like she couldn't control her hormones around him. It wasn't just that he was extremely good-looking. And built like a bodybuilder. No, it was something else that had her pulse racing.

It was the way his eyes said *Mine* when he looked at her.

Just like they were doing right now.

She took a breath to try to clear her head, but the breath was so shaky she almost didn't get any air in.

"Anna." He put his finger beneath her chin and tipped her chin up.

"Isn't this exciting?" she asked, trying to give him a confident smile.

"Yes," he agreed, and then, "Tell me what's wrong."

She forced herself to say, "Nothing's wrong," the same thing she'd been saying to everyone her entire life, whether or not it was true.

His finger moved from her chin up her cheek. "I can handle the truth, sweet Anna."

And the thing was, she suddenly believed him. Unable to look away from his dark, hot gaze, she said, "It's not that I don't want to do this. I mean, you asked if I wanted to get married and I said yes, so we're here and I'm sure it's going to be really great, but then when you started asking about paperwork, I—"

Well, it had just seemed so cold. So businesslike. So far from the heat that had driven them here.

"I kind of started to freak out." She sucked in a breath. "But I'm okay now." And it was the strangest thing, but just telling him what she really felt went a long way toward dissolving the knot in her stomach.

"What's your last name, Anna?"

Finding it difficult to focus past the fact that his fingertips were now traveling along the outside of her earlobe, she said, "Davis." His fingers ran down the side of her neck and it made so many wicked and wild desires jump to life inside that she had to close her eyes for a minute to try and keep her balance.

"Want to know mine?"

Anna opened her eyes in surprise. "Of course I do," she told him. "It's just that when you're doing that, I can't concentrate."

His full, masculine lips curving into a sensual grin, he ran his fingers across her collarbone and down the underside of her upper arm. "Good."

More moisture flooded her panties and she couldn't hold back a soft moan of pleasure.

"So sweet, Anna. So damn sweet."

The desire that rippled through her at his heated words sent her reeling. Needing desperately to ground herself in something, anything, she buried her face against his chest. But instead of grounding her, when she breathed in the heady scent of him—a clean, male scent that drew her in even deeper and made her want to rub herself all over him like a cat in heat—she could barely focus on anything other than how much she wanted Cole. No, this wasn't simply wanting, this was something else entirely, a desperate craving that ate away at her.

And then she felt his hands on her shoulders, pushing her back far enough that he could hold her gaze again. "You'll be Anna Taylor soon."

Her breath caught in her throat. It was a heck of a way to tell her his last name.

Before she could get her lungs or brain to cooperate again—was she really about to leave Anna Davis, the woman she'd been for nearly thirty years, behind?—the chapel's front door opened and an attractive gray-haired man walked in.

She felt herself flush as he quickly took her in, head to toe. He kept his face expressionless, save for the slight surprise lingering in his eyes.

"Introduce me, please," the man said to Cole.

Cole's eyes hadn't left her, not when his friend had walked in, not now that he was making the introductions. "James, this is Anna Davis. My fiancée."

Anna's heart rate leapt at the word *fiancée* and she worked to school her face into a normal smile of greeting. "It's nice to meet you, James."

The man's eyebrow lifted slightly. "It is very nice to meet you, Ms. Davis."

The next thing she knew, he was opening up a velvet case, much like the one the chapel attendant had under the counter. She gasped at the rings inside this one.

"No," she said, shaking her head and shooting a panicked glance at Cole. "You can't—I shouldn't—"

"Are these the biggest ones you could find?" Cole asked his friend in a clearly irritated tone.

Ignoring him, James told Anna, "Of course you will look beautiful in any of them. But now that I've met you, I think this one would be perfect."

He held out the only ring that had caught her eye, a princess-cut diamond surrounded by a circle of smaller diamonds. Still, she didn't reach out to touch it.

Frowning, Cole said, "Damn it, these diamonds aren't big enough." He pulled out the biggest one, so big she wasn't sure she'd be able to lift her hand with it on, and said, "How about we use this one tonight and then tomorrow morning we'll trade it in for something better?"

Standing in a Las Vegas wedding chapel, staring at a diamond that had to be at least five carats in the hands of a man she'd met approximately sixty minutes earlier, Anna stopped processing.

And starting laughing.

Both men stared at her as if she were completely off her rocker. She supposed they were right. After all, she was here, wasn't she?

"Cole," she finally said when she was able to speak, "these diamonds are all way too big."

"Too big?"

Cole looked utterly confused and she could have sworn his friend made a sound that was something between a cough and a barely-swallowed laugh.

"*Way* too big." Her gaze swung back to the one James had pointed out. "But that one's pretty. I guess I could get used to wearing it."

"Leave the ring."

James turned a bemused gaze to Cole. "Of course."

He put it on the counter, then closed the velvet box. He caught Anna by surprise with his smile, so friendly and genuine. "My best wishes to you, Anna." He left before wishing Cole luck.

"Wonderful, the ring has arrived!" The attendant returned, holding a clipboard and a pen. "I just need to see photo IDs and have you fill out your addresses, social security numbers, and signatures and we can get straight to the ceremony."

"We'll tell you when we're ready," Cole bit out.

The man's eyebrows rose. "Oh, I'm so sorry. I just remembered one more thing I need to take care of. Excuse me."

Cole practically carried her over to a small sitting area in the corner of the room.

"You scared him," she said.

"I don't care about him. I care about you."

Her stomach fluttered. *He cared about her?*

Oh my.

"You're overwhelmed."

No question, he was a man of few words. Still, he managed to say everything that needed to be said.

"Who wouldn't be?"

Before she knew it, he had pulled her onto his lap. "I don't want to hurt you, Anna."

He was so big and warm and hard beneath her thighs, against her chest, her hands. And when she was close to him like this, suddenly everything became so much clearer.

He hadn't forced her to come here. He'd simply asked her to marry him and she'd agreed. Because, for the first time in her life, she wanted to see what it felt like to really live.

"You're not hurting me, Cole. And you don't need to apologize."

"Good," he said in that low, rough voice of his that heated her up beyond reason, "because I'd rather kiss you." And then his mouth was on hers and her insides were lighting up like the Fourth of July.

"Sweet," he murmured against her lips, between kisses. "Sweeter than sugar."

Her body ached to get closer to his, to shift so that she wasn't sitting sideways across his legs, but straddling him instead.

When he finally let her up for air, she had to say, "You taste good, too."

"Nowhere near as good as you, Anna," he said, his eyes still on her lips, which were throbbing from his passionate kiss.

"Kiss me again, Cole."

She didn't have time to take another breath before he was there, stealing it from her lungs, shifting her so that her breasts were pressed hard against his chest, her arms wrapped tightly around him.

It didn't make any sense, not just being here in a wedding chapel with a man she hardly knew, but the fact that every cell in her body wanted to become part of him—and never, ever let go.

Every day, every minute of her life had made sense up until now.

And none of that sense had ever felt as good as this crazy did.

"Let's get married, Cole."

He stilled at her whispered request, before saying, "Anything for you, sweet Anna."

From that point on, everything happened in a blur. Cole lifting her off of his lap, the two of them walking over to the counter hand in hand to fill out the paperwork, realizing that they both lived in San Francisco as they wrote out their addresses; listening to the officiant say, "Do you, Cole Taylor, take Anna Davis to be your lawfully wedded wife," hearing Cole say "I do" in his low, rough voice; realizing she was being asked, "Will you, Anna Davis, take Cole Taylor to be your lawfully wedded husband?" and the words "I do" coming before she could let herself second-guess them; sliding the platinum band onto Cole's ring finger; watching Cole slide the diamond ring onto her left hand as the words "I now pronounce you husband and wife" were spoken...

...and then kissing the stranger she'd just married.

* * *

Cole didn't want to ever stop kissing Anna.

She was addictive, her taste, the feel of her soft curves, the breathy sounds of pleasure she made as he swept his tongue against hers and nipped at her full lower lip. Unfortunately, making out with his new wife to the sound of a throat clearing—loudly and repeatedly—wasn't exactly what he had in mind for his wedding night.

Not that he'd ever thought about his wedding night.

Or ever pictured himself with a new wife.

His heart rate kicked up, the ring Anna had put on his finger feeling strange as the officiant said, "Congratulations, Mr. and Mrs. Taylor."

Anna leaned closer into him as if she were trying to keep herself from falling. Fuck, he felt the same way even though getting hitched had been his idea, the perfect way to make sure Anna stayed with him at least long enough to meet his grandmother. And make her final wish come true.

Guilt knocked around inside his chest. At the same time, his dick was so hard he could pull it out and pound nails with it.

"Thank you," Anna replied to the officiant and the witness, whom Cole guessed were probably a married couple themselves.

"You're very welcome, honey." She lowered her voice. "I shouldn't be saying this, but after thirty years of owning Cupid's, we've seen our fair share of couples come through our doors. Enough to know which ones are going to make it, and which aren't."

He could feel Anna's intake of breath against his chest. "You can tell just from looking at the couple?"

Shit. Why hadn't he dragged her out of the chapel as soon as the rings were on? If this woman told Anna that their marriage was doomed—not thirty seconds after closing the deal—Cole was going to be pissed. There were plenty of half-crippled football players out there who could vouch for the fact that it was never a good idea to piss off Cole Taylor.

"Oh yes. We certainly can," the woman affirmed. "I can tell that you two are going to be among the lucky ones."

"We are?"

He would have laughed at the surprise in Anna's voice if he hadn't been more than a little insulted by it. Why the hell had she married him if she didn't think it was going to work out? He was the only one in this "relationship" with an ulterior motive, wasn't he?

She couldn't be that good an actress, could she? Hell, she was all but dripping innocence, and hadn't so much as reacted to learning his full name. Then again, for such an innocent girl, it hadn't exactly taken a hell of a lot of work to convince her to marry him.

Suspicion began to ride him as the woman said, "So many couples come in here on a spur-of-the-moment decision and just don't have what it takes to make it. But you two." She beamed at them. "I can almost see your bond. Strong and true. Real love. But you don't want to spend your wedding night gabbing with an old lady. Not when I can see how much you both are looking forward to celebrating your marriage."

Anna blushed furiously at the woman's comment, but for Cole it was a welcome splash of truth. The true love stuff was all bullshit. But the woman was dead right about one thing.

If his cock got any harder, he was going to bust a zipper. He wanted Anna, and he wanted her now.

He took her hand in his. He'd never been a big hand-holder before now, not even with long-time girlfriends, but holding her hand in his felt so right, so natural. He led her out of the chapel and down the back streets he'd learned as a kid, back to the hotel.

The warm night air was a shock after the air-conditioned chapel, especially considering Cole already felt overheated. Not just because he'd gotten hitched. But because holding Anna close like this did something strange to his insides.

Taking the back door he used when he was trying to go unnoticed, they got on the special elevator that went up to the Wynn's penthouse. The doors were closing as she said, "Wait a minute. The button for my floor isn't on here." She frowned at the elevator wall. "Why is there only one button on this?"

He put in his key and turned it before pressing the button. "This elevator only goes to my suite. And someone can get your things later."

Still clearly confused, she said, "It will just take me a few minutes to get them myself."

But Cole was all out of patience. He'd wanted her from the first second he'd set eyes on her. He'd been burning for her from the first taste, the first touch. Their wedding had pushed him way the hell past the point of reason.

Five more minutes to get her things wasn't an option.

Circling her waist with his hands, he dragged her into him.

"I don't want to wait a few minutes, Anna. I want to have sex with my wife." He all but growled the final word. "Now."

Chapter Four

"I want to have sex with my wife."

Wife. She was a wife.

Cole's wife.

How she wished the words, *Oh no, what have I done?* were coming out of Carrie Underwood's mouth right now via stereo speakers, instead of right between Anna's ears.

At least, she thought with barely repressed hysteria, unlike the character in the country song, Anna knew Cole's last name.

Even if she didn't know much else.

Anna's legs went weak. She needed to sit down, preferably with her head between her legs and a brown paper bag over her mouth and nose.

But even though her legs had decided not to bother holding her up anymore, she wasn't in any danger of falling. Not with Cole's hands gripping her tightly around her waist, holding her so close it was almost as if he didn't want to give her any room to think or breathe.

Or change her mind...and start running.

Desire was dark and possessive on his face as he said, "Do you have any idea what you do to me, Anna?"

By the end of the sentence, he'd lowered his head so that the final words were barely more than a hot breath against her mouth. But instead of another one of those drugging kisses that took away her breath and swept her up into him, his mouth was gentle against hers.

Anna shivered at the sensations caused by that brush of sensitive lips.

And what he'd said.

She wasn't the kind of woman who spent hours looking into the mirror, searching for flaws or beauty. She looked like what she looked like. Plenty of people had called her *cute*, so eventually, that's what she'd decided must be true.

But *cute* couldn't possibly inspire a reaction like Cole's, could it?

Equally confused as she was consumed by unfamiliar desire, Anna found herself whispering, "I want you, too," against his mouth.

For the moment, desire was the one thing she was certain of. The one thing she could trust.

"Damn it, I'm not going to take you in the elevator," Cole said as he pulled away from her. A split second later he was bending down and slipping an arm beneath her knees.

She was short, but not exactly stick-thin. No one had ever tried to pick her up before.

A thrill rushed through her at how effortless it was for Cole, at how protected—womanly—he made her feel.

Still, she wasn't used to being swept off her feet by a man who easily weighed twice what she did. So even though she was excited—and aroused—by his actions, she was also a little bit scared. Because the truth was, he could do whatever he wanted to her, and she wouldn't have a prayer if she tried to fight back.

Moisture shouldn't be pooling between her legs at the shocking thought.

More than a little freaked out at the way her body seemed to be utterly disconnected from her brain—as barely rational as it was right now—she said, "Cole, what are you doing?"

God, she sounded like a shocked fifties movie star in a black-and-white movie, but she couldn't help it. Nothing had gone like she'd thought it would tonight. She should be alone in bed right now wearing her flannel PJs, watching an old movie about a couple getting a quickie wedding in Vegas.

Instead, here she was, living the drama in full color.

Cole's response came with a grin that took her breath away. "Enjoying the hell out of carrying my bride over the threshold."

She couldn't help but smile back. Cole was one of the best-looking men she'd ever seen, up close or in pictures. Gorgeous and forbidding. Dark and hulking.

But when he smiled...his smile made her insides light up like a beach bonfire.

"Keep looking at me like that and we aren't going to make it past the front door."

He wasn't smiling anymore. Instead, he looked dangerous.

Sexy.

So sexy she wasn't sure she *wanted* to make it past the front door.

"I've never had sex up against a door."

The sound that came from his throat was half-growl, half-moan. "I wouldn't tease me right now, Anna." He kicked open the door.

"I'm not teasing."

And she wasn't. She was desperate.

Desperate for something she didn't understand.

Desperate for something she'd never felt before.

A heartbeat later, Cole had her back pressed into the now-closed door, her dress up around her waist and her legs wrapped around him. She didn't know how he'd done it, but she didn't care, not when the only thing that mattered was getting relief from the intense heat, the throbbing between her legs. She felt swollen and sensitive against him, where her underwear rubbed against the zipper of his pants.

His hands were wrapped around her butt cheeks and as he lowered his mouth to hers and kissed her hard enough that it almost hurt, she couldn't stop herself from thrusting into the thick bulge. A moment later, his mouth was moving across her face, down to her neck and she was baring herself to him, submitting to his dominance in the most elemental of ways.

"Cole," she moaned, begging for more, for some relief from the exquisite pressure, the intense sensations building higher and higher.

And then she felt it, the brush of his hand against her inner thighs, and she whimpered her pleasure, biting her lip as tremors of anticipation ran through her.

His fingers found her wet folds at the same moment that his mouth came down over one satin and silk–covered breast. Anna had never made sounds like this before—a cross between a scream and a moan, she was well and truly shocked at herself.

Shocked enough that she found herself pushing at Cole's chest with her open palms and gasping, "I can't. Not yet. Please."

Despite his own arousal, Cole's response to her abrupt shift was instantaneous.

Lifting his head from her breast, a large damp spot staining the center, he looked at her with honest concern. And no small measure of remorse.

"I was hurting you."

His completely unwarranted self-reproach tore at her

heartstrings. "No, you weren't," she said, rushing to reassure him.

Yes, he'd been killing her, but not with pain.

With pleasure.

Not knowing how to explain what had happened, she finally said, "Everything is moving so fast."

And she'd been on the verge of begging him to fuck her. Her. Anna Davis.

Oh, God. Not Davis. Anna Taylor.

Cole put her down on her feet, helping to smooth her dress back over her hips. Looking down, she couldn't take her eyes off his erection. Even bound by his clothes, it was like a living, breathing thing between them.

A second later, she noticed the dark spot in front of his zipper and froze. Was the patch of fabric that she'd been pressed against actually damp? Had Cole really made her that wet—wet enough that she'd soaked through her underwear, all the way to his clothes, with nothing more than a kiss?

And his fingers sliding between her legs.

Her freak-out jumped to a whole new level.

As if he sensed her sudden fear, Cole took another step back. But even as he gave her some room to breathe, he threaded his fingers through hers.

"Come on in. I'll show you around."

For the first time since they'd come inside, she realized they were in a strikingly luxurious living room, with floor-to-ceiling windows that looked out on the Vegas strip.

"This is your hotel room?"

"Like it?"

"Are you kidding? It's amazing. Have you stayed here before?"

"Since they opened in 2006."

Every question she asked—and every answer he gave—only highlighted just how little she actually knew about the man she'd just married.

Married.

The diamond ring on her finger felt heavy and strange. Her throat tightening up around the words as if her body and mind were shutting down one piece at a time, she asked, "Do you always stay up here when you're at the hotel?"

"Usually. My things are all here," he replied with a thread of amusement in his voice, at odds with the concern still written on his face when he looked at her. "I'm going to get us a couple of drinks." He left her alone to let herself out of a sliding glass door onto a deck.

She could hardly believe her eyes. There was a huge swimming pool surrounded by a rooftop garden. The pool alone was almost bigger than her entire apartment. Renting it would be one thing—one amazing thing—but owning this penthouse suite?

No way.

She was too busy gaping—and wondering just how Cole had enough money for a place like this—to notice him returning from the kitchen.

He pressed a cold glass into her hands. "Drink that."

The liquid was sweet and sugary, just what she needed after a day of too much champagne and too little food. She drank until it was empty.

"Thank you."

"You looked pale."

She had? Was that why he'd been frowning? Because he was worried about her, rather than angry that she'd put a halt to having sex up against the door?

"I play football. It pays well."

Here she'd thought she was playing it cool, but he'd obviously read the question in her eyes.

Because she had the exact opposite of a poker face.

"I don't know much about football," she admitted.

"I guessed that," he said with another one of those heart-thumping grins.

"I'm a quick learner, though."

Heat reflected back at her from his dark eyes. "I'm glad to hear that. Very glad."

A couple of sentences shouldn't be able to melt her insides, should they? Sure, when he was touching her, of course she melted. But just words—and that tone of voice—were doing just as good a job of arousing her as his kisses and caresses had.

His voice was gruff as he asked, "What about you?"

"I teach first grade."

"That's perfect."

It was?

"My sweet little schoolteacher."

His response struck her as strange, but she couldn't figure out exactly why. Especially when he was still looking at her like he wanted to lick her all over, head to toe.

Her body was responding to that look with intense arousal. But at the same time, the more physically aroused she become, the more it seemed her brain—and heart—were fighting that desire. Back in the club, even before he'd proposed, Cole had made it perfectly clear that they were going to spend the night together. Obviously, now that they were husband and wife, it was a slam dunk.

Still, it seemed that there was a difference between knowing something was going to happen and actually being there when it happened.

And there was definitely a difference between deciding she was going to be brave and actually being brave.

His eyes, still dark with desire, were fixed on her and she felt as if he saw all the way into her soul. It was too much, too soon. She tried to walk inside, but he grabbed her before she could take more than a step, and pulled her against him.

"You don't need to run from me, Anna."

Her breath was rising and falling too fast. "I don't want to run, but I don't know how to do anything else."

His mouth found hers and she tried to lose herself in his kiss the way she'd been lost in all the others, but panic was riding her too hard now to be able to let go. His hands moved down her back, rubbing, massaging from shoulder to hips, but instead of relaxing, she only tensed up more.

He lifted his head and she immediately said, "I'm sorry. I don't know what's wrong with me."

"No apologies."

Grateful that he wasn't pressuring her into anything—even though she was now his lawfully wedded wife—she said, "I want—"

Oh God, she was such a novice at all of this that she didn't even know how to get the words out.

"You want to sleep with me."

Thankful that he clearly didn't have the same problem, she nodded.

"But something is holding you back?"

Again, she nodded.

"How many lovers have you had, Anna?"

She flushed at his question. "Two," she said in a voice that was barely more than a whisper. "But being with them wasn't like being with you."

The words were out before she realized they were coming and her flush flamed even brighter.

"You're special to me, too," he said softly against her lips and this time when he kissed her, she was able to sink into it a little more. "I want to give you pleasure, Anna, more pleasure than you've ever known. Will you let me do that for you?"

His heated words shot through her veins like a drug. "I want to, Cole." And she did. God, how she did. "But what if I freak out again?"

"Will you trust me to make sure that doesn't happen?"

She had no reason to trust him, not when she didn't know any more about him than his name and profession. And yet, there was something in his eyes, in the way he'd touched her so far tonight, in the way he'd kissed her, that had her feeling cherished.

Adored.

No one had ever made her feel that way before. Not just the sexual part, which was way off any chart she'd ever had, but the safety part.

Cole made her feel protected.

"What we've had so far tonight is only the beginning. There's so much more, sweet Anna. Let me show you how good I can make you feel."

She couldn't hold back a shiver at his words. His arms were still around her, light enough that she could walk away at any moment, but she didn't want to go. His erection throbbed hard and thick against her belly even through his pants, and she wanted what he promised.

Badly.

But now she knew for sure that she couldn't do it on her own. Not without him helping her. Guiding her. Leading her.

Not without trusting him.

She'd thought a quickie wedding would be the craziest thing she'd ever done, but now she knew she was wrong.

Sleeping with Cole, trusting him enough to give her body over to him, letting him learn what gave her pleasure—learning it for herself—was far crazier.

"I'll trust you, Cole."

The relief that flashed across his features was quickly replaced with a darker, deeper desire than she'd seen yet.

He was halfway to kissing her when she found herself saying, "But please, don't betray my trust. Please don't hurt me."

He stilled a breath away from her mouth. "I don't want to hurt you, Anna."

Her brain tried to tell her it wasn't the promise she was looking for, but before she could fully hold onto the warning, he was picking her up again and kissing her as he carried her back inside.

Into his bedroom.

Chapter Five

Cole didn't throw her on the bed, didn't crawl over her and keep kissing her. Instead, he set her on her feet again and said, "Turn around."

Anna's eyes flashed a combination of desire and that uncertainty she couldn't shake at his command. But she did it.

"Good girl," he said as he slid her zipper down and pushed her dress off her shoulders to the floor.

The fine hairs along her spine rose as his fingers followed the dress down. She moved to turn again to face him.

"Stay right where you are."

"But I can't see what you're doing."

"I know."

Again, despite her reluctance to give up control, he hoped she was tempted enough by what he was offering to give it.

After taking a long moment to appreciate how good she looked from the back in nothing but a bra and panties, all soft curves and smooth skin—the anticipation of seeing her from the front nearly killing him—Cole said, "Don't move a muscle."

He could see how hard it was for her follow his instructions, even without seeing her face. She was all but bristling with anxiety as he walked over to his dresser and pulled it open.

"Tell me what you're doing," she begged.

God, how he liked to hear her beg.

"You'll know soon enough," he said, teasing her with his response. Despite what she thought she wanted, the fact was that not knowing what he was doing would make her even hotter.

And would help her let go.

That need to let go was exactly why he gently slid one of his silk ties across her eyes.

She reached for the blindfold, but he didn't stop her. "I thought you were going to trust me, sweet Anna."

Her hands stilled on the soft fabric. "But I didn't think you'd be...blindfolding me."

He had to press a kiss to the spot where her neck curved into her shoulder. But just the press of his lips wasn't enough, he had to rake her skin with his teeth, had to begin to mark her as his.

His.

"Don't think, Anna. Just feel." He finished tying it behind her soft hair, tight enough that it wouldn't slip, but not tight enough to hurt. "The blindfold will help."

"How?"

Her whispered question made his cock so big it almost hurt. Because she was trusting him.

And he didn't deserve that trust.

Damn it, he couldn't go there. Not now. Not when he had a feeling the greatest pleasure he'd known yet was right in front of him, wearing his tie as a blindfold. Along with his ring on her left hand.

When she'd asked him not to betray her trust, they'd been talking about sex. He told himself that his answer had been totally honest. Enough justification that nothing was going to stop him from giving her the ultimate pleasure.

"No decisions. No choices. Just pleasure."

He heard her breath catch, saw the flutter of excitement in the upper curve of her breasts where her heart was beating hard enough that he could see it jumping beneath her skin.

He picked her up again, her arms going around his neck to steady herself a moment before he laid her down on the bed.

With the blindfold covering her incredible eyes, he found himself enthralled by her mouth, a sweet and sexy cupid's bow that was made for kissing. A vision ambushed him of Anna's soft, red lips wrapped around his cock as she sucked him deep into her throat.

"You're beautiful, Anna. So damn beautiful."

Those perfect lips curved up into a tremulous smile. She blindly reached up for his face, running her fingertips across his jaw, over his lips. "Thank you," she whispered.

Leaning down over her, he licked her lips, a long stroke from one side to the other. She opened up to him on a whimper and for the hundredth time that night, he lost sight of his plan.

Because just kissing this woman was better than fucking any other.

As her curves went soft and pliant beneath his, as he settled his erection against her wet heat and she bucked up into him, it took everything Cole had for him to remind himself that they'd been to this point before, where she was open and wanting, and she'd frozen up. If he kept at it like this, not using any finesse at all, odds were high that it would happen again.

Not because she was a tease.

Not because she didn't want him as badly as he wanted her.

But because she was good girl.

And pleasure this extreme frightened her.

"Have I mentioned yet how much I love kissing you?"

"I love kissing you, too," she said in that soft voice that was as warm and sweet as the woman beneath him.

"I want to kiss you everywhere, Anna."

Her soft smile froze on her face at the exact moment that he took hold of her wrists and lifted her arms over her head.

"Cole?"

"Just relax, sweetheart."

He'd never been one for pet names, had never bothered to force them out to get in a girl's pants, but with Anna he wasn't forcing it. She *was* sweet. So sweet he ached with the need to kiss her. To taste her. Working quickly, he drew another silk tie from where he'd been storing it around his neck and bound her left wrist to the right bedpost.

"How can I relax when you're tying me up?"

Her earnest question had him smiling down at her. The kind of woman he usually slept with would be playing it up right now, moaning and putting on a show for his benefit.

But not Anna. Instead, she was telling him exactly what she was feeling every step of the way with beautiful honesty.

"Like this," he said a moment before he ran his tongue lightly across the delicate skin on the inside of her wrist. "And this." His mouth ran kisses from her palm around to her shoulder.

By the time he made it back to her face, he had to drop in for another taste of her sweet mouth. Her nipples were a hard press of heat against his forearms.

"Better?"

Her breath was coming in harsh pants. "No."

"Maybe this will help." With her limbs still rubbery from his kisses, he quickly moved her other arm into place and secured it to the bedpost. Moving back to stare down at her beautiful, half-bound body, he asked again, "Better now?"

"No, Cole. Please. I don't know how to do this."

"You don't need to know, sweetheart. Not when your body already does."

Gently spreading her thighs with a hand on each leg, he inhaled her scent, more sweet than musky. His mouth watered with the urge to bury his face in her soft, wet folds, and taste her.

"Can you feel how wet you are for me?"

Her pink panties were soaked against her pussy lips. He pressed two fingers against her wet heat and she gasped, clamping her legs together around his hand.

Leaving his hand pressed in tight against her silk-covered lips, he asked, "Do you have any idea what you're doing to me?"

"But you're the one touching me."

Jesus, she had no idea how much her innocence inflamed him. Hell, he was as surprised by it as she was.

He hadn't been sure about tying up her legs. Now he was.

Anna's reserve went so deep that if he gave her any chance at all to protest, to try and fight what her body so desperately wanted, she'd use it.

Leaning over, he lowered his face to her groin and slid his hand out of the way, only to replace it with his mouth. Knowing he'd have to use the element of surprise to his advantage if he was going to have any chance of prying her thighs apart again without hurting her, a split second after he planted a hard kiss against her soft, aroused flesh, he was drawing her legs apart and securing her ankles, one after the other, to the foot board.

* * *

Anna reacted instinctively to her imprisonment by pulling and yanking at her silk bindings. But although they weren't tight, they were firm.

"Cole," she begged, "please untie me."

"Let me look at you first," he murmured. "I've never seen anything so pretty. You should see how sexy you look all spread for me, so wet and aroused, so ready for me to love you."

Without touching her—even though she was frightened by how

vulnerable she was now—his words of approval sent her to new peaks of arousal. Especially when he'd used the word *love*. Because even though the rational part of her knew there was no way they could be feeling more than lust—and like—for each other after meeting only hours before, her heart clearly wanted to believe in the fairytale of love at first sight.

Feeling the heat of his stare, even though she couldn't see him looking down on her through her blindfold, she could feel her breath coming too fast, knew she was actually shaking within her bindings.

The next thing she knew, his warm breath was brushing against her earlobe. "You're being so brave, sweetheart."

But she wasn't. She was begging him to release her at every turn, telling him she couldn't do what he was asking her to do.

Just like she'd been doing her whole life.

He sucked the fleshy lobe of her ear between his teeth and she arched up off the bed as far as the bindings would let her. Her nipples brushed against one of his thickly muscled arms.

"Touch me, Cole." She was still begging, but in an instant what she wanted had changed.

No, that was a lie. She'd wanted him to touch her from the first. All that had changed was she had finally stopped getting in her own way.

His mouth moved from her ear to trail a hot path down her neck. "Here?"

"Yes," she said as her head fell back to give him better access to her sensitive skin. But the way her breasts were aching for his touch had her changing her answer. "No."

She heard him chuckle, felt his soft laughter against her skin a moment before his tongue dipped into the hollow in front of her shoulder.

She gasped at the delicious pleasure racing through her and pulled at the bindings at her wrists. Only, this time she was pulling because of the pleasure, rather than trying to get away from it.

"Is this where you want me, Anna?"

His mouth moved across her skin with the question, lingering behind with a lick and a nip when the words were done.

Knowing how close he was to her breasts—and yet so damn, frustratingly far—she said, "My breasts. Please, Cole. Touch my breasts."

"Sweet Anna," he said, that surprising thread of humor lacing his response, "you should have just asked."

But he'd known she couldn't, that she didn't have the words, the sexual experience to play the kind of games he probably played every single night with beautiful women.

And then, just as it had before, humor turned to instant heat as his mouth came down over one breast, his tongue laving her nipple beneath her bra in hot and heavy strokes.

It was good, so good, better than anything she'd ever felt before. But she wanted more.

Oh God, she wanted more.

Cool air rushed over her when he lifted his head. "Am I doing it right?"

His question would have been funny if she weren't lying there burning up, wanting things that had her all but squirming with embarrassment. Not the sexual act itself, which she'd done before, but the verbal element of their sexual interaction, something he was clearly insistent that she try.

Anna was surprised to realize that putting voice to her desire was almost more scary than being tied up and vulnerable to his every touch.

So many times in one short night, Cole had asked her to be brave. To take a chance by dancing with him. To marry him. To let him tie her up. And, now, to tell him what gave her pleasure.

He was the first person who had ever looked at her and seen someone who might have guts.

A woman who might be willing to take a risk.

She'd been so afraid of falling her whole life that she hadn't ever known the feeling of leaping and not knowing where she'd land.

But Cole had taken her hand and given her the opportunity to jump.

The chance to take a free fall and feel the wind in her hair.

Sucking in a breath, she told him something she'd never thought to say to anyone. "My breasts are really sensitive. Good sensitive."

She felt the air go still in the room, realized neither of them were breathing. And then, his fingers found the clasp at the front of her bra and cool air was rushing over the heated tips of her breasts.

"Anna." Her name was almost a prayer on his lips. "Sweet

Anna, no one should be this beautiful."

She thought—prayed—that he was going to drop his head down to her breasts, especially when she felt the soft ends of his hair brushing against the super-sensitive flesh.

"Tell me what you want me to do to your perfect breasts, sweetheart."

Before she could say a word, his hands came around the undersides of her breasts and cupped them together.

"Lick them."

His hair brushed against the outside of one breast, his tongue laving between her soft flesh and her rib cage. "Like this?"

She couldn't believe she was smiling, but it was such a surprise that the big, hard man she'd married loved to tease.

And, oh, was he good at it.

"What if I said yes?" she found herself teasing back.

After a bit of a pause that only served to ratchet up her anticipation, his tongue came down over her again, laving small but intensely sweet circles of pleasure against the side of her breast. And then, after a quick sweep of his soft hair over her chest, he found the mirror-image spot on the other breast.

She knew what he was doing, that he wasn't going to take another step on his own without forcing her all the way to the edge, but not off. Jumping was all her own responsibility.

She knew that now, understanding it for the first time ever.

"My nipples, Cole." She felt him lift his head slightly, pressing a soft kiss to her skin before moving away completely. "Lick my nipples."

She was instantly rewarded for her bravery by the wet flick of the tip of his tongue against the rigid points. His hands were wonderfully rough on her as he pushed her breasts close enough together that he could lick first one hard tip and then the other, again and again in such rapid succession that she never had a chance to recover.

Just Cole's tongue on her skin was better than any other sexual encounter she'd ever had. And still, it wasn't enough.

Not nearly enough to satisfy the need he'd made her feel.

And, oh God, the things she was feeling, white-hot flames rippling across her skin, pulling her into a maelstrom of heat...and boundless pleasure.

"Suck them."

Again, her request was instantly granted, and she couldn't possibly contain her cry of deep, dark delight as Cole's strong lips pressed around a nipple, as his tongue flattened against the underside so that it dragged along the roof of his mouth.

She'd heard women say they could come like this, but she'd never believed it, not for a second. None of her previous lovers—it wasn't even fair to put the men she'd slept with in that category, she suddenly thought—had given her what she needed. No amount of foreplay had taken her to this place where Cole had so effortlessly brought her.

While his mouth found sweet purchase on one nipple, his hands and fingers didn't neglect her other breast, rolling the sensitive peak between his thumb and forefinger so that she wasn't able to focus on just one spot, not when it felt like her entire body was on fire, her cells molten heat beneath Cole's talented fingers and mouth.

She sucked in one breath and then another around her moans of pleasure and just when she thought she was getting a handle on the incredible sensations coursing through her veins, he surprised her with something she wouldn't have been able to ask for, simply because she didn't know that lovers could touch each other in such a way.

The scrape of teeth against sensitive flesh had moisture flooding at her core, her stomach tightening down when she was unable to push her thighs together to try and drive herself over the edge. She couldn't control the arch of her back into his mouth or the sounds coming from her throat, a cry of wonder as she rode the edge of pain and came back around to the most incredible ecstasy.

And then, he was moving to her other nipple, and she was saying, "Do that again, Cole," but he was already there, already scraping against the tight tip with his teeth before laving the small hurt away with the tip of his warm, wet tongue.

Her limbs yanked against her binds as she tried to press herself up, higher, harder against his mouth. But then, her breasts were free, his mouth and hands moving down her torso as she opened her mouth to complain, his tongue dipping into her belly button and stealing away any words that might have been on her lips.

One of Cole's fingers slid beneath the upper edge of her panties and all of her awareness suddenly centered on the slick, aroused flesh between her thighs. She could feel the silk of her panties sticking to her labia and where she'd previously been afraid before to let a man she hardly knew see her naked, now all she wanted was for the final barriers to be pulled away.

"Anna, baby, tell me what you want. Tell me what you need."

His words brushing warm air against her belly almost had her coming. God, what would happen when he finally touched her there? If he loved her vagina with his mouth as well as he'd loved her breasts?

Amazed that she could actually feel her clitoris swell at the same moment another gush of arousal spilled out from between her thighs, she breathed, "Just touch me, Cole. With your hands. Your mouth. Your tongue." She shuddered. "Your teeth."

With her sight taken away by the silk blindfold, the sound of fabric ripping was loud enough to make her jump, but a second later, as thick, warm fingers moved through her bared, damp curls to part her naked flesh, she forgot everything—that she had married a stranger, that she was blindfolded and bound to his bed, that she was frightened by the strangely powerful desire eating her up from the inside—everything but how desperate she was for release.

Air blew across her clitoris and she bucked up an inch—all her bindings would allow.

Oh God, he was teasing her.

Had she actually enjoyed his teasing before? Didn't he know that it would kill her if he teased her now? That she couldn't take any more of this pleasure, not when it was all coming at her so fast, so hard, stealing her breath—and her senses—away.

Second by second, she was disappearing into a swirling storm of ecstasy. Breath by breath she was on the verge of losing the Anna Davis she'd always been against Cole's hands as they slid slowly against her slickly aroused skin, his mouth as it dropped softly to her clitoris, drawing the tight, hard bud into his lips so that he could drag his tongue over it.

And then, just when she thought he was going to give her what she wanted, one more swirl of his tongue against her, over her—all she needed to crest the peak and come apart—he pulled away and blew out another hot breath over her delicate skin.

"Don't tease me, Cole. Please don't tease me anymore."

His tongue came out to flick against her drenched skin and relief swept through her as pleasure spiked and she tried to grab onto the wave and let it take her over.

But then he was blowing on her again, the light rush of air so good, too good, and yet, not nearly enough.

"You like what I'm doing to you."

His words weren't a question. They were a statement of truth.

"God, yes," she gasped. "I love it." And she did. But, "I need to come, Cole." And then maybe she could survive this pleasure. Maybe she could stop it from racing away with her. Maybe she could return to being the woman she'd always been.

"How bad do you need it?"

"Really bad," was all she could manage as he tongue swept between her folds again, this time dipping into her. But even though she tried to buck into his mouth, his tongue didn't slide in far enough to give her any satisfaction.

She'd never survive his teasing.

"Well, now," he said slowly, letting his lips rake across the top of her mound, "doesn't sound to me like you need it all that bad."

If she'd been able to move her arms and legs, she would have launched herself at him, would have pinned him down to the bed and crawled up over his face and forced him to take her where she desperately needed to go.

Instead, all she could do was wait for him to give her what he wanted to give, when he wanted to give it. They were on his schedule, his plan.

Not hers.

With the thought came another inexplicable flood of arousal. Almost as if she liked being tied up and captive to Cole's every whim. And then his mouth covered her at the same moment he slipped a finger into her tight sheath and a small tremor worked through her.

"Just a little more. I only need a little more to get there."

His laughter took her by surprise, his lips and tongue and teeth rocking against her, his fingers shifting against her delicate internal walls. Another mini-tremor shook her.

"If you were expecting little, sweet Anna, you're going to be sorely disappointed."

Instead of being afraid of splitting apart beneath him, the vision of his erection stretching her wide as he forced her to take all of him catapulted her into a bigger, stronger tremor.

His tongue moved slow and soft against her again, from perineum to clit. She could feel herself perspiring from the combination of pleasure and frustration. From anticipation.

And desperation.

"I can't survive any more of this." She didn't have the will to keep her voice from shaking anymore.

His laughter came again, warm and almost loving, even as it was full of the same deep, dark desire that she'd been riding since the moment he'd kissed her for the first time.

"You'll not only survive it," he promised her, "but you'll wonder how you lived this long without it."

His words, the slight press of his mouth against her sensitive folds as he spoke, along with the tight clench of her inner muscles, were almost enough to get there. Holding her breath, she focused, willed herself to come, to escape the torture of Cole's teasing.

"Poor sweet baby," he murmured against her as she flopped back against the bed, frustrated and more aroused than she'd even known it was possible to be. "You really do need to come, don't you?"

But she was long past begging at this point, her cells were too wrapped up in the needs of her body for her to even attempt to form coherent words. She'd trusted him to give her pleasure and instead, she was frustrated and—

His tongue slid into her hard, thrusting once, twice, three times.

Oh God, yes! This was what she'd been waiting for, this was what she needed, a good tongue-fucking. She was riding his tongue like a hard shaft when his fingers moved over her clit again and swirled with dangerous precision.

Still riding his tongue, she rolled against his hands, fighting her bonds to try and get closer, but he was two steps ahead of her, increasing the pressure with delicious intent. And then Cole reached up with his free hand and found one hard, aroused nipple, and her entire body crashed in on itself, her clit and breasts dual epicenters for the massive earthquake rolling through her. She'd never come like this, so hard that she was certain the bed was splitting apart beneath her, the walls crashing in around her.

Her orgasm went on and on as Cole's tongue stroked new and shocking sensitive spots along her inner walls, his fingers magic on her clitoris and breasts.

Finally, when she was utterly spent—more tired than she'd been after running that 10K last year—Cole shifted on the bed.

"My wife has such a sweet pussy," he said before placing a soft kiss over her labia.

Shivers racked her as his stubble raked across the too-sensitive flesh.

"Such gorgeous tits."

Even knowing the kiss had to be coming, she couldn't prepare herself for the sweet heat of his mouth over first one nipple, then the other. A moan escaped her as he rolled her around on his tongue, then raked across the tips with the very edges of his teeth.

"And such a pretty, fuckable mouth."

Anna's mouth watered despite herself, despite the shock moving through her at the knowledge of what was coming, that she was going to be returning the favor by taking Cole's penis into her mouth.

The bed shifted again beneath his heavy weight and she felt her heartbeat kick into overdrive again.

"If I'm hurting you, if anything doesn't feel good, I want you to pinch me."

He slid his hands into hers and linked their fingers. Oh God, she'd thought she loved holding hands before. But now, feeling the slide of his wide, calloused palms against hers, a new warmth bloomed in her chest.

And then, before she could find the words to reply to his instructions, the flared, hot crest of his penis brushed softly against her lips.

Anna had given blow jobs before, but not very often. She'd never really seen the appeal of male genitalia, but the way Cole was teasing her with his erection, his skin soft against her mouth, had her salivary glands kicking into overdrive. His arousal was a clean, masculine scent that made her breathe in more deeply as he slowly painted her lips, from corner to corner, with the tip of his penis. It was pure instinct to taste him with her tongue.

Cole stilled as she made contact with him, a deep groan of pleasure seeming to come from all the way down in his chest. Spurred on by both his reaction to her touch and the surprising pleasure she was finding in being with Cole this way, she swiped her tongue all the way across his broad head, greedily licking up the spurt of arousal that resulted.

"Jesus, Anna, nothing has ever felt this good."

Even as his words resonated, she wanted to make him feel so much better.

In the end, Anna wasn't sure who moved first, if she was already opening up her lips to take him inside or if he was the one who pushed her open. All she knew was that she was glad, so incredibly glad, to be able to taste him like this, to open her mouth wide and stretch her lips around his hard, heavy shaft. She wasn't afraid of being captive to him, knew he'd never ever hurt her.

Using her tongue to explore him, she licked at every part of his shaft she could get to, using the suction of her lips to pull him in deeper.

His hands tightened on hers, another rumble of pleasure sounding in the room, and then he was rocking into her, so deep that her gag reflex kicked in.

Pulling all the way out, he said, "Your mouth is so hot, baby. I can't control myself."

Realizing he was sliding his hands from hers and shifting away from her mouth, she clamped down on his fingers as hard as she could.

"I want to taste you again, Cole." She forced herself to overcome her shyness and say it. "I loved licking you. Sucking on you."

"I don't want to hurt you."

"You won't," she insisted, promising, "I'll pinch you if I need a breather."

"Do you know what you're asking for, sweet Anna?"

His question was low, full of barely leashed desire.

"No. But I want it anyway."

That was all it took for Cole to drop the leash and give her what she was begging for. The press of his shaft against her lips drove her mouth open and she gratefully suckled his hot, hard flesh. He rocked into her several inches at a time, in then out in a rhythm that had her heating up again between her thighs, her belly tightening with renewed need as she tasted his arousal on her tongue, in the back of her throat.

But then her gag reflex kicked in again, and he bottomed out before she was anywhere near the base of his penis. She tried to relax her throat, but he was such a big, unfamiliar presence that she couldn't.

Tears pricked her eyes behind her blindfold, but they weren't tears of pain. They were tears of frustration. Because on some elemental level, she knew she had more to give him.

She just couldn't figure out how to do it.

One of his hands came untangled from hers, then, and he gently ran his fingertips along her exposed throat. "Tilt up and back, sweetheart."

He slid his hand around the back of her throat to help her, and then he was sliding in, and past the point he'd hit before. She could feel the muscles in her throat opening up to take him deeper, could taste the musky heat of him in her mouth. Again and again he moved in, then out of her mouth, her throat, and even though he wasn't touching her breasts or vagina, giving Cole pleasure had her right on the edge of release again.

Unable to hold back her own moan of deep pleasure, she felt Cole's penis twitch against her tongue, a large spurt of his pre-come coating her tongue and throat as he pulled all the way out of her on a curse.

A split second later, the bindings on her wrists and ankles were gone and she had to reach for Cole to steady herself. His shoulders were broad and hard, his skin slick with sweat, and she was relishing the unexpected thrill of being able to touch him, when he pulled her blindfold off.

She gasped at the passion, the desire, the need in his dark eyes. She opened her mouth to try and give voice to the emotions ricocheting around inside of her.

"I didn't know it could be like this," she whispered.

He tucked the head of his condom-covered penis against her folds. One thrust had him inside, and Anna lost her breath at the incredible pleasure.

"Tight," he ground out, sweat dripping from his chest onto hers as he worked to steady himself above her. "So damn tight."

He was right. She was small. And he was enormous. But she loved the way he was stretching her open, loved knowing that he was taking her someplace she'd never been before.

"Take me, Cole."

His eyes flashed something new, a bigger, richer emotion that even his desire, but before she could try and figure out what he was feeling, he thrust all the way into her, settling so deep inside her that she swore he was pushing into the base of her womb. And then his mouth was over hers and he was kissing her and she was kissing him back and wrapping her arms and legs around him to pull him in closer, to take him deeper.

"My sweet Anna. You're all mine," he rasped out against her lips.

"And you're mine."

Until that moment, she could have sworn he was still holding something back, that he was still worried about hurting her. But after her own possessive declaration, something in the man holding her changed.

A moment later, her hands were back in his, pulled over her head, and he was levered above her, driving into her with such heat, and power, that she not only lost her breath with every thrust, but as the pleasure coiled tighter in her belly, in the tips of her breasts, in the vee between her thighs, she actually begged for him to take her harder, faster, deeper.

And he did, each thrust taking her higher, closer to the peak.

She'd thought he'd been big when she'd first taken him into her mouth, when he'd pushed between the folds of her vagina. But now, on the verge of his release, he was a throbbing mass of veins and heat and male arousal. Anna swore she could feel her body actually react to his impending climax by both relaxing and clenching her inner muscles. Relaxing to let him in even deeper. Then clamping down on him to keep him inside, to keep the incredible sensations roaring through her.

"Anna."

The rough, ragged sound of his voice as he came sent her flying over the edge with him. And then his mouth was on hers again and she was thrown into another climax, spiraling off and just barely holding on to the edge of reason.

Chapter Six

Anna woke up curled within Cole's strong arms. One of his hands was threaded into her hair, the other on her chest, his open palm resting directly over her heart.

They weren't sleeping like two people who'd had a one-night stand. Anna wasn't trying to figure out how to squeeze out from beneath Cole without waking him up. She wasn't berating herself for her foolish behavior.

Instead, she was relishing the comfort of being held by a man who had given her not just pleasure, but something else that she hadn't even realized she needed: A window into the woman who had been waiting inside her all along, a woman who was at least a little bit brave and adventurous.

And, boy, had she been rewarded for that bravery again and again with his mouth and hands—and then his penis.

Thinking back on everything he'd done to her the night before made her body heat up again, her skin pricking with intense awareness. Comfort shifted to arousal, and with that shift came the realization that Cole was hard and throbbing against her hips where he was spooning her.

Even after he'd climaxed, his penis had been larger than any she'd seen before. Erect, it was mind-blowing, both in length and girth. Somehow she'd been able to stretch for him. As the memories of what they'd done came back to her the morning after with perfect clarity, her stomach clenched and arousal spilled through her. Readying her for his touch, just as it had the night before.

Only this time, she didn't want to be tied up. She didn't need it. Not when she knew just what Cole's touch, his kisses, did to her. Not when she wanted to touch him, kiss him, lick him, nip at him, the way he'd done all those things to her when she'd been his silk-bound captive.

Pure feminine instinct had her threading her fingers through his hand on her breast and shimmying her hips into his hard heat.

A low, almost inaudible groan came from behind her and she smiled. Until last night she hadn't known that there was a super-sexual woman lying in wait inside her. But now that she did, she found that she wanted to expose her more fully in the arms of the man to whom she'd inexplicably given her trust.

Trusting him wasn't something that should have made sense, but maybe, she thought, as the pad of his thumb rubbed light circles around her areola, that had been her problem all along.

She'd wanted everything to make sense. Had insisted on it. But maybe love didn't make sense.

Not that she was in love with Cole. She liked him. She lusted for him. But love? No. She wasn't there yet. Not after only ten hours together.

But could she fall in love with him one day?

If he always treated her the way he had last night, as though she were a precious gift to be cherished, worshiped? Then, yes, she probably wouldn't be able to stop herself from falling in love with him.

A hairy, muscled leg pushed between hers as Cole used his thigh to open her up to him.

Anna could now feel exactly how wet she was as her slick flesh—he'd called it a *pussy*, and instead of being horrified, the word had only aroused her more—rubbed against him. Her clit was already swollen and she loved the way the hair on his leg rasped against the hard nub where all of her pleasure seemed to be centered.

Before she realized it, she was riding his thigh, grinding into it harder and harder as his hand on her breast stopped teasing the puckered nipple and started squeezing it in earnest.

Oh God. She couldn't believe it. She was going to come.

After the way Cole had drawn out her climax the night before, after experiencing the exquisite release, she had thought she'd be sated for a while—longer than a handful of hours, certainly. Never in a million years did she think she'd be getting herself off against his leg first thing in the morning...or that the pleasure would be even greater for the slightly wicked nature of it.

Reaching for the peak, Anna squeezed her eyes shut and arched into his hand at her breast. Her breath caught in her throat as the first explosions started to rock through her. The shockingly wide, hard pressure of Cole's cock head against her labia stilled her. But then hard-tipped fingers came down over her clit, throwing her into an even harder climax, just as Cole pushed into her snug channel.

Still slightly sore from the previous night's lovemaking, her internal tissue tried to protest the invasion, but her continued desire for the man now taking her so roughly—so wonderfully—overpowered that protest with a flood of moisture to ease his passage.

"Open up for me, sweet Anna," he urged her in that sinfully hot voice that would have turned her insides into a puddle if they weren't already there.

She could feel how tightly her internal muscles were squeezing his hard shaft despite how much she wanted him inside of her. She tried to take a deep breath, but all that did was tighten her down on him further.

"I want to," she whispered, and she did. "I'm trying," she said, and she was. "Help me," she begged him, still pleading with him for her pleasure, even past the night hours.

Holding himself perfectly still inside her, not nearly all the way there but still so big she thought she might burst from the exquisite pressure, she felt his tongue move across the top of her shoulder, one long, smooth, wet stroke all the way up her neck to her earlobe. Without any effort on her part at all, her muscles unclenched and let go of their tight grip on him.

"That's it, sweetheart," he praised as he slid deeper, her muscles and flesh separating for him. "So tight. So hot." His tongue found her neck again. "So soft." She tilted her head back so that her mouth could find his and he murmured, "So sweet," against her lips.

His tongue found hers and then he was slipping out of her and repositioning them so that she was flat on her back, with her legs spread wide open. He found a condom in the bedside table and she watched with rapt fascination—and desperate desire—as he slipped it over the crest of his erection, then all the way down the thick, long shaft, shiny with her juices.

"You're beautiful, Cole."

He went suddenly still between her thighs, a heartbeat away from plunging back into her wet heat. "You're not scared anymore?"

She blushed to remember how worried she'd been last night, how frightened she'd been of his size, his sensuality. When he'd undone her blindfold, the size of his erect penis made her blanch with shock, with the sure knowledge that she couldn't possibly take him inside without being torn in two.

It didn't occur to her to be anything but honest. "How can I be scared when you make me feel so good?"

His pupils, already dark, nearly doubled in size as he looked down at her nakedness, the way her thighs were spread open for him, the way her breasts shook and bounced as she reached for him.

"You make me feel good, too, Anna. So good I'm surprised the pleasure isn't killing me."

No one had ever wanted her like this. No one had ever looked at her with such dangerous heat. No one had ever tied her up and played with her body until she was begging, pleading, crying for release.

No one but Cole.

Her husband.

At the exact moment that she pulled his head down for a kiss, he drove into her pussy, hard and deep. She lost her exhale to his lungs and he took what was left of her breath with a searing kiss.

"Again. Just like that," she begged against his mouth.

But instead of granting her this wish, he took long, slow glides in, then out of her, one after the other.

"You're still too sore, too swollen." He grimaced as he pushed back inside. "I shouldn't even be taking you now. It's too soon. You aren't used to me, to my size."

Anna knew she should appreciate the care he was taking with her, the way he was trying to protect her from pain, but the pleasure streaking through her system had pain turning to ecstasy, need turning to desperation.

Last night when she'd been bound to the bed frame, she hadn't been able to control any part of their lovemaking. And Cole had been right—it was just what she needed to force herself to let go and embrace the greatest pleasure she'd ever known.

But this morning, the rules had changed.

She had changed.

And she would take what she wanted whether Cole thought she could handle it or not.

Reaching her hands around to hold onto his tight rear muscles, she thrust her hips up with all her might.

"Anna," he all but shouted as she buried him to the hilt, so far in that she could feel his balls pressing in tight to her butt cheeks. Both of them stilled completely, panted, moaned.

Oh God. He was in so deep, deeper than last night, and she suddenly realized just how much he had held back his own needs on their wedding night.

"Don't hold back, Cole." Her voice was as dark and heavy as his now.

"I don't want to hurt you, sweetheart."

She loved that he cared enough for her to want to protect her, but not now.

Not from this.

"Take me, Cole. Make me yours."

She emphasized her demands with the strong, tight pull of her arms and legs wrapping around his body.

He cursed, grimaced, obviously tried to fight for control. "Sweet Anna."

The heavy, hard weight of Cole's body rammed into her, pushing so far down into the mattress that she could almost feel the box spring beneath it. But instead of being frightened, instead of regretting her impulsive, fevered request, she relished their lovemaking, every thrust, every groan, the hard slap of damp flesh as they came together and pulled apart in perfect rhythm.

Her inner muscles were clenching down on him again, harder than ever before, but instead of any pain there was nearly impossible pleasure, so deep and pure she could do nothing more than close her eyes and hold on as Cole gripped her hips and rammed his thick shaft into her, pulling her nipple into his mouth to rake his teeth across the stiff peak.

The muscles across his back and hips were drawn tight, the tendons taut and bulging as she gently scraped her nails across his skin.

Her belly tightened, her breasts arched into his mouth, her clit swelled.

And then she exploded, every muscle in her body seeming to tighten, then release, as she flew higher and higher into the blinding sparks that Cole was shooting off all around her.

The power of her orgasm shocked her into opening her eyes and that was when she realized he was propping himself up, one strong arm on either side of her face. He was staring down at her with such wonder, such amazement, that her heart almost stopped beating.

"Cole."

She whispered his name, reached up to cup his beautiful face in her hands. Just as their lips touched, he stilled, tightened, grew even bigger within her slick walls. She wanted to feel him explode, wanted to know that she'd made him feel as good as he'd made her feel the night before.

"Come for me, Cole."

The same words from his lips had sent her over the edge only hours before. And now she was the one taking him there.

* * *

Cole hadn't thought anything could top the previous night, certainly not first-thing-in-the-morning sex. But feeling Anna's hands on his skin, her arms and legs wrapped around him, knowing her desire —rather than his knowledge of all the things he planned to teach her— was leading their dance ... hell, it was like nothing he'd ever known.

Cradling her in his arms, he rolled over to his back. Looking down at her, he saw that her eyes were closed and there was a smile on her lips.

"That was incredible."

He stroked her back and she moved closer, her head in the crook of his shoulder, breathing soft and even. He was amazed by everything about her. Her sweetness, how she managed to retain her innocence even after he'd been fucking her hard and deep, but especially the way she'd given him her trust.

All he'd been looking for was a good girl. Somehow, he'd gotten so much more.

Sunlight streamed in the windows. He didn't want to wait much longer before taking Anna to meet his grandmother. She was going to love his new wife. Who wouldn't?

The thought stopped him cold, his hand mid-stroke on Anna's back.

He couldn't spend all day—or even all morning—in bed with Anna. He needed to get them up and out the door ASAP. His grandmother had looked tired and pale the previous morning. How quickly could cancer spread? How much time did he have left?

Cole abruptly threw off the covers and got out of bed. Anna stared at him, the furrow between her eyebrows speaking to her confusion.

"We need to get going soon." He pulled her out of the bed,

more roughly than he intended. “Let’s go shower.”

Anna tugged her hand from his. “Why are you acting like this all of a sudden? Especially after we just ...” Her flushed cheeks filled in the rest of the sentence.

Fear and worry for his grandmother suddenly taking precedence over everything, he said, “I want to introduce you to my grandmother. She’s better in the morning.”

Anna’s face—which was even prettier in the light of day—immediately softened. Coming toward him, she put her hands back in his.

“I’d love to meet her, Cole.”

Using the moment to his advantage, he drew her across the room into the large, tiled bathroom. He couldn’t wait to spend some time with Anna in the huge Jacuzzi tub, was practically salivating at the thought of turning the jets onto her, watching her come apart beneath the pulsating streams of water he’d aim directly at her clit. But that ridiculously potent fantasy would have to wait.

He turned the shower on and when the water was warm enough, brought Anna under the spray. She reached for the shampoo and even though they needed to hurry, he plucked it from her fingers.

“I’ll wash you,” he said, each word gruffer than the one before.

His dick grew bigger with every stroke of his fingertips against her scalp, as he tilted her head back slightly and watched the soapy water stream down her spine and over her luscious ass.

“My God, you’re beautiful,” he said as he picked up a bar of soap and ran it over every inch of her soft skin.

She shivered against him, moaning softly as he soaped and rinsed her breasts, her arms, her belly, her legs, and then—finally—her sweet pussy.

Cole barely held onto his control as he grazed her clit with his fingertips, then pushed the soap all the way along her labia, from clit to anus.

Her legs all but buckled beneath her as he stroked her clean and he had to catch her in his arms to keep her from falling.

“How can I still want you?” she whispered into his chest. “How can I still need you after everything we’ve just done?”

There was no hope for it. Hating himself for taking any longer than he had to before bringing her to his grandmother, Cole simply couldn’t resist what Anna was offering.

Still holding her in his arms, he moved her so that her back was flat against the tiles. She gasped as she felt his erection pressed hard and thick against her belly.

"Hold onto my neck," he instructed her.

Her hands trembled as she complied, but he knew it wasn't nerves this time that had her shaky. It was pure, unfettered lust.

"Why?"

"Because I'm going to fuck you right here, right now, up against the wall in the shower."

Her tongue came out to lick at her lips, her teeth biting down on her full lower lip in uncertainty. Somewhere in the back of Cole's brain he knew he was pushing her too far, too fast, but he couldn't stop himself.

Not when he wanted Anna this badly.

Not when he'd been almost incoherent with lust since the moment he'd set eyes on her.

Not when even the previous two times he'd taken her hadn't done a damn thing to slake that desire.

"Wrap your legs around me and hold on tight, sweetheart."

Without waiting for her agreement—because he wasn't asking, he was demanding—in one swift move, he put his hands on her ass, and as she opened her legs to him, he lifted her up and slid her down onto his throbbing shaft.

Her head fell back, a moan of pleasure escaping her lips. Thanking God that she was such a quick learner, the next thing he knew, she was riding him like she'd been having stand-up sex in a bathroom all her adult life, her clit rubbing against his pelvic bone, her breasts against the hair on his chest.

"Oh God, yes, yes, yes!"

Cole had to grit his teeth to ride out her orgasm and keep from shooting into her as her pussy clenched and pulled at his cock.

His balls pulled in tight to his body, his abs tight, Cole knew he couldn't hold back his release another second. Pulling out of her wet, clasping heat on a roar, he thrust himself into her belly, streams of ejaculate coating her once-clean skin.

When it was all over, when he realized she was trying to get back down on the floor but he hadn't loosened his grip, Cole gently lowered her and washed her clean. She leaned against the wall, still panting as he quickly shampooed and soaped up. Turning off the water, he handed her a towel.

"Thank you."

Despite the fact that she'd been fucking him like a wild woman in the shower not five minutes ago, she sounded just as prim, just as innocent as she had the night before.

He was about to tell her how mind-blowing fucking her was when she made a sudden sound of dismay.

"My clean clothes are all back in my room."

"They were delivered last night."

"When? I didn't hear anyone knock on the door." Her eyes went big. "Oh no. They didn't come while we were..."

Cole barely hid his grin in time at her clear embarrassment. Still, he couldn't stop himself from teasing, "Come to think of it, we were pretty loud last night." He lowered his voice, made sure she held his gaze. "Especially when you were begging me to make you come."

Her face flamed again and he had to press a kiss to her sweet mouth.

"You're too easy, sweetheart."

Shooting him an irritated glance, she said, "I'm going to get dressed."

After she'd left the bedroom, Cole realized it was the first time he'd been alone since last night. Normally, when he was done fucking, he couldn't wait for the woman to go home and leave him alone. But even though Anna was only a room away, even though he could hear her unzipping her suitcase and pulling out clothes, she was too far away.

He didn't just want her in the same room.

He wanted her in his arms.

As he dressed, Cole forced himself to face what had happened on their wedding night, despite how much he'd rather keep his head in the sand over what Anna was making him feel.

Of course he'd wanted to give her pleasure. And he'd taken the responsibility she'd given him to show her true pleasure seriously. But at the same time, he'd been fighting against the strange feeling in his chest—a warmth he'd never felt for any other woman—and had thought that tying her up and doing kinky things to her would put some separation into sleeping with her.

But it had backfired.

Big time.

Because even as she'd been begging and pleading with him for release, he'd been the one dying. Just thinking about the way she'd been naked and stretched out and bound and blindfolded—and so damn sweet, through it all—had him hard again.

Because he hadn't known it could be like that either.

And he wasn't just talking about the sex.

Cole hadn't known he could feel that close to anyone.

Not until he'd met Anna.

Chapter Seven

"My grandmother is probably going to ask you all sorts of questions, like how we met. Let's change around a few of the details."

Still trying to catch her breath from the way Cole was shooting through the streets of Las Vegas in his sports car as if he were trying to win a race, Anna somehow managed to get a reply out through her clenched teeth.

"Which details?"

Cole shifted gears again and knocked the air she'd just sucked in back out of her lungs. "Most of them. I'd like to get our story straight before we get to the hospital."

They hit a straightaway and she was finally able to think clearly enough to hear the warning bells clanging in her head. A hundred questions shot through her mind all at once. She started with, "We need a story?"

His face was the picture of innocence—her first clue that something wasn't right. Until now, Cole had been nothing but wicked. And she'd loved every second of it. Innocence looked all wrong on him.

"My grandmother is from a different generation and I think it might be easier for her to accept our relationship if she thinks it's more than a quickie Vegas wedding."

The words *quickie Vegas wedding* grated at her, made her feel like nothing more than a cheap slut all of a sudden.

"Are you saying you want me to lie to your grandmother?"

A muscle jumped in Cole's jaw and his hand tightened on the gear shift. "Look, Anna, she's really sick. Stage four melanoma."

"Oh, Cole." Even though what he was saying wasn't sitting right with her, she had to put her hand over his, had to try to give him comfort.

"She raised me. Took care of me when anyone else would have put themselves first. All she's ever wanted is for me to be happy. To have a good life."

"She sounds amazing."

"She is. That's why I've got to fulfill her dying wish, Anna."

There was no logical reason for her to feel as if ice had just settled over her heart. Not when she was out in the middle of the desert with a man who had taught her the true meaning of pleasure. All she wanted was to rewind an hour, to go back to being in Cole's arms beneath the covers.

"What's her dying wish?"

Cole looked as tense as she'd ever seen him. "Jesus, there's no good way to say this." He grimaced, blowing out a hard breath. The muscles along his forearm were taut. "She wanted me to fall in love with a good girl. So I told her that I already did and that I was going to bring you to meet her this morning."

An icicle speared her chest, going so deep that for a moment she half expected to find blood on her shirt.

Pulling her hand from his, she turned away from him and focused her gaze on the flat road. His words from the night before came back at her: *Perfect. My sweet little schoolteacher.*

"Oh my God, that's why you picked me last night."

"Anna, sweetheart, don't take it like that."

She whirled to face him, her seat belt cutting into her skin. "Don't take it like the truth, you mean? God, I'm so stupid. So unbelievably, idiotically stupid. Of course you wouldn't have come over to me without an ulterior motive. You could have had anyone in that club." Her throat swelled, caught on her next words. "But you had to find a good girl for your grandmother—and I was the only one in the room wearing a halo."

Without warning, Cole drove off the side of the freeway into the dirt, causing a huge dust storm all over his previously shiny car. "Fine, so I picked you out of the crowd because you looked innocent." He was clearly angry, frustrated. "But that doesn't change what happened between us last night. That doesn't change the fact that we can't keep our hands off each other."

"Wrong. It changes everything."

"No. It doesn't change this."

He had their seat belts off and his mouth on hers so fast she couldn't stop her reaction to it, couldn't stop her tongue from mating with his, couldn't stop her whimper of desire from sounding into his car.

"Last night you said you didn't know it could be like this. It isn't, Anna. Not with anyone else. It's never been this hot. It's never been this good. Just with you."

She had to force herself to push away from his seductive words, from the heat that was wrapping itself around her all over again. The pain of what she'd just learned still spreading through her chest helped.

She'd trusted him.

And he'd betrayed that trust, even when he'd promised not to.

"I want to go get a divorce. Right now."

A possessive growl rumbled through his chest, reverberating off the walls of the car. "No."

"I'm not going with you to meet your grandmother."

"Like hell you aren't."

He moved to turn the key in the ignition, but fury made her faster and she ripped it from beneath his fingertips.

"I thought you were marrying me for me, that I was special in some way!"

His jaw jumped. "Jesus, Anna. I did. You are."

"No, you didn't. And I'm not. You picked me out of a crowd and took me to a wedding chapel so that you could give me to your grandmother as some sort of prize. The *perfect little schoolteacher* on a pedestal." She didn't bother to hold back the sarcasm in her words, simply didn't care anymore.

"I didn't force you to marry me, Anna." She started at the sudden change in his voice, from raw and frustrated to coolly calculating. "We'd just met. Barely done anything but kissed. So tell me, did you marry me for me? Did you marry me because I'm special in some way?" He paused, let his questions sink all the way in. "Or did you marry me for another reason entirely? Did you marry me because you wanted to put one over on your sisters? Because you were sick and tired of people thinking you didn't have any guts? Because you hated the fact that you'd never done anything crazy?"

She narrowed her eyes, knowing exactly what he was trying to prove. Well, it wasn't going to work. He'd hurt her. Badly.

And she wasn't going to forgive him, even if she already knew she'd never come apart like that in anyone else's arms.

"Don't turn my words around on me. You want me to lie to your grandmother. You want me to tell her that we're in—" She couldn't say the word, couldn't bring herself to voice such a huge lie.

Unfortunately, Cole had a scarily one-track mind. "You didn't want your sisters to meet me, did you? And you were so angry about everyone thinking you were innocent. We both know why you married me, don't we, Anna? But I'm not angry with you, am I? I'm happy, pleased that we both were able to get what we wanted. And that it was so damn good between us, so much better than I ever thought it could be."

"Take me back to the hotel."

"Be reasonable, sweetheart."

She suddenly hated the sound of the endearment that she'd once loved so much. "Don't call me that."

As if she hadn't said anything, he said, "We both had our reasons for marrying each other. How about we rejoice over our incredible chemistry instead of splitting hairs over the details?"

She looked at him as if she were seeing him for the very first time. Which, she supposed, she was. "You're serious, aren't you? You really think that's all it's going to take to get me to stay with you?"

His eyes narrowed. "No, I guess I should have known better. Fine. After we visit my grandmother, I'll take you to Tiffany and you can pick out anything you want. Money is no object."

She reeled back as if he'd slapped her. And the truth was, he might as well have for the pain his "offer" had just sent through her.

"I can't believe you just said that."

"Jesus, Anna, what am I doing wrong now?"

"You're an asshole. That's what's wrong." The curse felt strange on her tongue, but there was no other word for Cole, for the way he was behaving, for what he was implying. "But you know what the really amazing thing is?" Steam all but blew out of her ears. "Not that you just treated me like a whore. But that you don't even seem to realize you've done it."

An instant later, cool calm came over her, sealing her cells from Cole's heat. And from the pain. She should never have taken a risk with Cole, should never have let him take her to the edge, should never have jumped off while holding his hand.

She'd never make that mistake again.

Never.

In a perfectly rational voice, she said, "I understand if you'd like to see your grandmother this morning. I'll wait in the car, and when you're done we can go get a divorce." She put the key back in the ignition and waited for him to pull on to the road.

The air grew heavy and still as the seconds ticked down in silence. She wouldn't let herself notice the bright blue sky, the jackrabbit running across the empty road, wouldn't let herself feel anything at all.

"I'm sorry, Anna."

She forced herself to shrug as if she didn't care either way. "Okay."

It wasn't, of course. How could it be? But she absolutely refused to break down in Cole's car. At least not until he went into the hospital to see his grandmother and she was alone, with enough time to repair the damage before he returned.

"No, it isn't."

His words were soft and so genuine that they almost scaled the walls around her heart before she could halt their progress.

"You're right. I'm an asshole. The biggest one on the planet. And I hope one day you'll forgive me for saying what I said. Especially when I've never, not for one second, thought of you that way." He bit off a curse. "I know that your forgiveness will probably be a long time coming, but my grandmother can't wait for that."

She had to close her eyes and tighten her hands into fists if she was to have a prayer of resisting the plea she knew was coming.

"I'll do anything, grovel any way you want me to, if you'll just come see my grandmother with me this morning. Please, Anna. Not for me. Not because I deserve it. But because she's one of the best people I've ever known. And because she didn't deserve to be stuck with a grandkid like me."

It was his last sentence that broke her.

"I'll go," she said. "And then I want a divorce."

Chapter Eight

"You're even prettier than I thought you'd be." Anna was immediately enveloped in Eugenia Taylor's arms. "Such a beautiful girl for my little boy."

Thinking that Cole was anything but little—everywhere—Anna blushed and said, "It's very nice to meet you, Mrs. Taylor." Despite her illness, his grandmother was very pretty, with dark skin and exotic eyes. Anna suddenly had a flash of a baby girl with those same eyes in a tanned face.

No! She was only faking this meeting for his grandmother's sake and then they were going to get an immediate divorce. What was wrong with her, dreaming of children that looked like Cole's grandmother?

"We have a surprise for you, Grandma."

He reached for Anna's left hand and threaded his fingers through hers so that her diamond ring shone through. Despite everything he'd said to her in the car—despite the way he'd repeatedly hurt her—her body instinctively reacted to the brush of his skin against hers.

"We're married."

His grandmother's eyes flashed. "Why didn't you tell me yesterday?"

Anna could see where Cole got his fearsome scowl.

"We didn't plan it. But we just couldn't wait another day, Grandma."

His grandmother's intelligent eyes moved from his face to hers. "Are you pregnant, Anna?"

Anna shook her head so fast the room spun. "No. I couldn't be."

"What she means," Cole said quickly, "is that we both wanted to make our union legal before we started our family."

Anna could barely swallow the bile rising into her throat at the lies he was spinning out one after another to this wonderful woman in the hospital bed. God, if she'd only known how good he was at lying when she'd met him, she never would have married him.

At least, that's what she tried to convince herself.

Because the alternative—that she wouldn't have been able to resist him, no matter what—wasn't something she wanted to believe about herself.

"Isn't that right, sweetheart?"

Anna tried not to flinch at the endearment. "Yes. Right." She forced something she hoped resembled a smile.

His grandmother's eyes narrowed slightly, but then she smiled. "I want to hear everything. How did you meet? When did you know that you were meant to be together forever?"

Anna swallowed hard at *forever.* Cole was a heck of a lot better at lying that she was. She didn't dare respond first.

"I saw her across a crowded room."

Well, that much was true. Anna barely held back a snort.

"She had the most beautiful eyes I'd ever seen. The same blue-green as the ocean."

Anna couldn't stop herself from looking at him, then.

"But so much prettier. I knew right then and there that I wanted to marry her."

Cole's grandmother sighed with pleasure. "How lovely."

Anna silently cursed herself for falling under his spell again. He was too good at this, too good at making it all sound so romantic.

"Our first kiss sealed the deal."

His grandmother raised an eyebrow. "Is that so, Anna?"

Stuck between a rock and a hard place, unable to deny it, but not wanting to confirm it either, Anna simply said, "Your grandson is very persuasive."

Especially, she thought with a flush she couldn't contain, when her wrists and ankles had been bound and he'd been driving her wild with more pleasure than she'd ever thought she could feel.

"Tell me about yourself, honey."

Anna could almost feel Cole's silent sigh of relief that his grandmother had bought his story and was moving on. Barely restraining herself from elbowing him in the ribs simply for the pleasure it would bring her to hear him grunt in pain—but that would be immature and she was never immature—she said, "I'm a first-grade teacher."

"Isn't that perfect, Grandma?"

There was no helping it. Anna's eyes rolled. And she snorted aloud. And she said, "I hate it when you say that. Like I'm some sort of prize instead of a flesh-and-blood person."

"That's right, honey, he needs someone to give him hell. Women have been coddling him for too long, giving him everything he wants. You tell him."

Anna's eyes widened at his grandmother's approval and she quickly said, "I'm one of five girls."

His grandmother's smile nearly broke her heart. "I wish I could see Cole surrounded by little girls." Anna found herself blinking back tears as Eugenia turned to him. "I always knew you'd be a wonderful husband and father. The very best, just like your grandfather. Just like your father was before the accident."

And in that moment, as Cole's mouth tightened in pain, as sorrow filled his eyes, it didn't matter what he'd said to her in the car. It didn't matter that he'd lied to her every moment since they'd met.

All that mattered was comforting him.

She brushed his jaw with the fingertips of her free hand and he turned into it just enough that she could feel the pressure of his cheek against her palm.

"I'll take care of him for you."

The promise left her lips before she could stop it, before she'd even known it was on its way.

His grandmother put her hand on top of their entwined fingers. "Thank you for loving my baby, Anna. It's all I've ever wanted."

* * *

"Oh God, I shouldn't have done that." Anna wrapped her arms around her waist. She felt nauseated. Dizzy with remorse. "Your grandmother didn't deserve any of those lies, but especially mine."

Cole pulled her out of the hallway and in through the nearest door, a linen supply closet.

"You did a good thing, Anna. You made her happy. Just like I knew you would."

"But none of it was true."

"All of it is true."

"You just twisted your story to fit the situation."

"Damn it, Anna, I did see you across a crowded room. You do have the most beautiful eyes I've ever seen. And we really are married."

And she supposed he was right, all of those things were true. Especially since not once had he mentioned *love* anywhere in there, not to her, not to his grandmother.

So, then, why was she still stupid enough to long so desperately for his love?

"I can't do that again, Cole. I can't stand pretending to be someone I'm not." She hugged herself tighter. "I made good on my side of the deal. Now it's time to make good on yours." She lifted her gaze to his and held it. "I want a divorce. Today."

"What if my grandmother finds out?"

Anna shook her head. "No one knows we're married, so no one will know we got a divorce. I'm sorry. I know how hard it must be for you, but I can't keep bending my moral code for you."

"You're right. You shouldn't make the decision to stay married to me for her. Or even for me." He paused, dropped his gaze to her mouth with such desire her traitorous lips actually tingled. "You should do it for yourself."

"How could I possibly want to stay in a fake marriage to you for myself?"

The supply room suddenly seemed too small as he moved closer and she backed into a laden metal shelf.

"Remember what you said to me last night, sweet Anna, about how you'd never even had the chance to do something crazy that you could regret in the morning?"

"Well, I sure have now."

"And was it enough?"

"Yes."

"Now you're the one who isn't telling the truth, aren't you?"

"You don't know what you're talking about."

He didn't come any closer, didn't press his hard body against hers, simply brushed the back of one hand against the side of her neck.

"Now that Pandora's box is open, you're wondering what else there is in there, aren't you?"

Yes.

"No."

"Tell me, sweet Anna, how has lying to yourself about what

you need worked so far? How many nights have you spent like the one we had last night? How many do you think you'll have if you run now?"

Her breath was coming too fast. Her body was heating up too much. Her brain was scrambling, leaving her without a retort.

Without the strength to do what she knew she needed to do.

Without the will to do the right thing.

"You want to know crazy. I know crazy." Now his voice was a low, seductive whisper against her skin. "Last night was nothing, Anna."

Unbidden, a movie reel of their lovemaking played in her head. God, the things he'd done to her so far had already blown her mind.

There was more?

She'd never survive it.

"All I'm asking is that you stay until—" He obviously couldn't finish his sentence. "If you stay—if you let my grandmother think that our marriage is a real one—I promise to make it worth your while."

"I told you, I don't want your money or jewelry."

"I'm not talking about those things, sweetheart. I'm talking about pleasure. About coming so hard you black out. About finally experiencing everything you've been waiting for and wondering about."

"No."

She pushed away from him and blindly fought for the door. He was asking her to become a slave to her body. To reckless desire. He was asking her give up her morals in exchange for more pleasure than she could imagine.

And she'd been about to say yes.

"Wait a second, Anna. Don't go out there. Not yet. We need to talk first, figure things out."

Did he really think she was going to turn around and let him "convince" her some more? She was done talking.

She pushed through the heavy door and walked into a wall of photographers...and suddenly realized why he hadn't wanted her to leave the building.

She'd forgotten that Cole was a famous football player.

And their marriage was big news.

Big enough news that if they went straight from the hospital to the courthouse to get a divorce, his grandmother would be reading about it on the front page of the newspaper's afternoon edition.

Frozen in place, Anna was actually glad to feel Cole's warm arms encircle her waist from behind. The way she sank into the relative security of his body wasn't an act for the cameras.

He pressed a kiss to her cheek and she heard his faint urging, “Smile, baby,” a split-second before he told the crowd, “Last night, Anna made me the happiest man on earth.”

And then, as flashbulbs blinded her and journalists pelted them with questions, Cole maneuvered the two of them across the parking lot and into his car.

Chapter Nine

"I need to go home, Cole."

"I thought we had a deal."

Anna blew out a frustrated breath. As they'd driven back to the Wynn, they'd agreed that she'd remain his wife for as long as she had to. Now they were back at the hotel and she was staring down the barrel of who-knew-how-long as Mrs. Cole Taylor.

"We do have a deal," she said. Although neither of them had spoken again about what he'd said to her in the supply room.

I'm talking about pleasure. About coming so hard you black out. About finally experiencing everything you've been waiting for and wondering about.

"But I have a job." And a family that was going to demand an explanation.

"Tell the school you're on your honeymoon. They can get a sub."

More tempted than she would ever admit—especially to herself—she said, "Maybe that's how things work in your world, but for us normal people we either go to work Monday through Friday or they give our job to someone who will."

"I don't want to leave my grandmother."

Every time she'd convinced herself to be good and irritated with him, he said something that pulled hard on her heartstrings.

"I'm sorry, Cole, I would stay if I could." Sadly enough, she was telling the truth. Fake marriage or not, she was powerfully—stupidly—drawn to the man standing in front of her.

His phone rang. "It's her," he told Anna, before picking up. "Yes, I know she's beautiful. Very sweet, Grandma. I knew you'd love her."

His eyes ate her up as he spoke and the only way to hide her flush—and her growing desire—was to bend over her bag and pretend to pack. Even though she'd finished earlier that morning.

"The team will survive without me."

She lifted her head at his abrupt change of tone.

"I'm staying here." He paused, listened, frowned. "It's my life, Grandma, not yours."

Anna lifted her hand to hide her smile. It really was something to watch such a big, strong, tough man be such a softie. All for a woman he loved dearly.

"Fine, I'll play the damn game Sunday. But I'm flying right back."

Another pause, one where he looked like one of her first graders who knew he'd spoken out of turn.

"Sorry, ma'am," he said, and then, "Well, if you want me to stay in San Francisco with the team for practices, then I want you transferred to a nearby hospital." His face was like thunder. "We'll talk about this again soon."

He all but threw the phone down on the couch.

"Grandma is sending me back to California."

Anna knew she shouldn't be happy to hear it.

But she was.

* * *

It was all too much for her. The flight home in first class. The knowledge that she'd soon have to explain her rash marriage to not only her family, but also her friends and colleagues. All the while knowing that it would be coming to an end in the near future—and then she'd have to figure out how to explain her divorce.

But mostly, Anna was overwhelmed by being so close to Cole for so many hours. He was always touching her, a thousand little caresses that slowly but surely drove her out of her mind.

Tucking a strand of hair behind her ear.

Placing his hand at the small of her back to guide her through throngs of photographers outside both airports.

Brushing her shoulder and arm with his during the flight, despite the fact that her first-class seat was the size of a small ocean liner.

Thankful that James was already waiting for them just outside Arrivals, Anna was glad for Cole's large frame protecting her from the bulk of the flashbulbs.

"I didn't realize football players were so well known."

"Most women would be thrilled by my fame. And fortune."

She scooted as far away from him as she could in the backseat. "I'm a good girl, remember? We don't care about that stuff."

She didn't bother to hold in her bitterness. Why should she? It wasn't like she had anything left to lose.

Except for her heart.

Anna shoved the mute button down on the stupid little voice in her head. She could feel Cole's eyes on her, just by the way her skin was heating up.

"I know it's strange, but you get used to the fame after a while."

But Anna wasn't sure she would. Hopefully the pictures and the short statement Cole had given the paparazzi about Anna making him "the happiest man on earth" would be enough.

"Damn it. I expected them to figure out where you lived, but not this fast."

Anna realized a crowd of journalists were on the sidewalk in front of her apartment. "Why would they care about me? I'm a nobody. I'm not important."

He was in her face in an instant, gripping her shoulders in his strong hands. "You're beautiful. And sweet. And intelligent. You're very special, Anna."

Looking into his eyes as the rough tone of his words pummeled her, she realized he was angry. Because of what she'd said...about herself.

He rapped on the shaded window that separated them from James. "Keep going. We'll head straight to my house."

"But I need to go home." She poked a finger into Cole's chest. "And don't you dare say you'll send someone for my things again." His eyebrows rose at her no-nonsense tone of voice. "Please park outside my apartment, James."

James made a U-turn. "We'll be there in just a moment, Anna."

She straightened her shoulders, ran a hand over her hair, then opened the door and stepped onto the sidewalk. "Hello. Good afternoon. Excuse me."

She carefully walked past the camera-laden strangers, keeping her smile firmly on her face. She could feel Cole a step behind her, knew without looking that he was barely keeping a lid on it. She refused to let her hand shake as she put her key in the door.

She had barely closed—and bolted—her front door when Cole spun her around and pressed her against it. He hunkered over her, his eyes flaming.

"Damn it, you'll listen to me next time."

She could feel his thick erection pressing into her body and even though he had no right to treat her with such disrespect, her body instantly responded with a flood of arousal, her breasts peaking beneath her bra and shirt.

"No, next time you'll ask me what I want to do before making a unilateral decision. And you'll heed my answer."

His dark, sinful eyes moved from her eyes to her mouth, then back up again. "Are you talking back to me, sweet Anna?"

She couldn't stop staring at his mouth. "Get used to it." The throbbing between her thighs had turned into a deep ache.

"What happened to my good girl?" His mouth was now so close to hers that she could smell the mint from his toothpaste.

"Don't you remember?" she asked in a voice that was barely more than a whisper. "You tied her up and played with her."

Cole's mouth found hers on a desperate groan, his tongue pushing past her lips as he took her kiss. "I need you. Now." His hands were already on the button of her pants, his hands pushing down past her panties to the wet warmth that waited for his touch. Always. But he wasn't the only one ripping at clothes, because her hands were on his jeans, shoving down the zipper and then the waistband of his boxers.

She gripped his penis, thick and hard, thrilled at the feel of him in her hands, more aroused than she could believe simply at the knowledge that someone wanted her this much.

No, not just someone.

Cole.

Cole could have anyone, the most beautiful women in the world. But he wanted her.

She didn't know what possessed her to do it, but suddenly it was the most natural thing in the world to drop to her knees and put her mouth over him.

"What the hell are you doing now, Anna?"

His words were hard, but his fingers had already threaded through her hair. Who would have thought that she had it in her to turn a man like Cole inside out? Certainly not her. And, judging by his response to the slow swirl of her tongue under the rim of his head, the way he groaned like a man who couldn't believe he was giving in rather than leading their dance, definitely not him.

She would have smiled around his shaft if she'd been able to, but he was more than a mouthful and her jaw was opened as wide as it could go, her lips completely stretched around his beautiful penis.

She suctioned him deeply before letting him go with a loud pop. Licking her lips, she looked up at him mischievously.

"Just what it looks like. I'm sucking my husband's cock. And enjoying myself immensely."

His large hands came under her so fast she didn't have time to react. "Bedroom."

"Through the kitchen."

Her drapes were closed, but they were fairly sheer and she knew someone might see Cole carrying her through the house, their pants partially undone.

But as he held her against his chest, and she pressed her palm to the strong, steady beat of his heart, she simply didn't care. The only thing she cared about was making love to her husband. The fact that it was only a temporary marriage made her even hungrier for him, made her want to squeeze every second of pleasure out of being with him.

"Don't forget our deal."

"Which one?"

She pressed a kiss to his Adam's apple. "The one where you make me come so hard I black out."

He dropped her onto her bed. "Get those clothes off before I rip them off."

She tried her best, but it wasn't easy to focus on herself when he was revealing his perfect, muscular body as one piece of clothing after another fell to the floor. She was still trying to get her jeans off when he came at her and yanked them off. Her shirt was next, the rending of the thin silk the only sound in the room apart from their heavy panting.

"So damn gorgeous." His mouth came down over her belly, his tongue dipping against the small indentation. "So damn soft." One quick yank and her panties were gone. "So damn sweet."

And then his tongue was there, licking, tasting, teasing, swirling, and she was arching into his mouth, already so aroused that it took nothing more than the pressure of his lips around her clit and the smallest suction to send her flying over the edge.

She was still flying when he came over her and pressed her thighs further apart with his knees.

But her orgasm hadn't taken the edge off her need. It had only made her hungrier, more desperate for Cole.

Not to mention slightly disappointed that he hadn't let her finish what she'd started, on her knees, with her mouth and hands on him.

"I wanted you to come in my mouth, Cole."

Using his surprise to her advantage, she used every ounce of strength she had to twist and roll them over so that he was the one on his back looking up at her. He gripped her hips and tried to lift her over his shaft. The head of his penis slipped just inside her slick opening and it felt good, so incredibly good that she almost gave in to his lead.

But something had snapped inside Anna in the car on the way to the hospital, when she'd realized that Cole had lied to her. Or maybe it was before that, when he'd tapped into her secret desires in his bedroom.

She was sick and tired of letting everyone else take the lead in her life.

From here on out, she was taking charge.

"Here's how it's going to be," she said in a deadly serious voice. "You are going to let go of me and I am going to finish what I started in my foyer."

His fingers tightened on her hips.

"Later, Anna. I need to be inside you. Now."

His demanding words caused a new flood of arousal to pool between her legs.

No, damn it. She was going to hold firm, for once!

"Move your hands, Cole."

His cock twitched against her and she almost sank down onto him out of pure feminine instinct, but then he said, "Yes, ma'am."

She could still feel the imprint of his hands on her skin even after he'd removed them. "Put them above your head and keep them there until I tell you otherwise."

He didn't move for a long moment and she felt a smile move on her lips. She'd never played with anyone like this in bed, had never fought for dominance with a man, had never even known the need to be on top.

And in charge.

"This won't happen again, Anna. So you'd better enjoy the hell out of it."

"Oh, yes, it will," she replied, and then, "And I'm sure planning on it."

Very reluctantly shifting herself from his groin, she leaned down and pressed a kiss to his shoulder, moving slowly down his chest to the faint dusting of hair over his nipple. She'd never paid much attention to men's nipples before, but the dark circles on Cole's chest demanded her attention, her appreciation.

She licked across the already taut tip and it came alive beneath her tongue. He gripped her back, his thumbs working to find her nipples.

She lifted her head from his chest. "I'm going to get something to tie you up pretty soon if you're not careful."

His reaction was instantaneous. And fierce. "Like hell. You're not tying me up."

She raised an eyebrow. "Wanna bet?"

He groaned and pinched his eyes shut, his hips seeming to move off the bed on their own. "You're killing me."

"Too bad." She moved up the bed and picked up one of his hands. She wrapped his fingers around a section of her pewter bed frame. "If you need to hold onto something, hold onto this."

"You're pushing it, sweetheart."

She shifted back over him, letting her hair brush over his neck and shoulders and chest, loving the way his muscles rippled in response.

"Ooooh, I'm scared."

And the fact was, there was a little fear there. Just enough to keep her on the edge of her seat. She had no idea how far he'd let her push him. Just as she had no idea how far she could push.

But boy, was it fun figuring all of that out. Shockingly so.

She swirled her tongue around the nipple she'd thus far neglected and the entire bed moved and groaned as he gripped at the bed frame with both hands. Using her tongue to guide her explorations, she roamed down his body, tasting the indentations between his incredible abdominal muscles.

Every muscle, every sinew, every tendon was tensed.

"Seems like you're having a hard time relaxing," she murmured against the dark line of hair that trailed from his belly button down towards his cock. "I'm thinking maybe I should blindfold you."

When his growl came, she didn't bother hiding her smile of pure feminine pleasure. How had she gone this long without knowing the thrill of holding a man sexually captive?

It was beyond incredible.

"You don't like that idea very much, do you, Cole?"

"You have no idea how close you are to the edge, sweet Anna."

The unveiled threat in his voice sent a wave of intense desire through her. "Close enough to make you black out, I hope."

She knew he would try to grab her. But before he could, she opened her mouth wide and sucked his cock inside. Using what she'd learned the previous night about bypassing her gag reflex, she tilted her neck slightly and relaxed the tight muscles until her nose was pressed into his pelvic bone.

She was mesmerized by his taste—his pre-come was salty and sweet all at the same—and his scent. So clean, so distinctive. Again and again, she took the long, thick length of his shaft into her mouth and throat, working the base with her hand on every outward thrust.

She'd loved sucking him last night. She loved it even more now, hearing his wild groans of pleasure, his heated praise at how wet and soft and tight her mouth was around his dick.

A hot splash of fluid erupted from his thick head and she greedily licked it up.

"It's too damn good," came a split-second before he pulled her mouth off his cock and lifted her pussy onto it.

She'd known all along that he wouldn't let her take him all the way over the edge in her mouth—not yet, anyway—so instead of fighting him, she gladly sank down onto his thick, throbbing shaft with a deep sigh of pleasure.

"So perfect," he said as his hands moved from her hips to cup her breasts. "So damn pretty."

Using her thigh muscles to propel her up and down over his cock, she rode Cole like a star jockey. Sweat dripped between her breasts and he lifted his head to lick at a rivulet in the center of her chest, along her breastbone.

The rough stroke of his tongue in such an unexpectedly sensual spot sent her into a climax she hadn't even realized was coming. Her inner muscles pulled and clenched at his thick shaft and she ground her clit into his pelvic bone to prolong the incredible waves of pleasure.

Somewhere in there she realized he was growing even harder inside of her, that he was thrusting harder.

At the very last second, he pulled out of her, his semen spurting against her belly as he ground himself against her. But Anna hadn't forgotten what she'd wanted earlier—what he'd taken away from her when he'd had her ride him instead.

A moment later, she had him in her mouth. And this time, instead of pushing away, he helped her take his still rock-hard shaft deeper into her throat.

It was the first time she'd ever tasted herself on a man's flesh. Her musk was all mixed up with Cole's essence, but instead of being disgusted by what she was doing, she was filled with a surprising satisfaction instead.

"Anna."

Her name was a plea on his lips, and she was shocked to realize that his cock was actually growing between her lips, against her tongue.

Spurred on by this realization, she was just getting down to business when she felt his hands on her hips again. She fought to resist him—this time she was getting what she wanted, no matter what—but then she realized he wasn't pulling her off, he was simply rearranging her so that his cock was still in her mouth.

And her pussy was directly over his face.

Despite everything she'd done with him over the past twenty-four hours—oh God, it hadn't even been that much time, had it?—despite the fact that she was sucking on his penis as if it were a popsicle on a scalding hot day, being exposed to Cole in this way pushed every one of her shy buttons back into overdrive.

Quickly sliding her mouth off his shaft, she said, "Cole, you don't have to do that," at the same time that she tried to move her thighs from where they were pressed against his ears.

"Oh yes, I do."

His response came a split second before his tongue swept between her folds. Part of her wanted to jump off the bed and lock herself in the bathroom in embarrassment. The other part wanted to grind down onto his lips, force him to plunge his tongue deeper.

His hips lifted as she tried to decide, his cock-head probing her lips, and she instinctively opened back up for him, taking him onto her tongue. And then, as if he knew she was still on the verge of running, he took the decision away from her with a long, slow slide of his fingers inside of her, curling them into a vibrantly sensitive patch of flesh deep inside her vagina.

She whimpered around his cock and arched into his fingers, inadvertently pressing her clit harder against his tongue at the same time. Apprehension quickly morphed into nearly unbearable excitement as he captured the swollen bud between his lips and sucked.

Blood rushed between her legs, making her lightheaded and gasping around his cock. But instead of letting her up for air, he only thrust deeper down her throat. And amazingly, that out-of-control feeling was what sent her over the edge yet another time. Her third climax was so powerful that the firm pressure of a large hand on her thigh holding her still was the only thing that could have kept her where he had her, his tongue flat and hard against her clit, his fingers plunging deeply into her wet canal.

Contractions continued to rip through her when she got her first salty taste of Cole, one long shot deep in her throat. Frenzied sounds of licking and sucking and moaning reverberated through her small bedroom as she tried desperately to focus on pleasuring him the way he'd pleasured her, but, oh God, it was so hard to focus on anything other than the way his tongue and fingers were still tormenting her sensitive flesh.

Finally, she lifted her mouth from him and tried to move back into a normal position on the bed. But he wasn't quite done with her, holding her still for one more sinful kiss of his lips against her pussy.

"Cole," she begged, "please."

"Want another?"

He followed up the offer by a seductive lash of his tongue against her labia.

"Cole." She moaned his name this time and even she wasn't sure what she was asking for.

His chuckle was warm and evocative against her incredibly aroused, sensitive flesh. And then, finally, he set her free, shifting out from between her legs.

"Looks like I'm developing a serious sweet tooth."

His grin was wolfish—satisfied and full of ownership. Her heart clenched, even though she knew better. Yes, Cole made her feel good. Yes, she enjoyed being with him.

But that didn't mean she could let herself fall for him.

She needed to remember at all times that he was using her to make his grandmother happy.

She needed to make sure all she did was use him right back.

She needed to make sure she didn't fall in love.

She scrambled off the bed, grabbing a blanket that had fallen off the bed in their frantic lovemaking. "I have some things to get ready for school on Monday."

He raised an eyebrow. "You trying to kick me out?"

She started to shake her head, then realized that after the things they'd just done to each other, there really was no point in lying to him. "Yes."

He shifted off the bed and the quick swelling of disappointment in her stomach at the thought of him actually leaving surprised her.

"I'll help you with your suitcase."

Maybe it was all the brain cells she'd lost when her brain exploded from three intense orgasms, but she wasn't following. "I can unpack my bag just fine on my own, thanks."

"It's going to hurt my feelings soon, you know."

"What is?"

"The way you keep forgetting that we're married, sweet Anna."

She wrapped the blanket tighter around herself and took a step backward. "I haven't forgotten."

"Then why don't you seem to understand that you're moving in with me?"

"No."

Entirely without her permission, he opened up her closet, found a larger suitcase, and threw it on the bed. "People expect a new wife to live with her husband." He yanked open her dresser, grabbed a handful of her underwear, and tossed it into the bag.

"Stop doing that." She gathered up her underwear, accidentally loosening her hold on the blanket. "Has it even occurred to you to ask me first before you make a decision about something?"

"My grandmother would know something was up in an instant if the papers reported me leaving here without you."

"I'm sick and tired of you using your grandmother as your excuse for every stupid thing you do!"

She all but clamped her hand over her mouth, the blanket dropping all the way to the floor. Not only did she already know that Eugenia was the entire reason for their relationship, not only did she know that Cole would have never, ever picked her out of a crowd if he hadn't been looking for a good girl—but she also knew how deeply he was hurting over his grandmother's illness.

"I'm sorry." She wanted so badly to take back her careless words. "I know how much you love her."

She was surprised to find him standing in front of her, one finger tipping her chin up so that she was meeting his dark and serious eyes. She was naked, now, but he didn't look away.

"My grandmother has nothing to do with the fireworks between us, Anna. While we're married, you're going to be in my bed every single night."

Still trying to find a loophole, she pointed to the window where the last rays of light were still peeking through her blinds. "It's not night yet."

She waited for his stubborn response, waited for him to tell her it was nonnegotiable.

"I want you with me, Anna. More than I've wanted anything in a very long time." He looked as serious as she'd ever seen him, totally earnest. Honest in his desires, both prurient and otherwise. "Please come home with me, sweetheart. Stay with me. Let me take you back to my bed and give you all the loving you deserve."

Oh no.

Anna knew exactly how he meant "loving." He was talking about sex, about what they'd been doing in her bedroom and in his apartment in Las Vegas.

But her heart—her stupid, pathetic, rapidly pounding heart—was doing everything it could to ignore the truth.

And it was her heart, not her brain, that made her drop her underwear back in the suitcase and say, "I need the matching bras, too."

His answering smile was the most beautiful thing she'd ever seen.

Oh no.

Chapter Ten

Anna looked at his house and said, "You really should have had me sign a pre-nup."

Not only was Cole known as one of the meanest men in the NFL, he was also one of the surest footed. Nonetheless, Anna's crazy statement had him tripping over his feet.

"Say that again."

Clearly unaware of his dangerous reaction to what she'd said, she gestured to his huge stainless steel and granite kitchen, out the sliding glass doors to his infinity pool and sloping green lawn. "All this must be worth a fortune. When your lawyer or manager or whoever it is that works for you finds out about our marriage, they're going to lose it in a serious way."

"Well then, maybe I won't ever let you go."

Her eyes widened in surprise, making him realize what he'd just said.

He didn't want to let her go. Not now. Not ever.

Jesus, what the hell was he saying? What the fuck was he thinking?

Her taste, her sweet little whimpers as she came, the wonder in her innocent eyes as she took him into her mouth—clearly, they were all fucking with his head.

"We both know I'm going, Cole. After you don't need me anymore."

Yes, he knew that was their agreement. One he'd thought he was happy with.

"You won't even take jewelry, Anna. I'm not worried about you coming after my house."

But instead of agreeing with him, she frowned. "But you don't know anything about me."

He couldn't keep away from her, had to move closer. "You sure about that? Seems to me I've learned quite a bit about you since last night."

Her beautiful face flushed. "I'm not talking about sex."

"Sure you are, sweetheart. You can't hide from your sensuality anymore. I won't let you."

"I'm not hiding from anything." She thrust her chin up into the air, putting her lips even closer to his.

He moved even closer. "My sweet little liar. Don't you know you give yourself away every time you look at me like that—like you'll die if I don't kiss you in the next five seconds?"

Her eyes widened again, but this time desire trumped her surprise, and he had to kiss her. Her mouth opened for his, her tongue meeting him halfway.

Cole loved fucking as much as any other guy. More, probably, given the rampant opportunities in his line of work. But usually after he'd come a couple of times, he was pretty much done for a while. At least until the next day.

Not this time.

Not with Anna.

For some reason, just looking at her, just talking to her, teasing her, had him wanting her so bad he was about to bust through his zipper. She made him feel insatiable to the point that he knew he could easily spend the rest of the night taking her again and again. Hell, the only reason he could see to get out of bed at any point in the near future was because he had a job to do out on the field Sunday.

Which meant they had a good twelve hours to fill until then.

But the way she'd said, "You don't know anything about me," bothered him. "Where were you born?"

Her body stiffened in clear surprise. "Why?"

"Tell me, sweetheart. Where were you born?"

"Palo Alto."

Noting that she hadn't moved far from home, her apartment barely an hour from her childhood home, he asked, "College?"

"Stanford."

He wasn't surprised to hear that his sweet little sex goddess was carrying around a big brain too. Intelligence sparkled from her ocean eyes.

"Major?"

"Education."

"Favorite color?"

"Yellow."

He had to smile against her lips, where he'd been asking his questions. He loved talking to her like this, right on the verge of a kiss, knowing he could take her mouth, devour her at any time.

"Hobbies?"

"Reading."

"Any ex-husbands?"

She tried to pull away from him. "No!"

He tightened his hold on her, was glad to feel her relax back into his arms. "I know you have four sisters. Any brothers?"

"No."

He knew her age and birthday from the marriage license they'd filled out. "Favorite movie?"

"*Hoosiers*."

This time he was the one shifting in surprise. "A basketball movie?"

She grinned. "Basketball is just one facet of the story. It's actually a very moving portrayal of second chances and overcoming racism and finding real love."

He grinned back at the woman he'd married. She was just so likeable.

And so damn pretty.

"Your turn. But let's do it backwards. Movie?"

"*Pretty Woman*." Her eyes sparkled. "Are you laughing at my answer?"

"No." A giggle erupted. "Okay, yes. A little bit. It was a great movie, but you're such a guy."

"What guy wouldn't like the part where Vivian waited for Edward at his dining table wearing only a tie and spike heels?"

"Perv." She smacked his chest, but she didn't try to move out of his arms. "Brothers or sisters?"

He shook his head. "I wish."

She paused for a moment, her eyes softening, her fingers unconsciously stroking his biceps. "Ex-wives?"

"Hell, no."

She raised an eyebrow at that. "Hobbies."

"Crushing the offense."

She cocked her head to the side. "What does that mean?"

"I'm a linebacker, sweetheart. My job is making sure no one

gets through the line."

"What about your spare time? What do you like to do when you're not playing football?"

He grinned wickedly. "How about I show you again right now?"

"Cole!" She smacked his shoulder. "Apart from that."

He shrugged. "Helping out a teammate's camp for kids and doing some reading with a literacy program."

Cole was used to people looking at him like he was a walking bank account. Like he was a hero, a sports god. But no one but his grandmother had ever looked at him like this, like she saw something inside him that pleased her.

Anna's mouth was a light brush of pleasure against his. "Favorite color?"

He licked the curve of her lower lip, made her shiver against him as her nipples hardened into his chest. "Green."

It sounded like she was having some trouble breathing evenly as she asked, "College?"

"University of Las Vegas."

"Major?"

"Football."

She gave him a hard look. "Do you ever think about anything else?" He shot her another wicked glance and she quickly said, "Never mind. Forget I asked. But apart from football, what classes did you like best?"

"Probability. Statistics." Jesus, why was he telling her these things? "It's one of the reasons I like football so much. Coming up with plays is a lot like the problems I used to do in class."

Her answering smile stole his breath. "I thought you all just ran around and jumped on each other."

"You're so sweet. So naïve. Good thing there's nothing I'd rather do than teach my sweet little schoolteacher all the things she doesn't know."

He cupped her ass and pulled her tighter into him, ready to move onto the next part of getting to know each other better.

"Wait," she said breathlessly, "I still don't know where you were born."

"Vegas."

"What about your parents?"

He gave her his standard answer. "I don't have that many memories of them."

"How old were you when they passed away?"

He'd been asked this question a thousand times at press conferences and interviews, but never with such palpable concern.

Never by anyone who really cared.

"Five."

"Cole." She stroked his cheek, her fingertips feathering pleasure across his skin. "I'm so sorry."

He forced a shrug. "My grandmother took care of me. She was great."

"You're great, Cole."

And then, finally, he was back to where they started, with his mouth a breath away from hers.

The chorus to *I Just Called To Say I Love You* played from her purse.

"Oh no. I need to get that."

She pushed out of his arms and pulled the phone out of her purse on the kitchen counter. "Hi, Mom. I was going to call, I swear. It all happened so fast." She shot him a wild look. "You want us to come over? Right now?"

Cole fought back panic. Meeting the parents wasn't something he did. Hell, there'd been no chance of that from one-night stands.

But he'd married Anna.

And her family wanted to meet her husband.

Fuck.

It had all seemed so simple in the club, when he was kissing her, and holding her, and looking for a Hail Mary pass that would fill his grandmother's dying wish.

First the paps. Now Anna's parents and siblings.

What would be next?

Anna looked so panicked—he hated to see her doing anything but smiling or crying out in ecstasy—that when she sent him a silent question with her eyes, he found himself nodding.

"Okay. Yes, we can come. Back in San Francisco. No we haven't eaten." Her eyes grew bigger. "Everyone's going to be there?" She swallowed hard. "Fantastic." She put the phone down. "We're having dinner with my family." She put her face in her hands. "What am I going to tell them?"

Shit. He'd asked her to lie to his grandmother. But he couldn't ask her to lie to her own family.

"The truth."

She lifted her head. "Are you kidding?"

"I know how important family is, Anna. I'm not going to ask you to lie to them."

One corner of her mouth lifted, but it wasn't a smile. It was a grimace. "I appreciate that, Cole. But I can't tell them the truth."

"Why? You think they'd tell the press that this isn't a real marriage?"

Pain flashed in her eyes. She blinked and it was gone. "No. They would never betray me like that. I can't tell them the truth because they'll think I'm a desperate fool who had to marry the first man who asked."

Hating to hear her talk about herself like that, he had to pull her back into his arms before he set her straight. "No one who knows you would ever think you were a desperate fool."

He felt her relax in his arms and let himself enjoy holding her. Until now, he'd been totally focused on sex. But this, the warm, soft comfort of her, knowing he was comforting her too, was surprisingly nice.

She lifted her head. "I have a feeling things could get pretty messy tonight. Can you follow my lead?"

Did she have any idea what she was asking him to do? Cole Taylor wasn't a follower. He was a leader. And yet, this tiny woman was asking him to hand over the reins.

Even stranger was the fact that he actually wanted to do it, wanted to help her, any way he could. Because she didn't deserve to have her life turned upside down by a football player with ulterior motives.

"I'll do it. On one condition."

Her sweet lips parted slightly, the plump lower lip slightly damp from where she'd been chewing on it. "You're making this a trade?"

"Oh, I think you'll like my terms."

Her skin flushed and her eyes gave away the desire she didn't have the first clue about hiding from him. "You're awfully sure of yourself."

"That's because I know I can deliver."

"Deliver what?"

"I want you to promise me you'll do anything I want the next time we're in bed."

Her body heated up against his, the vee between her legs the hottest of all, like a beacon drawing him in to her. "What could you possibly want to do that we haven't already done?"

He had to smile at the fact that she hadn't just said no. She was looking for details instead. Because she was interested. Because she wanted to say yes.

"Make you feel really, really good."

Her response came, honest and unfiltered. "You've already done that."

He slipped his hands around her incredible ass and tucked her up against his hard-on. "I'm very glad to hear it, sweetheart. But trust me. There's more."

"More?" Disbelief warred with anticipation on her beautiful face.

He had her.

"Is that a yes?"

She bit her lip again. "Yes."

He couldn't stop grinning—or thinking about how badly he need to fuck her right fucking now. Especially with the way she was pressing herself against him, little circles of sweet heat that had him a heartbeat away from ripping her clothes off and taking her on the floor in the middle of his kitchen.

"When are your parents expecting us?"

"Right away."

Meeting her family for the first time looking and smelling like they'd just been fucking each other's brains out was wrong. That was the only thing that could have stopped him from picking her up and making a meal out of her on the kitchen island.

Still, that didn't mean he couldn't kiss her, didn't mean he couldn't shift his thigh between her legs so that she was pressing herself into him with a desperate little moan.

On the verge of no return, he forced himself to pull back. "So, what's your plan?"

Her eyes were hazy with desire and he felt a deep sense of pride at how long it took them to clear.

"I wish I knew. I'm hoping I'll figure it out during the drive."

Cole surprised himself with the rumble of laughter that escaped his chest at her completely honest response. Usually when his dick was this hard—fuck, had it ever been this freaking hard?—he wasn't sitting around thinking how cute the woman was. He was just focused on fucking her.

Somehow, Anna managed to be both astonishingly sexy and cute as hell.

"Stop laughing. It's not funny."

But now that he'd started, he couldn't stop, and then, neither could she.

It felt good to hold her and laugh together.

Damn good.

* * *

"Cole and I have been together secretly for months."

Half a dozen gasps rang out throughout her parents' living room and Cole worked like hell to keep a straight face.

They'd literally just walked in the front door. Her father and her sisters' husbands were all clearly starstruck, which he hoped would work in their favor. Her sisters looked surprised, maybe even a little envious.

Her mother just looked mad.

No, he quickly realized, it wasn't anger. She was hurt. And disappointed.

Guilt knocked into Cole's gut. Last night at the club when he'd asked Anna to marry him, he hadn't thought about anyone else. Just himself. And now eight strangers were looking with confusion at the woman he'd dragged into his mess.

He hated the thought of anyone being upset with Anna.

She really was a good girl, in the best kind of way.

Whatever he had to do to make this up to her in the end, he'd do. It wasn't going to be money, he knew that now. Hell, even pleasure wasn't enough. He needed to give her something more, something bigger even than riches and mind-blowing sex.

But what?

What could he give her that she really wanted? And that could only come from him?

Clearly nervous, but determined to continue the riveting little story she must have concocted in the car, Anna said, "Cole wanted to meet you long before now. He practically begged me to come clean with everyone about us, didn't you, honeybuns?"

Honeybuns?

Shit, he couldn't laugh. Not now. Not when she was trying so damn hard to make it all sound real.

Obviously not realizing she'd just given him a totally ridiculous nickname—although he did have a pretty awesome ass—her expression was totally earnest as she reached for his hand, gripping it so tightly that her nails dug into his palm.

Crazy bastard that he was, he actually found himself hoping she'd mark him so that he could have a reason to bend her over later and "punish" her by spanking her sweet, round ass.

He somehow managed to get the words "I did" out with a straight face.

"It's just he's so famous and I really wanted him all to myself, at least for a little while."

Surprised to find himself wishing they'd actually had some time together out of the public eye, he agreed. "The press can be pretty hard to deal with."

"But Anna, how could you get married and not tell your own family?"

Anna's face fell at her mother's soft question and he wanted to jump in and save her so badly he had to grit his teeth together to keep his mouth shut. They'd made a deal. He was going to let her lead at dinner...then she was going to follow his lead in bed tonight.

His dick jumped to life in his pants. Crap, that was the wrong thought for a family gathering.

"I'm really sorry, Mom." She looked around at everyone, her lower lip starting to quiver. He pulled her closer. "You're right. You all should have been there. It's just—I didn't want to take away from Jeannie's special day." And then she looked up at him. "And I finally had a chance to do something special with Cole. I had to take it."

He couldn't look away from her, couldn't stop himself from leaning over to kiss her sweet, trembling lips.

"This just might be the most romantic thing that's ever happened." Jill was the first one to hold out her hand. "I'm Jill. It's so nice to meet you. This is my husband, Brian."

Cole shook hands with Jane and Alan, Joanne and Chris.

Anna's father moved out from behind his kids. "I'm not going to pretend that we don't wish we'd known about you before now. But anyone who makes my Anna happy is welcome in my book."

There wasn't understanding in her father's eyes, but neither was there condemnation. And when his gaze shifted to Anna, love shone out strong and pure.

What a shame there hadn't been time to ask her father for her hand. But that didn't make sense. Cole hadn't even known her yesterday, wouldn't have ever sought her out if not for his grandmother's wish.

"Thank you, Mr. Davis." He shook her father's hand, a strong handshake from the kind of man Cole would have loved to have had around when he was a kid.

"Call me John."

Anna's mother turned and walked into the kitchen and Anna stiffened against him.

"Go," he said in a low voice that only she could hear.

But when her hand slipped out of his, he found he already missed her. Not just the soft press of her curves, but the sweet pleasure of holding her hand in his, of knowing that he could fall back into pass coverage if she needed his support.

But he didn't have long to dwell on the thought, not with seven people he was now temporarily related to all peppering him with questions and compliments.

* * *

"Are you mad at me?" Anna asked her mother.

"Should I be?"

Anna's mother, Jackie, had always been there for her daughters with a hug and smile and chocolate. And, sometimes, when they needed it most, tough love.

Anna wished there was something for her to do in the kitchen, for some place to put her hands and eyes so that she wouldn't completely give herself away.

"I know my marriage is really unexpected, Mom."

"Do you love him, Anna?"

She met her mother's gaze on a swift intake of breath. It was the one question she'd hoped no one would ask, the one thing she'd hoped they wouldn't pick up on from her explanation.

"He's a wonderful man."

A man who would do anything for his grandmother—including finding a nice stranger and marrying her—couldn't possibly be bad. Even the fact that he'd lied to her no longer seemed all that bad. Not when she herself was doling out the lies by the bucketful.

"That wasn't what I asked." Her mother nailed her with a sharp glance. "Do you love him?"

Anna didn't know how to lie, not to one of the people who loved her more than anything else in the world.

But just as she was about to say, "I don't know," she realized it wasn't true.

Oh my God, she was falling in love with him.

She was only vaguely aware of her own gasp, of her mother's arms coming around her. "Oh, Anna. You always were different."

Anna's chest clenched. "And you've always felt sorry for me." At her mother's shocked look, Anna forced herself to step away. "The rest of your kids were all tall and blonde, they were all so popular, had so many dates, and won so many awards. I've never fit in, no matter how hard I tried."

"Anna, honey, I can't believe you think that."

But twenty-nine years was an awfully long time to hold it all in, and now that the dam had cracked, she couldn't keep it all from gushing out. "I picked out a new *J* name for myself when I was in first grade. Jennifer. But I never had the guts to tell you I wanted to change Anna so that I could be like the rest of you. Plus, I knew it wouldn't be enough. I'd still be me."

She hated the spike of tears in the corner of her eyes. Damn it, for once she was going to be strong. Cole had helped her leap last night, showed her the strength—and adventurousness—she hadn't seen in herself every time he made love to her. And no matter how much it was going to hurt when their marriage ended and they went their separate ways, she'd always be grateful to him for that gift.

Tonight she was going to have to take what she'd learned and trust that she knew how to fly on her own.

"You were Anna, honey, right from the start, right from the first time I held you in my arms. I'm sorry you didn't feel that you belonged. But you always did. Your differences have always been special. Precious to me and your father and your sisters."

Anna had needed to hear that for so long, she could barely take it in. And yet, at the same time, she couldn't just back down. Not this time.

"You're right, Mom. I am different. And this is how I want to live my life. Cole is my husband. I'm his wife. I'm sorry you didn't meet him before now, but he's here tonight."

The pain in her mother's eyes had her on the verge of an apology. And then her mother said, "Well, one thing's for certain. He's very good-looking," and Anna knew that her mother was trying to mend the hole in their relationship any way she could. This was her way of saying she'd accept Cole, if that was what her daughter wanted.

* * *

Cole stood in the doorway and watched Anna laugh with her mother. Tension rode him from what he'd seen, what he'd heard.

Her mother was right. Anyone could see that Anna was different from the rest of her family. Not just the first letter of her name, not just her looks, but her spirit.

So full of sweetness it took his breath away.

She turned and saw him, then, pleasure lighting her eyes as she held out her arm for him. And as he walked toward his wife and took her in his arms, he wanted her with an intensity he hadn't known he could feel.

But most intense of all, far more intense than his desire for her, was pride at the magnificent woman he held in his arms.

Anna was brave. Compassionate. Sexy as hell.

And all his.

* * *

Two hours later, they were back in his car. Anna hadn't said much through dinner and every minute that he'd been answering questions about his career, about the Outlaws' Super Bowl prospects this season, he'd been watching over her, keeping her hand safely in his whenever he could. She hadn't pulled away, but hadn't held on too tight, either. Still, he'd known that small connection helped.

"You okay?" He reached over, stroked his thumb across the

sensitive skin inside her wrist.

"I think so." The moonlight was just bright enough for him to see her small smile. "You were great, Cole. Thank you."

"You don't have to thank me for anything, Anna." Hell, he was the one who should be down on his knees thanking her. "And your family is great. Really great."

She made a soft sound of agreement, her eyes closing at the stop light. Cole sat at the empty intersection long after the light turned green.

They hadn't done enough sleeping the night before for him to get an opportunity to watch her like this. Her pretty face relaxed, her eyelashes long and curved across her cheekbones. The pulse moving evenly at the side of her neck.

His chest clenched at how beautiful she was. Desire was there—he already knew it would never be far from the surface between them—but it was another emotion entirely that had him unable to take his eyes off her. More than appreciation, stronger than respect.

He wanted to cherish her, wanted to devote himself to making her happy, to seeing her smile.

A car honked behind him and Cole stomped his foot down on the gas pedal, shooting them away from the light like it was a high-speed roller coaster ride. Anna stirred, but didn't wake up.

Twenty-four hours. He'd known her twenty-four hours.

It made sense that he'd like her. That he'd lust for her.

But all this cherishing and devotion crap? Hell, that didn't make a lick of sense.

Thirty minutes later, when Cole pulled into his garage, he had his head back on straight. No question about it, he'd lucked out by picking Anna as his temporary wife. But that's all their relationship was. Just a brief union that was never meant to be anything more. Sure, Anna had said she didn't want anything from him, that she would play her part solely for his grandmother's sake, but Cole was going to find a way to pay her back. In a big enough way to make sure they could both move on with their lives as they'd been before Vegas. No regrets for either of them.

He lifted her, soft and warm, out of the car, and even though she was still asleep, her arms went around his neck and she laid her cheek against his chest. Completely trusting, just as she'd been the previous night in his bed.

He carried her inside, up the stairs to his bedroom, kicked the covers open on his bed with one leg, then gently laid her on a pillow. She immediately curled up on her side and he had to smile as he looked down at her. The first time a woman entered his bedroom, she didn't usually just go to sleep.

Her mother was right—Anna was definitely different from every other woman Cole had ever known.

Sitting at the edge of the bed, he slipped off her shoes and pulled the covers over her. Ten minutes later, he slid under the covers naked. Reaching for his wife, he tucked her small body into his and fell asleep.

That damn smile still on his lips.

Chapter Eleven

"You need anything, sweetheart, let Veronica know, okay?"

Anna nodded at the woman, and forced a smile. "I'll be fine, Cole."

He was giving her one of those looks she was starting to recognize, the one that said he knew she was anything but fine. But the truth was, she was less freaked out by being in the family VIP box before Cole's game than she'd been earlier that morning when she'd woken up in his bed, fully clothed, after dreaming of being held in his strong arms all night long. He could have easily woken her up by undressing her for bed. And if he had, well, there was no doubt in her mind that they would have made love again.

Instead, he'd made sure not to wake her, had simply climbed into his big bed and held her.

He'd acted like a man who cared.

Her chest still felt tight whenever she looked at him. Not wanting to make a complete fool of herself in front of a bunch of strangers, she brightened her smile. "Have a great game!"

She leaned over to give him a quick peck and he said in a low voice against her lips, "We're newlyweds, remember," then slid his hands into her hair and kissed her.

Any embarrassment she might have felt at his very public display of affection was quickly lost in the pent-up desire from the previous afternoon in his kitchen. Without realizing it, her hands went around his neck, her pelvis pushed against his, and she whimpered softly into his mouth.

Finally, he pulled back enough to gaze down at her. She tried to catch her breath, but she was a long way from being able to control her response to his kisses. After he'd pressed one more sweet kiss against her lips, she gratefully sank into the chair behind her and stared out at the football field.

* * *

"Honestly, I didn't expect this from you, Cole."

Out in the hall, Cole nearly walked into his agent, Melissa, who was holding her phone up and shaking it in his face.

"Not only married, but your phone is clearly broken too, huh?"

Okay, so he'd ignored the half-dozen messages she'd left him since the news broke yesterday. Sue him. He'd been busy.

With his sweet wife.

"You were on my list."

"Sure I was." She rolled her eyes. "You should have given me a heads-up on this, Cole."

"How is my marriage any of my agent's business?" He crossed his arms over his chest.

"Last I saw you, I thought we were friends, too. I would have liked to meet the woman you're planning on spending the rest of your life with for that reason alone. I would have liked to have a chance to congratulate you rather than ream you for keeping secrets." Her expression hardened. "But if you just want to talk business, fine. As your agent, we both know that everything you do is my business."

As if on cue, Julie appeared in the corridor. Unlike Melissa, she hugged him. "Congratulations, stud." A bemused grin on her lips, she added, "Got quite a situation with the press going on outside there. All over little ol' you." She pulled a handful of clippings from her shoulder bag, a dozen different pictures of him and Anna. "She'd different from your previous girlfriends. Really cute." She raised an eyebrow, still smiling. "How'd you two meet, anyway?"

Cole looked over the two women's heads for their husbands, Dominic and Ty, but the hall was empty except for the three of them.

Fuck.

"I've got to get down to the field."

Melissa's eyes narrowed as Julie said, "Just be sure to come right back here after the game, Cole, so that we can work out our PR plan on this."

He stared at his team's PR rep—and one-time friend—with a look that would have had most people running. "She's my wife. I'm her husband. Our relationship is private. We don't need a plan."

Instead of looking scared, Julie simply shot one of her sassy little looks at Melissa, who suddenly looked less pissed off and more intrigued.

"Have a great game," they said in unison as they walked away, their heads tucked together as they conferred with one another.

Well, he'd fucked that one up royally. He wanted to follow them back into the VIP box and protect Anna. He wanted to make sure they didn't completely freak her out. But he was pushing it with his team as it was, should have been down on the field thirty minutes ago.

Dread drove every footstep he took away from his new wife.

* * *

"Congrats, buddy."

A hard slap sounded across his shoulders from yet another teammate. Only Ty and Dominic had kept silent, the two newly married guys who just shook their heads as they looked at him.

He'd never been happier to hear the whistle blow. After the past twenty-four hours, he needed these three hours playing a game that was so natural to him. It was as close as he was going to get to decompressing. He wouldn't give up a second he'd spent with Anna, but her family, the press, and all of the crap swirling around them was another matter entirely.

Football. That's all he was going to think about.

But even as he took his spot in the defensive lineup, he found his attention wasn't entirely on the game. He'd never paid much attention to who was up in the VIP box watching him. But today, Anna was there. What was she thinking? Feeling?

And was she okay without him there to protect her?

* * *

"Hi there. Are you Anna?"

Anna looked up to see two very pretty women standing in front of her. Getting to her feet, she hoped her legs weren't nearly as shaky from Cole's kiss as they had been a minute ago.

She smiled nervously. "Yes, that's me."

She was surprised when the slim blonde hugged her. "Wonderful. It's so nice to meet you. And such a surprise, too. Such a good surprise."

Completely off balance from the warm greeting, she was glad

when the curvy woman with the curly hair simply held out her hand. "I'm Melissa, Cole's agent. And this is Julie. She does PR for the Outlaws. We're also both good friends of Cole's."

"Or at least we thought we were." Julie smiled as she sat down next to Anna, more put together and polished than Anna could ever dream of being.

Melissa grabbed a seat on her other side, her business suit not nearly stark enough to hide her soft, sexy curves. "And then he goes and gets married to a woman we've never heard word one about."

Feeling neither as put together nor as sexy as either of Cole's female friends, Anna was trying to figure out how to respond when Julie said, "Honestly, getting hitched in Vegas is something I would have expected my husband to do." At Anna's shocked expression, Julie added, "Before we got serious, Ty used to be a bit of a player."

Melissa laughed at that, her initial businesslike demeanor quickly giving way to friendliness. She leaned over to Anna as if she were sharing a secret. "Actually, the truth is that the team had to hire Julie as Ty's personal PR rep."

Julie shrugged. "He's a bad boy. But he's my bad boy. Besides, you should know that Melissa met her husband, Dominic, when he hired her to be his agent." She waggled her eyebrows. "I've never seen an agent *that* interested in her client."

Anna had to bite her lip so she wouldn't laugh at the way the two women were ribbing each other. At the same time, she'd noticed they both seemed to have a glow about them, especially when they were talking about their husbands. A little pang of envy caught her in the chest, similar to the way she sometimes felt when she watched her sisters with their husbands.

"So." With unsettling abruptness, Julie and Melissa stopped teasing each other and turned their laser focus on Anna. "Tell us about yourself. What do you do for a living? How did you meet Cole? When did you know he was your forever?"

Oh God, what was with people and the word forever?

"I teach first grade." She paused, readying herself to lie to these two nice women. Just one more lie to add to the heaping pile. But she couldn't quite do it, not when they'd been so nice to her. "We met in Las Vegas. One of my sisters was getting married and he was visiting his grandmother."

She would have stopped there, but she already knew neither of these women was going to let her get away with leaving the "forever" question unanswered.

Dropping her voice, she lowered her gaze to her lap. "I knew it was forever the first time he looked at me."

Julie's soft gasp echoed Anna's own private reaction to what she'd just said.

To what she'd just admitted...to herself.

Oh God, had everything she was starting to feel for him already been there in that first glance, when he'd looked into her eyes and told her they were beautiful?

"It's clearly mutual."

Julie's surprising statement was quite possibly the only thing that could have pulled Anna out of her shocked self-examination.

"Cole is usually pretty even-keeled, but he almost bit my head off in the hall before we came in here."

Anna didn't understand. "Why? What happened?"

"I told him I wanted to give the press our version of your story, rather than whatever random misinformation they'll splash onto the Internet and the newspapers. I thought he was going to tackle me when he told me that your relationship is private. And that there wasn't any story."

Melissa agreed. "I've never seen Cole act like that about any other woman. I honestly never thought he'd find anyone he really, truly could care about. Not until you."

Anna couldn't believe how wrong these women were about Cole. He'd bit off Julie's head because he was trying to keep their lies from being revealed, not because he cared about his new wife.

"I still can't believe he managed to keep you a secret," Julie said. "When did you say the two of you met?"

Anna knew she wasn't a good liar. Not only did she preach to her first graders day in and day out about the value of honesty, but she simply didn't like the way lying made her feel, like gears were grinding together in her gut, pulling and tugging at her insides.

Thankfully, before she could answer, the game began and everyone's attention turned to the field. She peered out at the men in their uniforms. She wanted to ask which one was Cole, but it would be way too suspicious if she did. Fortunately, he wasn't hard to pick out. Not when she already knew how he moved, the broad set of his shoulders, his tight hips. He looked up at the VIP box between plays and she couldn't stop her body from reacting. From wanting.

Needing.

As she watched the players move on the field, she was glad to find herself quickly picking up on the rules. Time passed and she had almost started to feel comfortable, when suddenly Cole thundered into a player from the other team, knocking the huge man to the ground without even breaking stride.

"Oh, my God."

She was too stunned by what she'd seen, by the brutal way he'd stopped the other team from advancing down the field, by what she now realized was his job, to keep the words from leaving her mouth, to keep what she was sure was a clear expression of shock from her face. He was paid to be violent, given so much money for being huge and hard and unstoppable that he could pay for a mansion on the hill in San Francisco, for an expensive sports car, for a penthouse in Las Vegas, for the jewels he'd offered to buy her.

But bigger than her shock at what she'd just seen her husband do, was her shock at herself.

Because instead of being horrified at the violence, instead of wanting nothing more to do with Cole as the other man was helped, limping, off the field, her body had heated up...and she wanted her husband now more than ever.

She wanted all of that barely leashed violence unleashed over her. On her.

In her.

Realizing that both Julie and Melissa were staring at her, questions in their eyes, she shot to her feet. She had to get out of here, had to go somewhere she could be alone and pull herself together.

Somehow, she had to figure out a way to stop reacting with such pleasure every time she saw Cole, or said his name aloud, or even thought about him, about little things like how good he'd been with her family, especially her mother. He'd been perceptive enough to realize that her mother was upset and he hadn't pushed, hadn't tried to get Jackie to like him. He'd just been himself, been easy with all of them, telling them football stories he'd had to know they would like, and by the end of the night, Anna had caught her mother smiling at him despite herself.

"I have to go—" She paused awkwardly.

"The restroom is just out the door and down the hall to the

left," Melissa said, concern lacing her brows.

"Thanks."

Splashing her face with cold water in the bathroom, taking the time to repair her light makeup, Anna stepped outside a sliding door into the cool air off the Bay and tried to breathe deeply. But she didn't have enough time to figure out a way to deal with her response to Cole, to tamp down on it and contain it in a little box, one she would only let herself open for the sensual pleasures he'd promised her.

Still, no matter how hard it was going to be to hold firm, she couldn't give up the fight. Not when she knew with utter certainty that if she gave in to the insidiously soft emotions growing by the second behind her breastbone, she was going to be in a whole lot more trouble than just being caught telling a couple of lies.

If she deviated from their agreement to simply stick it out through his grandmother's illness, she was going to get caught wanting more. So much more that she could already feel herself drinking in every single one of Cole's touches, his kisses, his gazes.

If there was one thing she knew with utter certainty, it was that no man—especially one this rich, famous, and good-looking—would ever want his fake temporary wife to fall in love with him.

Finally, when she heard loud cheering and saw people beginning to file out into the parking lot, she made herself return to the VIP box. Cole would be worried if he couldn't find her. Besides, she might not be the most adventurous woman in the world, but she wasn't a total coward either. Not anymore, anyway.

Thankfully, neither Julie nor Melissa acted like anything was strange about her disappearing for so long. They introduced her to the other players' families and everyone was incredibly nice, despite their clear curiosity over her sudden appearance in Cole's life.

But all the while, she was waiting. For Cole.

"Sweet Anna."

His arms came around her from behind, his heat enveloping her, his breath warm on her cheek, and there was no force strong enough in the world—not good sense or any one of the ridiculously big men from his team who were now in the room with them—to stop her from turning around in his arms and lifting her mouth to his for a kiss.

His smile was the first and last thing she saw before his mouth covered hers and she closed her eyes to sink into the pleasure of being in his arms.

"I missed you."

He spoke against her lips, just loud enough for her to hear, and as pleasure lit her, inescapable and wonderful, she couldn't remember what she'd been so certain she needed to fight against just minutes before.

"You'll get her the rest of your life. Time to share your wife with the rest of us." The low male voice behind her was laced with barely suppressed laughter.

Feeling her face flame with embarrassment at the way she'd forgotten there was anyone else in the room, Anna tried to pull out of Cole's arms. But she should have known better. The man she'd married on a whim wouldn't let her separate herself from him like that—whether they were surrounded by a crowd or completely alone.

Turning so that he was still holding her to his side while they faced the two couples in front of them, he said, "Ty, Dominic, I'd like you to meet my wife, Anna."

Two of the best-looking men she'd ever seen live and in person smiled down at her. But as she shook their hands and said the appropriate things, instead of her heart beating and her skin tingling with awareness, she felt nothing.

Only Cole could make her heart feel like it was going to break through her ribs. Only Cole could make her skin heat and tighten with desperate need.

His hand lay warm on the small of her back, the only reason she felt at all secure in this strange new place.

She appreciated that neither Ty nor Dominic focused on her, that they both seemed to realize it would make her more uncomfortable than she already was. Melissa and Dominic moved away to talk to some of their other clients. As the conversation swirled around her about the game, about upcoming barbecues, about people they all knew, Anna was able to watch the easy way Ty made Julie laugh, her eyes lighting up every time her gaze landed on her husband.

They weren't a couple she would ever have put together just from looking at them. Ty was clearly a wild, dangerous bad boy to his core, while Julie was as polished as a woman could be. And yet, despite the fact that they shouldn't make sense together, their deep affection for each other was powerfully clear, even to a bystander, as was their desire for each other, just barely beneath the surface but visible in the way he was constantly touching her and she was touching him back.

Hope lit Anna's heart a beat before a bone-deep sadness settled in. It was all very well to wish that she could be as good a strange fit with Cole. But all it did to her was make the knowledge that it wasn't ever going to happen more painful.

She could feel Cole's eyes on her, dark with heat and concern. "Ready to go?"

They said their goodbyes, relief hitting her that she didn't have to try to play the role of Cole's wife anymore.

He took her out a door that bypassed the press and she got into his car. She had just put her seat belt on when he hit the locks.

"Finally, alone with my wife again."

That was when she realized she should have made every excuse she could think of to stay in that room with a crowd of strangers.

Because even as he called his grandmother to find out how she was feeling and fill her in on the details of the game, as unsafe as she'd felt in the VIP box, she'd been a million times safer then than she was now.

Chapter Twelve

“Nothing I like better than Sunday afternoons. Especially after a win.”

On the surface, Cole’s words shouldn’t have made shivers run up and down her spine, but she could easily read the subtext, especially when his hand moved to her kneecap. He wasn’t grabbing at her, wasn’t doing anything particularly sexual, and yet her body was responding as if he had put his big hand down her pants—flooding with arousal, her breasts peaking hard and tight beneath her bra and top.

She didn’t respond, not when the idea of an entire Sunday afternoon alone with Cole had her almost panting with anticipation.

She could feel his eyes on her, the heat in them, as he turned down a narrow alley and pulled over in front of a small storefront. Her brain felt fogged up by all the unfamiliar desire rushing through her synapses and she hadn’t been paying enough attention to realize he hadn’t been heading straight back to his house.

“There’s something I want you to do, sweetheart.”

His warm, gravelly voice, already so thick with need it took her breath away, wrapped itself around her body like a physical touch.

“I want you to go into this store and buy something.”

Her eyes moved from that dangerous heat in his eyes to the almost dark storefront. “Where are we?”

She’d never heard her own voice so husky and Cole’s eyes flared with possessive desire as he ran the knuckles of one hand down the side of her cheek.

“A toy store.”

“But it doesn’t look like someplace children would...Oh.” She licked her lips nervously. “It’s not that kind of toy store, is it?”

His mouth turned up at the edges, but she wouldn’t have called it a smile. He looked at her like she was a delicious meal that he couldn’t wait to dig into.

Cole clicked open the lock to her door. “Go.”

But she couldn't move. "I haven't ever—" She shook her head. "I don't know—"

His fingers moved to her chin and gently turned her face toward his. "But you want to."

It wasn't a question. And yet she knew he expected an answer.

She took a deep breath, feeling the way it shook inside her chest. And all the while, as she fought for the strength to tell him what he already knew, he watched her with that heat she'd never thought to see in a man's eyes.

Finally, she whispered the shocking, difficult truth. "Yes. I've always wondered what one of these stores was like inside." All the while knowing she would never find out.

He brushed his thumb against her lower lip and she couldn't stop herself from lightly tasting his flesh. A small moan of pleasure emerged from her throat at the rough texture of his calloused skin against her sensitive tongue. And then he pushed his thumb into her mouth and by pure instinct she sucked him in deeper, taking his thumb between her lips and teeth as she had his penis.

He groaned and shifted hard in his seat. "So sweet, Anna. So damn sweet."

She nipped at him, reaching up for his hand so that she could pull him in further and rain kisses and little licks all along his palm. He pulled away.

"No, baby. I'm not going to let you distract me." He brushed his damp thumb across her lips. "Not yet."

He reached over her, his hard muscles pressing into her in the most delicious way as he opened her door.

"You have five seconds to go or it'll be me picking out your toy."

His threat made her jump out of his car as if her seat were on fire.

But once she was outside, she didn't move toward the front door. He rolled her window down and she had to give one more little protest. "This wasn't what I meant when I said I wanted to be crazy with you."

"Five minutes, Anna." The window rolled back up.

She clamped her jaw shut as she pushed open the front door, trying to prepare herself for whatever shocking sights awaited her. But she was surprised to find herself in a perfectly normal-looking store.

The middle racks all held clothes that didn't look much different from what she'd seen adults wear to Halloween parties. One wall was full of books and videos, and while some of the covers were mildly titillating, they weren't anything she hadn't seen in her previous boyfriends' closets.

But it was the display on the far wall that held her interest: dildos of every shape and size and color. Anna knew her sisters all had one—heck, for all she knew, her mother probably had one—but Anna had never been able to get over her embarrassment enough to actually go into an adult store and buy one. Even the "massagers" they sold at drugstores made her blush.

None of her previous boyfriends had even suggested they use sex toys. Then again, none of them had ever made her feel particularly sexual. And not one of them had looked at her like they wanted to burn her clothes and have her walk around naked all the time.

The knowledge that Cole wasn't about to let her come back to the car empty-handed gave her the courage to walk across the store and study her options. Only, it was hard to concentrate on reading the descriptions of included features when she couldn't erase the image of Cole using each and every one of them on her.

Her heart pounded so hard she swore she could feel it between her legs, a steady throb of arousal that only heated her up more.

Thankfully, the very normal-looking man behind the counter didn't even seem to notice she was in the store. He wasn't coming over to offer suggestions or looking at her like she was a pervert. If anything, he seemed bored and tired as he flicked through a magazine.

The clock was ticking down on her five minutes—and Cole would surely buy the most shocking thing he could find if he had to come in after her. She grabbed the closest box and took it to the counter.

"Cash or credit?"

"Cash."

The man had no reaction to her slightly squeaky response. He simply told her the total. Anna quickly counted out the bills, then took the bag from him.

The heat of Cole's gaze immediately hit her as she exited the store, almost making her stumble off the curb. A moment later, she slid into the passenger seat, tightly gripping her new purchase.

"Not knowing what you've got in the bag, but knowing it's going to be damn good, whatever it is, is killing me, sweetheart."

She looked at him, realized his knuckles were showing white on the gearshift. All because she'd gone in and bought a sex toy.

For him to use on her.

She closed the bag tighter. The balance of power had shifted between them. Yes, he'd all but ordered her to walk into the sex shop and buy a toy, something she never, ever would have thought she'd want her husband to do.

But now she knew better.

It was exactly what she'd wanted.

He hadn't just had her do it for him, solely for his own pleasure. Instead, he was forcing her to face her secret desires, so deeply hidden she hadn't dared admit them even to herself.

He'd done it for *her* pleasure too.

Once more he was pushing her outside of her comfort zone. Not to a place she didn't want to go—she already knew he wasn't the kind of man who would ever do that. Instead, he'd walked hand in hand with her to another, higher ledge and told her it was okay to jump.

Her body was already so aroused, so sensitive to the slightest brush of fabric against her skin, that she hadn't thought it would be possible for her feel more. But the swelling in her chest had nothing to do with sex—and everything to do with her heart.

A heart she'd vowed to protect at all costs back at the stadium.

* * *

Cole hadn't come this close to losing it in his pants since early adolescence. But from the minute Anna had walked out of the sex shop holding that brown bag, he'd been using every mental trick he knew to try to hang on until they were back at his house, when he could put his mouth, his hands on her.

At this point, it didn't even matter what was in the bag. He just needed to possess her, to feel her warm and soft beneath him, to drive into the wet clench of heat between her legs and know that she was his.

Somehow he let her walk from his car to the house on her own, rather than just cavemanning her and dragging her in by her hair so that he could fuck her like the savage he really was. But once the door clicked closed behind them, once she turned around with that look in her eyes that was part anticipation, part apprehension, he was lost.

Completely fucking lost to wanting her.

"Take your clothes off, Anna."

Each word was clipped, his teeth clenched together so tight he was on the verge of chipping them.

She looked around the empty living room. "Here? But I thought —"

She stopped at the look in his eyes, at his slow approach. "Take them off before I rip them off."

The brown bag dropped from her hands. "Okay, but shouldn't we—"

"Not fast enough." He didn't have a prayer of keeping his hands off her, of stopping himself from ripping her silky shirt straight down the middle.

"Cole."

He took her lace-covered nipple in his mouth even as his name left her lips, the single syllable melding with a moan. He lifted his head from her sweet breast and rasped out, "I can't make it another second, baby," the only warning he could give before he yanked apart the zipper on her jeans and tore them off her legs, her shoes coming off along with them.

Somewhere in the back of his head he heard her little yelp of surprise, but he couldn't stop now, not when he was so damn close to what he wanted.

To what he needed so desperately he was going crazy with it.

She was over his shoulder a second later, then flat on her back on his wide leather couch. His hands moved without any help from his brain, ripping her panties and bra off, and then she was lying there, her eyes wide as she stared up at him, her thighs splayed open on the dark leather.

Cole could barely drag in enough oxygen as he stared down at the slick pink flesh between her thighs, her soft brown curls already slightly damp for him.

Maybe, he thought later, he would have been able to stop himself from taking her without any foreplay if he hadn't already seen the proof of her desire. If he hadn't known that she was just as desperate for this fucking as he was.

His zipper was down, his cock in his fist a moment later.

He positioned his throbbing head in the center of her drenched pussy lips and drove into her, high and hard, with such ferocity that she slid halfway across the couch.

"Cole!" Anna's scream ricocheted through the high-ceilinged living room.

He gripped her smooth, naked ass in his rough hands so that he could hold her where he wanted her, then drove into her again and again, harder and harder.

Lost to everything but the feel of her clenching heat around his cock, so damn tight he could already feel his balls pulling up tight, the buzzing sensation at the base of his spine moving around the front of his groin, it took him several seconds to realize that Anna's hands had come around his shoulders, that her fingernails were scratching down his back.

When had her legs come around his waist to pull him closer? When had she pulled herself up so that she could kiss him, driving her tongue into his mouth with the same pounding rhythm as his cock?

Her inner muscles contracted around him and then she was begging against his chest, "Please, Cole, oh God, more, more!" and then her tongue and teeth were scraping across his nipple.

The feel of her teeth flipped a switch inside, the one that meant he couldn't hold back anymore, couldn't protect her from his too-strong needs, his too-big body.

But just as he was about to unleash everything he was into Anna's soft body, he looked down at her, her slim arms and legs wrapped so tightly around him, and saw just how small she was compared to him.

Fuck. He'd never taken anyone this hard. No matter how good the sex had been, he was always aware of how big he was. Knew how much damage he could do to a small, feminine body. Which was why, subconsciously, he'd always dated tall women, women that could handle him.

But Anna, his small, sweet Anna, was pushing him harder, and faster, than he'd ever let himself be pushed. His cock had never been this hard, on the verge of total obliteration. Jesus, it was going to kill him to pull back. But he had to.

Because he couldn't hurt Anna.

Sweet, innocent Anna.

Stilling, he held her hips tightly in his hands. She tried to buck into him, but when he wouldn't let her move, she looked up at him, confusion warring with desperate desire on her sweat-dampened face.

"Cole?"

“So small and sweet.” He had to lick at her lips, tasting the salt from her skin mixing up with her own sweet essence. “I don’t want to hurt you.”

He’d been saying the same thing to her since practically the first moment they’d met, and damn it, he didn’t think he could live with himself if he ever hurt her, if he accidentally ripped her apart because he’d needed her too bad to think straight.

“Then why are you hurting me now?”

His chest clenched with instant regret. “Jesus, Anna, I didn’t mean—too rough on—you’re too small for—” He was trying to force himself out of her wet heat as word fragments fell from his lips, but fuck, even knowing what he was doing to her, he couldn’t manage more than an inch.

“I love it when you’re rough, Cole. I love it when you can’t control yourself.”

He blinked hard, his brain working to convince him that he’d heard her correctly. “But I’m hurting you.”

“The only time you hurt me is when you stop.”

And in that moment as he looked into her eyes and knew she wasn’t saying what he wanted to hear, but was speaking the truth—he let the switch go.

All the way up.

The next heartbeat had him driving into her so hard that the entire couch slid across the floor. The knowledge that he hadn’t imagined her answering smile of pleasure had him ravaging her mouth with his lips and teeth and tongue even as he ravaged her pussy with a cock that was as hard as steel and so thick that he could feel her sensitive tissue working to stretch around him.

And then, through his own crazy thrusting and pumping into her, he felt it...the telltale way her muscles all clenched around his cock, the way her ragged breaths came to a momentary stop, hitching in her chest, the way her nails dug in deep along with her heels, the way her thigh muscles tightened on his hips. Any other time he would have focused on her pleasure, would have made sure she hit her climax before he did, but now that the beast was out, there was no locking him back into his cage.

Rearing up over her, he roughly cupped a breast in each hand, her hard nipples searing the centers of his palms, and he rode her like he’d never ridden anyone. Her head was thrown back, her eyes closed tight as she held onto his forearms and let him take her, riding the wave that he'd become. And instead of pain or fear, in that moment when a gasp left her throat as she began to climax and she opened her eyes and stared straight into his soul, he saw his own pleasure mirrored in those ocean depths.

A pleasure so deep that he wasn't sure how either of them were going to survive without it.

His roar shook the windows as he exploded, her muscles milking him, and if he might have thought that he should pull out, that they weren't really married and he shouldn't be shooting his come deep into her womb, he didn't hear it, wasn't aware of anything but riding out the biggest, strongest orgasm he'd had in thirty-four years.

* * *

Cole shifted them so that he was lying beneath her on the couch and Anna was plastered over his big, hard body, still holding on for dear life, still trying to figure out how to breathe, how to think. She was still trying to figure out how it was even possible for anything—or anyone—to make her feel so good.

To feel so much.

If she were smart, if she had any sense of self-preservation at all, she'd be sliding off him, putting space between them, making sure she didn't let him take her over, body and soul.

But that last orgasm must have obliterated a huge chunk of her brain cells. Because she couldn't have left Cole's warmth, the comfort of his arms around her, if someone had been holding a gun to her head.

Not when she was finally right where she'd wanted to be for so very long, held in the arms of a strong man who knew exactly what she needed, even when she hadn't known it herself.

He pulled her tighter and she willingly curled into him, closing her eyes, her muscles relaxed, her breath coming more evenly as she realized just how much all of that crazy, extremely physical sex had worn her out.

* * *

Cole hadn't thought anything could top the wild sex they'd just had on the couch.

He was wrong.

So goddamned wrong.

It didn't make any sense that anything could be better than fucking Anna, especially not when they repeatedly had the most explosive sex of his life.

But Anna's warmth, the soft press of her curves against him as she fell asleep in his arms—holding the sweet trust of a woman he was starting to really care about in the palm of his hands—was good.

Too good.

Way too good.

So good that a man could lose his way if he wasn't careful.

Chapter Thirteen

Anna woke in Cole's big bed. He was stretched out beside her, watching, obviously waiting for her. Even though he wasn't touching her, she felt her skin come alive beneath his gaze.

He was naked now, too, and as she ran her hungry gaze down his tanned skin, over the deeply sculpted muscles over his shoulders and chest and stomach to the thick erection jutting out from his body, she realized what he was holding.

The dildo she'd bought.

Amazingly, in their frantic coupling in his living room, she'd forgotten all about it. Now, looking at the thick flesh-colored plastic penis she'd chosen made her blush. She reached out for a nonexistent blanket to pull up over her nakedness.

Cole's gaze was full of heat and such deep possession it stole her breath. "Why don't you put those hands above your head, sweetheart?"

It shouldn't be so tempting to follow orders. Her hands and arms shouldn't automatically be rising above her head, but the truth was, she'd already given up trying to make her reaction to this man fit into a tidy little box.

There was nothing tidy whatsoever about any of this. Not their quickie marriage, or the fact that instead of cursing the way he'd manipulated her into marrying him as a gift for his grandmother, she felt almost ... thankful.

"You look so pretty like that, Anna. Your skin all flushed, your sweet breasts arching closer to my mouth." He bent over her then, his tongue a flat press of heat over one peak.

Anna instinctively moved her hands to thread into his hair and he lifted his head from her sensitive skin.

"Did I tell you to move your hands?"

She bit her lip. "No." When he simply held her gaze, but didn't say anything more, she realized he was waiting for her to put them back up by the headboard. She swallowed reflexively. "Aren't you going to tie me up?"

"Oh no, sweetheart." He grinned at her, his eyes sparkling with humor in addition to that intense heat that never seemed to go away. "This time I'm going to expect you to keep your hands right there all on your own."

His words shouldn't have been a compliment, shouldn't have signified anything more than dirty verbal play, but they still felt like a big deal.

Like he was trusting her to own a heck of a lot more of her sexuality than she had during their first night together.

Searching within herself, she decided he was right—she wasn't going to freak out this time. Instead, she was going to trust herself, trust her body to know what felt good. Rather than fight it when it all got to be too much, she was going to relish every single sensation.

Moving slowly, sensuously, she moved her hands back into place, where he wanted them.

Approval lit the desire in his eyes. "Good choice."

Belatedly, she realized he was talking about more than the position of her hands. He was holding up the dildo between them, slowly moving it toward her chest, rubbing the soft plastic between her breasts, the head dragging along her breastbone.

She knew she should have been shocked as she lay there watching Cole caress her skin with the toy. The night she'd met him, she would have been. Even yesterday, she knew she would have made some protest.

But in less than forty-eight hours, Cole had almost effortlessly broken down walls she hadn't even realized she'd built.

Instead of being shocked at the renewed arousal throbbing at the tips of her breasts, between her legs, she reveled in the glorious heat.

Instead of being anxious about what Cole was planning to do with the dildo, she was practically panting with desperate anticipation, could feel herself creaming, readying herself for whatever he wanted, for whatever he was going to do.

Still, she wasn't prepared for him to lift the toy to her mouth, for him to say, "Lick it," or for her own tongue to automatically obey.

"Look at that sweet little tongue," he murmured as she bathed the thick plastic head with her saliva.

Her gaze followed his to the plastic shaft that he was moving across her lips so that she could wet the top half. Her womb clenched at the way it glistened with her saliva, not because the toy itself turned her on, but because she was imagining Cole's cock in its place, feeling him hot and throbbing against her lips as he slowly let her taste him.

She was so lost in her delicious vision that the next thing she knew, he was swirling the head over her nipples, using his forearms to push her breasts together, so that he could drag the wet plastic across both in a sinful figure eight that had her arching her back up into his touch, almost forgetting her promise to hold her arms and hands in place at the headboard.

"So damn sexy."

Cole's reverent words moved across her skin like a whisper, pulling the tiny hairs all across the surface of her body up and toward him, and then he was blowing a puff of warm air over her tightly puckered nipples. The skin across her breasts had never felt so tight. She'd never been this close to coming with nothing more than breast stimulation.

"Open your legs, sweetheart."

That first night, as soon as she'd agreed to trust him, he'd taken choice from her. He'd protected her from her own lack of faith in herself. But now, he was asking her to trust not only him.

He was asking her to trust herself, too.

Aware of every movement, even the slight flutter of her eyelashes on her face, the way her chest was rising higher, falling deeper with every breath, she separated her thighs, opening herself up to Cole.

And the toy in his hands.

"Anna." Cole dipped his free hand between her legs, slowly moving two fingers through her arousal before bringing them to his mouth and sucking them clean. "Sweet, sweet Anna."

"Touch me again, Cole." She didn't need any prompts from him this time to tell him what she wanted. She was learning how to listen to her body's signals, was gaining courage in putting voice to her desires.

Oh, and how he touched her, the same two fingers not only sliding between her slick folds, but sliding all the way inside, driving so high inside her that she had to arch into his hand to try and take him even deeper. But then she could feel his fingers curling, stroking, settling against a shockingly sensitive place.

"Cole?" Her breath caught on his name, turning one syllable to two.

In lieu of an answer, he slid his fingers from her and positioned the head of the dildo at her entrance. For a moment it was all too much for her again—this shockingly beautiful man lying naked on the bed with her, a sex toy in his hands, wicked promise in his eyes. She closed her eyes and worked to suck in air, to locate her courage once more.

"Watch with me, Anna."

The low words rumbled across her belly, her breasts, and brought her back to him. Back to the incredible pleasure he was not only promising, but was already giving.

He lifted her upper body to tuck a pillow beneath her head and shoulders and she opened her eyes just in time to watch as the head pushed her open. He left the toy there, let them both stare at her labia, glistening with her arousal, stretching open over the thick intrusion.

"Does that feel good, baby?"

She knew he knew exactly how good it was, but just thinking about telling him had another flood of arousal coating the tip, had her inner muscles clenching around the plastic as her body tried to pull it deeper inside.

She turned her gaze from the toy to the man who was wielding it with such perfect precision. "Oh yes."

His pupils dilated. "Let's see if we can make it even better."

He left her no time to respond, pure sensation taking over every part of her as he gently, slowly started spinning the toy inside of her. Even without pushing it in further, he was making her feel so ridiculously, incredibly good with the way the latex rubbed and pressed against her sensitive inner walls. And then, just when she thought she was getting a handle on her arousal, he filled her up.

This time she didn't need him to tell her to watch. Not when she couldn't have taken her eyes off the shiny latex shaft as he slowly slid it out from between her legs and then sank it back in on a groan. Her thighs fell further apart as she opened herself up to him, to the toy, to the sinful pleasure taking her over. Not once had he touched her clit, and yet she could feel—and see—how swollen the tender tissue was.

She opened her mouth to ask him to touch her there, to put his lips and tongue over her, but before she could get the words out he made a request of his own.

"Get on your hands and knees."

Everything inside her stilled with shock. And that was when she realized just how naïve she really was. Had she really thought that she was brave enough to do whatever he asked her to do? Had she really been innocent enough to think that simply plying her with a dildo while she lay spreadeagled on his bed would be as far as he would push her?

He didn't ask against again, he simply kept her trapped in the dark heat of his gaze.

And he waited...waited for her to realize that she was less shocked by his command than she was by the impossible excitement that swamped her at the thought of moving into the oh-so-vulnerable position.

Her limbs were too shaky for her to even try to move in a sensual manner, but when she finally got into position, resting her weight on her palms and her knees and shins, and looked over her shoulder at Cole, he was looking at her as though she were—

"A miracle. You're a goddamned miracle."

The look in his eyes, the reverence in his words didn't just make her wet, didn't just make her ache for his touch.

It made her heart pound harder, swell bigger.

It made her fall deeper than she should.

And it made her get way too close to the one thing that would rip her apart and tear her previously fine life to shreds when their temporary marriage ended.

Thankfully, there was no way for her thoughts to spin any further toward the danger zone, not when he was stealing them away with the firm press of the toy's head against her folds. Sliding easily into her wetness, it felt so good that she had to arch into it, had to tilt her head back to try to take in enough air to fuel the desperate need taking her over.

"I wish you could see how beautiful your ass looks, so round and soft and sweet."

His lips moved over her bottom and even as his kisses there shocked her, especially when she felt his teeth lightly score her skin, she whimpered her pleasure.

"I knew watching you take this would be good, Anna," he murmured as his mouth moved down over the curve where her bottom met her thigh.

She gasped as he licked at the seam of incredibly sensitive skin, bucking herself even harder into his hand, the heel of his palm landing hard and heavy against her aching clit with every thrust of the toy.

"But I had no idea it would be this good."

She could feel the heat of his eyes on her pussy, on the wet clench of her muscles against the toy.

"Nothing has ever been this good, baby."

He moved before she could react, sliding his head beneath her open thighs, his tongue reaching out to lave her clit, his free hand pulling her down onto his mouth.

She came that quickly, her climax a lightning bolt that ran from her clit to the tip of her toes, the top of her head, the tips of her fingers. Even her earlobes tingled. And all the while, Cole's tongue on her clit was driving her crazy. All the while, he never lost his rhythm with the decadent, sinful toy in his hand. All the while, she was gasping her pleasure into the pillow, grinding herself down onto his face, onto the wonderful pressure of the toy inside her.

And then the toy was gone, making a loud thud as he threw it across the room. Cole slid out from under her and came around her back, covering her hips with his, her back against his chest. Thank God he held her up as he drove into her, taking her in a position she'd never let another man take, with her up on her hands and knees, her breasts in his hands, his mouth kissing, sucking, inhaling the skin along her neck and shoulders and back, his hard flesh driving, stretching her open as far as she could go.

She'd never heard sounds like the ones coming out of her mouth as he drove into her. But it wasn't a one-way street, wasn't a world where he put her where he wanted her and she gave him pleasure despite herself.

No, it was the exact opposite.

Anna was taking at least as much pleasure from Cole as she was giving to him. She pushed back into his hard shaft, into the rock-hard muscles of his thighs and tight hips, with everything she had, used up every last ounce of energy to find her way back over an even higher peak than the one she'd just crested barely moments before.

"Come again for me, baby."

The raw command came with the sudden press of rough, calloused fingers over her clit and this second unexpected hit of extreme pleasure had her crying out with what was left of her voice. Her entire body exploded around his, black spots appearing in her vision as Cole roared out her name, his out-of-control thrusts pushing her flat into his mattress, his fingers never once losing ground on her pulsating clit, wet with her arousal and his come. But even after she came down from the heady pulses of her climax, she loved the way Cole continued to drive into her, his cock still hard as steel against her swollen, sensitive inner walls, as he continued to stimulate her clit.

It should have been impossible—her body couldn't possibly sustain this level of pleasure, could it? —but before she knew it, she was right back in the place she thought she'd just left behind, on top looking over the edge.

"Again, sweetheart. One more time. For me."

His thrusts were more measured now, his touch more concentrated on the stiffening bud between her legs. But it was the warmth, the adoration, the sheer need in his tone that had her crying out one more time.

Holding her steady until she rode out the astonishing waves of pleasure, Cole shifted his weight slightly off the side, just enough to cover her still without crushing her.

Anna's mind worked to right itself, but Cole's nearness had always made clear thinking difficult. More so now than ever before. No matter how she tried, she couldn't think past—no, couldn't ignore the question that had been there since his first kiss in the club: *Who was she letting herself become?*

And was there any way she would ever be able to go back to the woman she'd been before Cole?

"Sweet Anna."

He moved onto his back and effortlessly lifted her so that she lay across him rather than the mattress. She relaxed into him, utterly sated now, and realized with a small smile against his chest that they were no longer strangers. Two days of almost constant togetherness meant that she could recognize the sounds of desire and arousal, anger and frustration, in his voice. And now, the way he almost dropped the last syllable of her name as exhaustion took him toward sleep.

He pressed a soft kiss onto her hair. "You're the best thing that's ever happened to me."

His sweet words were on the verge of being slurred and she wasn't surprised when his breathing became slow and even. Just as she wasn't surprised by the truth staring her in the face as she lay there with his heart beating steadily beneath her palm.

There was no going back from the way she felt about this man.

Not just because they'd made love without protection twice in a row and she might have already conceived their child. Not just because being with Cole made her happier than she could ever remember being. Not just because he'd spent every minute of their short relationship cherishing her, worshiping her. Not just because of his fierce love for his grandmother.

No. It was all so much simpler than that.

Cole was the key. The key to the prison in which she'd been locked her whole life.

In two days, he'd managed to not only set her body free.

He'd set her heart free, too.

And as Anna reached for the covers and pulled them over their naked bodies, she knew she wasn't just losing the fight to keep her heart from her husband...she was chucking it onto the field with both hands.

Chapter Fourteen

"Now that's a pretty sight for a Monday morning."

Cole stepped into the shower just as Anna was rinsing the shampoo out of her hair. Even with her eyes closed, her body instantly responded to his nearness.

"Let me do that for you." He moved behind her and his hands went to her hair, lightly massaging her scalp as the warm water washed the suds down her back.

He hadn't been in the bed when she woke up and she'd instantly missed him. But the numbers on the alarm clock had her rushing into the bathroom to get ready for work.

When he turned her around in his arms and kissed her all the way awake, late or not, she couldn't keep her hands off his hard muscles.

She stopped at his biceps. "You're bigger than you were before."

"It's always like that after I lift weights."

"Oh." She couldn't keep the murmur of appreciation for his incredible, ridiculously perfect body to herself.

His hands ran down the sides of her spine before cupping her bottom. "Other things are bigger now too. Wanna see?"

Oh yes, she really did. "I need to hurry and get dressed or I'm going to be late for school."

Still, even knowing she didn't have time to do anything more than throw her clothes on at that point—blow drying and makeup weren't in the cards today—she couldn't stop herself from pressing her lips to his big, broad chest and licking across a nipple.

"What will happen if you're late?"

His hands roamed from her hips to her breasts—and the already slick flesh between her thighs.

"My first graders will worry that something happened to me."

His hands paused on their trip across her erogenous zones. "Those kids owe me big time for this." When she didn't immediately move away, he said, "You'd better go before I change my mind, sweetheart."

Her body throbbing with unsatisfied desire, she had to force herself to step out of the shower and grab a towel.

She was surprised when he emerged sixty seconds later, threw on some clothes, and picked up his keys. "Ready whenever you are."

"Wait a minute. If you work on Sundays, shouldn't you get today off?"

"Most guys do, but as defensive captain I need to look at game tapes while it's still fresh." He leaned against the door, twirling the keys around one finger as he watched her put on her shoes. "So, where am I taking you?"

She looked up at him in surprise. "You don't have to take me to school. I usually take the bus."

His grin made her heart beat faster. "Not too many bus stops in this neighborhood."

She frowned. "I hadn't thought about it."

Clearly. Of course, not having a plan to get to her job on Monday morning was only one of a hundred things she hadn't given any thought to when she'd agreed to marry Cole in Las Vegas on Friday night.

"You saw my office, Anna. Now I'd like to see yours."

He called his grandmother from the car's built-in speakers to check on her, and this time Anna said a quick hello, too. She smiled all the way through town, right until they turned the corner to her school.

"Sorry, Grandma. I'll have to call you back later." Clicking off the phone, he said, "Damn it. They shouldn't be here."

Anna craned her neck. "Who's here?"

"The press."

She put her hands in her still damp hair. "I look horrible."

"No way. You're the prettiest thing I've ever seen."

A fake husband didn't have to say things like that to his fake wife. Just as he didn't have to touch her the way he did, or give her so much pleasure that just thinking about all the things he'd done could have heated her up in a snowstorm.

Knowing she was blushing from his compliment, she clarified. "While I know they want pictures of you, not me, I'm really afraid I'll be late if we have to run into them now. There's a back entrance, just around that corner."

He frowned, but made a quick right turn before they were seen.

"I don't like dropping you off on a street corner."

His clear concern was very sweet, and definitely deserved a kiss. "You're a very sweet man, Cole."

"Good thing my boss doesn't agree with you," he grumbled against her mouth, but she knew he appreciated her words by the gentle way he kissed her back.

Working to catch her breath, she was grabbing her bag and clicking the door open when she felt his hand on hers.

"What time should I pick you up?"

Warmed by the fact that he wanted to go out of his way to come get her—her school was on the opposite side of town from both his house and the stadium—she said, "Again, very sweet. But on Mondays, after I meet with the other K through 2 teachers, my friend Virginia usually gives me a ride. I should be home no later than six."

Seeing the way his eyes warmed at the way she'd naturally called his house *home*, hope swelled inside her chest again. Maybe their fake marriage could turn into a real one in the not so distant future. She went out on a limb by giving him another kiss.

"I had a great weekend with you, Cole."

"Only great?" He nipped at her lips, teasing her as much with his mouth as he did with the question.

"No," she said softly. "It was phenomenal."

And as she jogged away from the car toward the elementary school campus, making it just in time for the bell, she realized she still couldn't stop smiling.

Because of Cole.

* * *

"Miss Davis, my mommy said we should call you Mrs. Taylor now. Why did you have to change your name?"

"What's it like to be famous?"

"Can you have Cole sign this for me and my big brother?"

Anna was suddenly hard-pressed to keep smiling. Okay, so she was getting slightly more comfortable with the fact that she'd fallen head over heels for a man she hadn't known last Thursday. But everything that came with him...frankly, she wasn't sure when she'd get used to it.

Some people were made for fame. Some definitely weren't.

It was pretty darn clear which check box her mark belonged in.

Knowing it was perfectly natural for her students to be excited about the news of her marriage, she carefully answered each and every one of their questions. Somehow it got to be recess. After she let her kids out to play for fifteen minutes, in lieu of her usual cup of coffee in the teacher's lounge, she was about to close the classroom door when a well-manicured hand pulled it open.

"Anna. Congratulations."

Biting back a sigh that she wasn't going to get the tiny bit of quiet time she desperately needed to get her head on straight, Anna accepted her principal's congratulations.

"I've been thinking," Celeste Manning began, and Anna forced herself to keep smiling, even as her gut told her to be wary. "As you know, we've really had some trouble getting the community to contribute to our fundraiser this year, what with the current economic climate. But, that was before I found out we have a celebrity in the Cougar school family."

Anna couldn't imagine Cole at one of their little school fundraisers.

"I'm sure my husband would really love to help the school out, but—"

Celeste's clapping hands cut Anna off mid-sentence. "Wonderful. I have to hurry back to my desk to let not only our parents, but also everyone in the city know that we will be auctioning off a special dinner with Cole Taylor."

Anna gripped her boss's wrist before she got away. "Celeste, you don't understand. He's very busy."

"He couldn't possibly be too busy for his wife. Besides, our phone lines have been clogged all day with calls from the press. At least now I'll have something to say to them that will benefit our school." Celeste glanced down at her wrist and Anna released her. "Although I do have to say, we all feel rather taken by surprise. You should have let us know you were engaged. We would have thrown you a party with cake."

Cake.

They would have fed her cake.

Anna could barely hold in her laughter until she got the door closed. And if it was slightly tinged with hysteria, well then, at least she had the rest of recess to get ahold of herself.

* * *

Before he went to the tape room, Cole stepped into Julie's on-site PR office, knowing she often started her day at the stadium before moving to her office across from the Bay Bridge.

"We have a problem."

Julie frowned as he told her about the paps waiting outside Anna's school. "Fortunately, Cole, they aren't legally allowed on a school campus."

"She feels trapped." And he hated seeing that fear come back into Anna's pretty eyes.

"Of course she does. Marrying an Outlaw is definitely not for the fainthearted." Julie pinned him with one of her trademark no-bullshit gazes, always a little strange on such a classically attractive face. "Look, Cole, I know you wanted to keep your relationship private, but the fact is, if you want them off your back, you're going to have to give them something."

The thought of exposing Anna, his sweet, innocent Anna, to the craziness of fame made his gut churn. "No."

"I'm not talking about a press conference. One interview." She held up her hand to stop him from telling her where to shove her suggestion. "I'll handpick the journalist. Trust me, she'll be thrilled to get the scoop on the surprise marriage of the season."

"Anna never asked for this."

"Speaking from personal experience, loving an Outlaw has always been worth the price that sometimes needs to be paid."

Cole knew he hadn't done a damn thing in his life to deserve a good, sweet woman like Anna—especially with the bonus that she'd turned out to be a wildcat in bed. But despite the way he couldn't stop thinking about her, couldn't stop touching her—despite how good just being with her made him feel—he had to keep reminding himself that there was no way she was going to fall in love with him.

Unlike Julie, who was willing to make sacrifices in the name of love for her husband, Anna wasn't in love with the man who'd tricked her into marrying him. She didn't know about his past, about the fact that while he might be acting sweet around her now, he'd been anything but sweet before.

Anna didn't deserve to pay any price at all.

Unfortunately, none of that made a damn lick of difference to their current situation. A situation that was entirely his fault.

"Should I make the call?" Julie held up her phone, her eyebrows raised.

"Make the damn call."

He'd hit the tape room later. First, he needed to beat the crap out of some tackling dummies.

* * *

Anna couldn't believe the way her day had gone. If she'd been smart, she would have gone with Cole's suggestion to have the school get a substitute—and stayed in his bed all day.

Instead, she'd naively walked into a situation so far beyond her control, she didn't have the first clue about how to get it back in line. She'd never seen so many parents come to pick their kids up, especially the fathers of girls and boys who usually took the bus. By the time the last of them cleared out, it felt like she'd been smiling that pasted-on smile for hours.

After hiding out in her classroom at lunch, her colleagues weren't any better when she got to her weekly planning session. Between the squeals over the size of her ring to the not-so-veiled questions about what it was like to be married to a big, strapping Outlaw—they didn't care about the married part, just the marital relations part—Anna's budding headache turned into a biting migraine.

Only her friend Virginia acted like a normal human being. Feeling much as she had with her mother, as soon as they were in the car, Anna said, "I'm really sorry I didn't tell you about Cole."

"You don't need to apologize for anything, Anna. I can see exactly why you felt you had to keep your relationship private." Virginia snorted. "I've never seen people act so crazy." Then she smiled. "You look different today."

Anna had to laugh at an assessment that was all too accurate. "You mean because my hair is standing up on end and my eyes are bloodshot?"

"No. You look happy. Happier than I've ever seen you." Anna shot her a surprised look as Virginia added, "Almost like you're glowing."

Glowing? She could actually glow after the day she'd had?

The thing was, despite her exhaustion, just thinking about Cole had a smile moving to her face—and heat coursing through her veins.

He's worth all of this.

"Anna, can I ask you something?"

Virginia's hesitant words had caution riding her again. "Sure." She forced herself to add, "Anything."

"I remember seeing a picture of Cole in a magazine a couple of weeks ago and—" Her friend grimaced, shook her head. "Never mind."

But Anna wasn't stupid. She knew without being told that her new husband was a lady-killer of serious proportions.

"He was with another woman, wasn't he?"

For a moment she thought Virginia was going to cry. "You're married now. You're happy. I shouldn't have said anything, but you're one of my closest friends. And I can't stand it if he hasn't been honest with you."

Hating herself for being the dishonest one, Anna said, "Thank you for being my friend."

She wanted so desperately to come clean to someone. And she hated lying to such a close friend, one who cared enough about her to risk their friendship by warning her about possible trouble with her husband.

"Honestly, Cole and I are doing great. And I know that this is going to sound really strange, but if you see any other pictures—" She was a hundred and ten percent positive Virginia would. "—please remember that appearances can be deceiving."

Finally, Anna thought, she'd said something true.

Chapter Fifteen

Virginia followed her into Cole's huge house. "Smells great. Does he have a cook?"

Anna made a sound that she hoped could be construed as either a yes or no, depending on what the right answer turned out to be. But when they turned the corner to the kitchen, she had to stop and brace her suddenly weak legs.

Was there anything sexier than a man who knew how to cook?

Cole's back was to them as he stirred food in several pans, then leaned over to check the oven. Anna was starting to realize how much money her husband had. He didn't need to cook to feed himself. And he certainly didn't need to do a damn thing—like cooking dinner—to try and charm himself into her pants. One hot look was all it ever took.

He was picking up a knife and turning to his cutting board on the kitchen island when he saw them. "Anna, sweetheart, you're home."

Her name on his lips—along with the endearment and the intense heat in his eyes as he drank her in—made thrill bumps run all along her skin.

"Hi."

She suddenly felt shy, but Virginia was going to get suspicious pretty soon if she didn't act a heck of a lot more comfortable with her husband than this.

"Honeybuns," she said brightly, "this is my friend Virginia."

His mouth quirked up into that wonderful half-smile she couldn't get enough of. After turning down the burners on the gas stove, he moved forward with his hand outstretched.

"I really appreciate you bringing Anna home, Virginia." He reached out to Anna and threaded his fingers through hers as he pulled her close and pressed a kiss to her forehead. "There's plenty of food. Stay for dinner. I'd love to get to know one of Anna's friends."

Virginia looked between the two of them. "Thanks. And everything smells great, but I don't want to interrupt your plans."

Selfishly, Anna was desperate to be alone with Cole. How, she suddenly wondered, had she gone so many hours without touching him? Without kissing him? Without being held against his heat? Without breathing in his clean, masculine scent?

But at the same time, the dinner invitation felt so normal. Like he was really her husband.

And she was really his wife.

Hope was carving out another notch inside her chest as she said, "We'd love for you to stay, Virginia."

"Well, if you're sure, then I'd love to."

As they set the dining table and helped plate and carry in food, Anna loved the way Cole made Virginia so comfortable. And she was surprised to find out that her friend was a pretty big football fan. But although he could have easily kept the conversation all about him, he was truly interested in getting to know Virginia better. How had she not known that Virginia had lived in France for several years after college?

From the way people talked about Cole and the part of the game she'd seen on Sunday, Anna understood that Cole was a great football player, but every moment she spent with him made it clear to her that he was so much more than just a spectacular athlete.

He was a great person, period.

As she all but licked her plate clean, she had to laugh at herself. He could have won her love on dinner alone.

"I can't believe you made this," she said for approximately the hundredth time as she debated taking thirds of the salmon and scalloped potatoes.

"Anything for you, sweetheart, although pretty soon Virginia is going to think I've never cooked for you before." His smile was indulgent, tinged with a warning only she could see.

He was right. She needed to do a better job of playing her part. "Oh, of course you have. It's just that this is so darn good." Really trying to play it up, she added, "In fact, this meal is worlds better than the last dinner you made for me."

Anna almost groaned as she saw Cole's eyebrows go up at her back-handed "compliment," his lips quirking up before he forced them flat again.

After Virginia excused herself from the table to find the powder room, he softly said, "Remind me to paddle your ass for that last comment after your friend goes home."

Anna flushed hot at the thought of Cole's hands on her bottom. Liking the thought far more than she thought she should, she ignored his comment.

"You've been so great tonight. Thanks for being so nice to my friend."

He did just as good a job of ignoring the change in subject. "You don't think I'm serious about spanking that sweet ass of yours, do you?"

"But you've never made me dinner before," she protested. "I was just trying to make it sound like we've done this before. It's not fair for you to—" She had to stop and breathe to get it out. "—to spank me."

His sensual grin stole her breath. "You want me to. That makes it fair."

She shook her head, but couldn't get the word *no* past her lips. Not when she was suddenly feeling all tingly. Not when she suddenly realized that she *did* want to see what being spanked felt like.

But only with Cole.

Standing quickly, Anna began to clear the table. He didn't take his eyes from her as he pushed his own chair back and stacked plates in the sink. They were done by the time Virginia walked back into the room.

"Thank you so much for dinner, Cole. It was really nice to meet you."

Anna linked her arm through Virginia's. "I'll walk you out."

"Wow," her friend said when they were standing outside on the front step. High on its hill, Cole's property had a 360-degree view of the city lights. "This place is really something."

"I know."

Only, Anna wasn't just talking about the lights. *Overwhelmed* wasn't even close to how she was feeling.

"I love him."

The words left her lips before she realized they were coming. She lifted her hand to cover her mouth before she could stop herself from giving herself away.

"I know you do." Virginia turned to face her, her head cocked to the side. "Although, honestly, I never would have picked a man like him for you."

Virginia didn't know he never would have picked her either, if it hadn't been for his grandmother. But Anna couldn't forget it. All she could do was try to convince herself that it had been fate. A lucky accident.

And that it was all going to work out perfectly.

Anna fought back a chill of foreboding at her hopeful thoughts as her friend joked, "Know where I can find a big hunk of my own?"

It felt good to laugh, to firmly push away the fear that kept bubbling up inside her.

Cole hadn't been in her plans. A husband hadn't been anywhere on the horizon. But maybe if she was really, really lucky, it would all work out better than even her biggest dreams.

"I'd love it if you'd come with me to the next game," she said. The VIP box would be way less scary with a friend by her side. "Maybe we can sneak into the locker room after the game."

Virginia's eyes widened with momentary shock before she laughed again. "It's great to see you so happy, Anna. Not just happy, but —" She paused, searching for the right word. "Free. You seem free."

Anna blinked back the sudden tears that wanted to fall. She did feel free. Happy. In love.

And scared.

More scared than she'd ever been before.

* * *

Cole didn't want to interrupt Anna's conversation with her friend, but he missed her like hell already. A full day away from her was way too long. And sitting with her at dinner, barely touching her because he knew if he started he wouldn't be able to stop, had only fueled the flames inside.

On the verge of going outside to claim her, he finally heard Virginia's car start up. Thirty-four years, he'd been as cool a fuck as they came. Now, he couldn't even begin to act like he wasn't waiting for his wife.

She stepped inside and he was about to go all Neanderthal on her again when he saw something that shook him: She looked like she'd been crying.

"What's wrong?"

She looked up at him, her eyes wide with surprise at both his question and the fact that he'd practically jumped over the couch to take her into his arms. Studying her carefully, he didn't see any tear tracks, but her eyes were glassy.

"Something happened to upset you. Tell me what it is."

The last thing he expected was for her to smile at him. "You always tell me how sweet I am, but you really are the sweet one." She went up on her toes and kissed him softly.

That one kiss had his cock growing from the hard he always was around her to downright uncomfortable behind his zipper. He needed to get her naked and taste her, take her, fuck her until they were both sweaty and panting. But even that, he was starting to understand, couldn't ease his need for her—or ease the strange ache in his chest.

Besides, he knew he had a bad habit of throwing her over his shoulder and ripping her clothes off within thirty seconds of her walking into a room.

"Tell me about your day, sweetheart."

"It was crazy."

She nestled into his chest and, sweet Lord, he wasn't sure how much longer he could hold out on the urge to take her upstairs and strip her down. He wanted to take her, Jesus, he'd never wanted it so bad, but he wanted to hold her just as bad.

Worse, maybe.

He was about to lift her into his arms when his too-thick brain finally clicked into gear.

"Crazy?" Was this why she'd been on the verge of tears? "What happened?"

"We didn't do word puzzles today."

He loved the feel of her soft curves against him, the vanilla scent of his shampoo on her hair, the sweet smell of her feminine heat. None of that, however, gave him the barest hint of what the hell she was talking about.

"You were crying over word puzzles?"

She pulled back just enough to look at him, her confusion mirroring his. "No. Why would I cry over word puzzles?"

"Hell if I know. I don't even know what word puzzles are."

Her smile was cute and sexy all at once as comprehension dawned. "My kids couldn't stop asking me questions about you. That's why we had to skip a few things today." She bit her lip, looked away. "I hope you don't mind, but they were all hoping you'd sign a few things for them. I wouldn't normally ask, but they're such big fans and—"

He stilled her excuses and apologies with a finger over her soft lips. "I love kids."

Relief swept over her pretty face—along with another emotion that had his gut tightening. "You do?"

"Yes. I do. Tomorrow when I drop you off, why don't I come in and sign them in person?"

Her eyes lit up. "My kids are going to be beside themselves. Although I'm pretty sure we're going to end up skipping word puzzles again."

"How about we do word puzzles first, autographs second?"

"Oh Cole, you're only making me feel worse about the other thing I have to ask you." She frowned. "I hate putting you in this position, so much I can't even tell you. But there's this fundraiser coming up soon and the district had been short of funds lately and—"

"Of course I'll do it."

As she looked up at him with surprise, he had to wonder, had anyone ever been this beautiful?

"You don't even know what my principal wants you to do."

"Will you be there with me doing whatever it is?"

"Yes, of course. I wouldn't throw you to the wolves like that. Not for anyone or any reason."

"Did you ever think for one second I wouldn't help you?"

"Of course not. I just felt so bad about the way my school is using your fame."

"You have nothing to feel bad about, sweetheart. Nothing at all."

"I don't get it." Another frown came, this one deeper. "You're so great. You shouldn't have had to go out looking for me—looking for a wife to bring to your grandmother. You should already have been married with kids."

She was looking at him so intently, it was almost as if she was trying to see all the way into his soul for the answers.

"Other people don't see me like you do."

All they saw was football and money—and what they could get from him.

"Then they're all wrong." She reached up, ran her fingers through his hair. "And stupid." She pressed her free palm against his chest. "And blind. Crazy blind."

Jesus, he'd never wanted anything, anyone, as much as he

wanted the woman in his arms, her ocean eyes so wide and loving.

Loving.

A sharp pang nicked him in the center of his chest, knocking loose a memory from his childhood. One of hundreds of afternoons he'd watched his friends' parents come and pick them up from school while he walked alone to the bus. He'd loved his grandmother more than anyone in the world, but he'd wanted a mom and a dad so bad that sometimes he almost hated her. Almost as if she'd taken their place, as though if she were gone then maybe they'd come back and he'd be whole.

And now, here he was, wanting a real wife just as bad as he'd wanted a real family back then. Fucking longing nearly tearing him apart again, nearly breaking him, the way it had tried to break him when he was a kid.

Didn't she know he hadn't gone looking for love? Or forever?

Anna was supposed to be temporary.

Not forever.

He wasn't supposed to want her to stay forever.

Good thing he knew exactly what to do, exactly how to make it seem like he didn't care.

"No, baby," he forced himself to say, "they're right. I'm not the wife and kids type."

He waited for her to push out of his arms, to walk away, to cry. Instead, she simply blinked at him. "Why aren't you?"

He was hit with another picture of himself as a kid, scrawny and smaller than the other boys in his class, a little kid who had to learn early how to protect himself.

Every day on the field, he practiced the defensive plays he'd learned as a kid. Protecting his back had helped get him where he was today.

He wasn't going make the mistake of dropping his guard. Not for anyone.

Not even for Anna.

"Some people want those things. Some don't."

Her eyes darkened, a storm rising over the ocean. "Okay." Her voice was measured. Too measured. "I've got another question for you."

He tensed, waiting for her to push him, waiting for her to try and force him to admit what he was feeling for her. Women had done a lot of desperate things over the years to try and bind him to them. Fake pregnancies. Crying. Begging. None of it had worked even the slightest bit. In fact, he'd only ended up losing what little respect he'd had for them.

"Are you done showing me crazy?"

Jesus, what had she just said? Was she talking about sex when every other woman would have been trying to yank out his heart?

"You don't want to go upstairs with me right now." His cock twitched behind his zipper even as he warned her, the words hard, low, raw.

He couldn't trust himself with her. Not when he wanted too damn much. Not when he wanted things a man like him had no right to want from a woman like her.

"Maybe you're right. We shouldn't go upstairs."

Pain speared him at her quick agreement, until he realized she was glancing at the living room, then back at him.

"Right here worked pretty good yesterday."

Fuck. No. She couldn't be saying what it sounded like she was saying. But the look in her eyes, the new sensuality he'd so enjoyed putting there, was definitely front and center now.

"Anna."

He could only warn her one more time before she pushed him too far. Especially when just being with her, just breathing her in and listening to her sweet words had already pushed him to the edge.

She stared right back at him. "Cole."

He heard a growl rip from his throat, and then his hands were on her, turning her, bending her over the dining table, pushing her skirt up to her waist. He knew his hand was coming down over her ass, but couldn't stop any of it.

The sound of his open palm again her panty-covered ass shot into the silent room.

But then another sound came. Anna's whimper.

Not of pain. But of desire.

He'd promised her crazy, but constantly ripping her panties off wasn't really what he'd meant. He'd planned to slowly introduce her to pleasure, had thought he'd tease her until she was begging for his lovemaking. Instead, he yanked her panties down to her knees and couldn't stop staring at the imprint of his hand on her flesh.

And as he lifted his hand and brought it down on her sweet, soft flesh again and again, he knew he wasn't just playing a sensual game, wasn't just trying to drive her higher as arousal dripped from her pretty pussy lips down the inside of her thighs with every connection of skin on skin.

He was spanking her for making him feel too damn much.

He was punishing her for making him fall in love with her.

He was about to actually hurt her because he was desperate to prove to her that she was wrong.

Furious with himself—with her—with the whole damn world, he yanked open his pants and positioned the throbbing head of his cock at her entrance. Instead of trying to get away from him, she squirmed against him, trying to take him inside her body.

No! The voice yelled at him not from his head, but from his heart. *He couldn't do it.*

* * *

Anna's body craved Cole's touch, any kind of touch at all. Hard or soft. Out of control or sweetly tempting. No question, there was something so wonderfully depraved about what he was doing to her.

And yet, even as she responded to him, even as her body begged him for more, for faster taps on her backside, even as she felt herself grow wetter, more open for him, she couldn't hide from the fact that nothing about this was right.

Not when pain was everywhere in the room. Not when pain was taking her over, top to bottom.

She didn't really feel the pain of his hand on her bottom. He wasn't hurting her at all with his little smacks. He simply didn't have it in him to hurt her. Physically, at least.

No, the pain she felt was all Cole. It was seeping from his cells, his veins, from his heart to hers.

On the verge of taking her, he'd sudden gone completely still, his fingertips digging into her hips so hard she knew she'd have ten finger-sized round bruises on her skin in the morning.

He moved away so abruptly she would have fallen if not for the table holding her up. She blinked back tears as she slowly pushed herself up so that she was standing, using the time to pull her underwear back up and smooth down her skirt to catch her breath. Finally, when she felt strong enough, she turned and faced her husband.

He'd righted his clothes too and now he was standing halfway across the room—*away from her*—his hands in fists, his eyes so dark and so bleak she had to choke back a sob.

"Tell me what you see now. Tell me if they're all blind now, Anna."

She knew what he was doing, that he was trying to force a monster into the room. But there wasn't one.

"I see a man who knows exactly how to touch me."

His jaw tightened, his biceps flexing as he clearly worked to control himself. "Fuck no, Anna, I was hurting you."

"We both know you weren't," she countered in a soft voice as she took a small step toward him. "We both know I was loving, craving your touch. The way I always do. The way I always will. The way I'm craving it right now."

She knew she had to be careful, that the big strong man who hadn't run from anything in his life was a heartbeat away from bolting. But she was so sick of being careful. She'd spent a lifetime being careful.

She'd taken her first risk on Friday night when she'd let Cole kiss her, and then one after the other since in his arms. Every minute with him the risks grew bigger.

But so did her courage.

"Do you want to know what else I'm seeing, Cole?"

Instead of answering her, he said, "Don't do this, baby. Don't try to convince yourself that I'm someone I'm not."

"Don't you dare talk to me like I don't know my own eyes. My own mind. My own heart."

And despite the way he was trying to push her away, she knew deep in her heart that she wasn't wrong about him.

"I know what I see. I see a man who loves his grandmother, who plays for his team with all of his heart, who treats complete strangers with respect." She took another small step toward him. "I know what I feel. I feel your innate tenderness. I feel the pure comfort of being in your arms. And I know, without a doubt, that you're the best thing that's ever happened to me."

His eyes flashed as she repeated his earlier, sleepy words back to him. His barriers had been down after their lovemaking, so different from the thick wall she was facing tonight.

"I see what you let me see, Cole. But I want to see so much

more. I want you to trust me the way I've trusted you."

"You know firsthand just how well I can lie, Anna. You shouldn't trust me. Not for one second, sweetheart."

Did he hear himself call her *sweetheart* even when he was trying like hell to push her away? She'd given him her body. Now there was only one thing left to give him.

And even though she knew it was the very thing he was fighting against, she couldn't keep it inside.

She wouldn't.

Not when he'd taught her how to take a chance, how to grab his hand and fly higher than she'd ever thought she could.

"I'm not an opponent you can tackle to get me out of your way," she told him. "If you want to try to push me away then you'd better be ready for me to push right back." She moved the rest of the way across the room, leaving only a couple of feet between them. "I thought I was the one who needed to learn from you. I thought I was the scared one, that you weren't afraid of anything. I thought you knew more than I did. I thought you were going to teach me crazy and I was going to learn everything I could. But only about pleasure."

She stopped, held his dark, dangerous eyes with her own. She wasn't scared anymore.

Even though her heart was completely on the line.

Instead, the strength of her feelings for the one man she never would have thought to fall for in a million years gave her the strength she'd always been searching for.

"You are the only person who's ever looked at me and thought that there might be strength inside. You are the only one who's ever held my hand and helped me fly." She held out her hand to him. "Let me do that for you, Cole."

His face was completely empty of expression and it took everything in her to keep her hand from trembling, to keep from backing away from the biggest chance she'd ever taken.

It took more strength than she even knew she possessed to hold steady, to know that she couldn't force him to feel something he didn't feel.

And to still say, "I love you."

Chapter Sixteen

Her bravery stunned him. The sweet girl he'd propositioned in Las Vegas was still there, just as innocent, her halo still hovering over her beautiful hair. But that Anna wasn't the only one standing in front of him, hand outstretched. An incredibly strong woman stood there, too.

Offering him something he didn't deserve: Love he didn't think he was capable of returning.

Cole didn't know what the fuck he was going to do about it. All he knew right then was that he couldn't let her go. Not like this.

Not fucking yet.

It was the fear of losing her that had him pulling his feet up out of the hardening cement, it was a vision of her dropping her hand and walking away forever that made him reach out and take it.

Their first night together, he'd held her hand, had loved the feeling of protecting her. But he didn't know who was protecting whom anymore.

He dropped his gaze to their linked hands, turned hers over and stroked his thumb across the base of her palm, along the very edge of her wrist.

"I—"

Cole had lied so many times. Lies had kept him on teams he should have been cut from. Lies had kept him in beds he shouldn't have been allowed anywhere near. One more lie shouldn't be so hard. One more lie would keep Anna right here with him.

He lifted his gaze to hers, watching her watching him as blue turned to green, then back again. The storm was still raging in her ocean eyes, everything swirling together—her love, her pain, her hope, the desire he'd taught her to crave.

There was only one other wish he'd wanted to grant so badly. Making that wish come true for his grandmother had brought Anna to him.

But he couldn't grant this wish for love as easily. Cole hadn't grown up in a home where he could watch how a man was supposed to love a woman. But Anna had.

"Don't, Cole." She gripped his hand more firmly in hers. "Don't say something you don't mean just to try and make me happy. That isn't what I want from you. That isn't why I said what I just said."

But even as she spoke, she moved closer and he could smell the storm on her, sweet and spicy and darker than ever. And he couldn't help but notice she hadn't said "I love you" again, just as he couldn't help the flash of disappointment at not hearing it fall from her sweet lips one more time.

Knowing himself for the bastard that he was, he said the only thing he could.

"I really, really, really, really like you."

Disappointment flared blue-green, before laughter filled her big eyes. Eyes that would haunt him forever.

"Wow. Four *really*s. That's a whole lot of like."

The words danced in her laughter, but all he could hear was the pain beneath them.

"Anna, I—"

But this time, she wouldn't let him finish, her finger moving over his lips. "Take me to bed, Cole."

And as he lifted her into his arms, instead of the relief he should have been feeling that she'd not only let him off the hook but still—miraculously—wanted to be in his bed, Cole couldn't escape the dragging feeling of discontent in his gut that told him he was on the verge of making the biggest mistake of his life.

* * *

Anna felt Cole's frustration as if it were her own. She'd never learned how to block out other people's emotions, especially when she cared deeply for the person who was hurting. She should have been the one in pain—the one who gave love and only got like in return. And yes, a part of her was smarting from that.

But for all of her fears, she'd grown up with a foundation of love. While she knew Cole had always been loved by his grandmother, she suspected that hadn't been enough. He'd needed a family of more than two.

If she could, she'd give him all the love he'd never had. Even knowing he might not ever give it back to her.

He laid her down on the bed, so gently she knew he was trying to make up for the way he'd been on the dining table. He moved away, but she was quicker, pulling him off of his feet so that he couldn't stop himself from falling onto her, the hard thud of his heavy muscles knocking the breath from her lungs.

"I keep hurting you," he said as he lifted his weight up over her.

Didn't he know she loved having all of him, loved knowing she drove him so wild that he lost control and took them both to the edge of reason?

"No, Cole. You would never hurt me. Never."

She took advantage of his surprise by pushing him with all her might so that he was lying sprawled on their bed. She swung her legs over his, tucking her groin against the hard length in his jeans.

He groaned and she threaded her fingers through his, holding them away from his body.

"I'm sure one day I'll need you to be gentle, to kiss me softly and stroke me, to whisper in my ear and take me slowly."

Pure lust flared in his eyes at her soft words, his hips grinding into hers as automatically as hers came down onto his.

"But I've had gentle my whole life." She let her lips move into a wicked smile she hadn't known was a part of her. Until Cole. "Right now, I like it—" She leaned down, the tips of her hair brushing against his chest, his neck as she put her mouth to his ear. "—raw." She nipped at his earlobe. "And rough." She licked over the small bite. "So, are you going to keep apologizing to me—or are you going to give me what I really want?"

And just as she'd hoped he would, he immediately answered her demand with one of his own as his strength overpowered hers, flipping her onto the mattress. But then, she saw him pull back, watched as his hard-won control came back down over them.

"You don't know what you're saying." His nostrils flared, his jaw jumped. "You don't know what you're asking for."

Excitement, anticipation, desire, along with the swirling darkness surrounding Cole, shuddered up her spine, made her nipples even harder, sent blood racing between her thighs.

"Everything." She could be just as stubborn as the beautiful man she'd fallen so deeply in love with in such a short time. "I want everything you can give me." She wrapped her legs around his hips, pushed herself into him. "Just like this, Cole, take me just like this. Show me how much you want me. I need to know how much you want me."

Still fully clothed, he thrust against her as hard as he ever had, his hands dropping hers to grab her hips instead. She gasped as he roughly gripped her still-tender butt cheeks, but instead of pulling back he gripped her harder, grinding her sensitive, almost painfully aroused flesh against his erection. The covered zipper against her clit drove her crazy with need, but it was his words—"You have five seconds to come or you're going to feel my hand on your sweet ass again"—that had her pussy clenching. And oh God, how she held out those five seconds, as he ground out, "Five. Four. Three. Two," pausing far longer than he needed to before saying, "One," she didn't know.

And then she wasn't thinking anymore, couldn't get any part of her brain that wasn't connected to sex to work, because he had flipped her back over, one hand in her hair to keep her face down against the mattress, the other shoving her dress up, her panties down. And then he was lifting her hips up so that she was on her knees and she could almost feel it, the sweet burning of his palm across her skin.

Nothing happened. The air was still. She held her breath, then had to let it out when she didn't have enough oxygen.

Whack!

Nothing could have prepared her for his hand coming down over her pussy. She cried out, the sound more pleasure than pain, partially swallowed by the thick comforter. There was no time to get used to the new sensations wracking her, no time to try and anticipate his next move, no time to get her head around the fact that she was being spread open by thick fingers, that they were driving high and hard inside of her.

She'd asked for rough and he was giving her things she'd never known she wanted, never could have guessed that she needed. Every second, he took her higher, showed her something new and wonderful. Like now, with his teeth against the raw, tender skin of her bottom, his thumb a hard and wonderful press against her clit.

The beginnings of a climax crawled down her spine, one heavy throb of pleasure after another, slower to build than any other orgasm he'd given her, but promising to be so much bigger, so much better. Anna gloried in deeper, darker pleasure than she'd even known was possible.

And then, as she felt Cole's hips behind her, his cock pushing her open so much farther than his fingers had, as his chest covered her back, as he turned her head to the side and his mouth found hers, Anna finally understood what love could do.

Love could take pleasure and make it thrilling bliss, blessed ecstasy. Love could throw her into the midst of luscious heat. And through it all, through every rough and raw and overpowering release, even as she lost not just her control, but the entire thread of who she was, Cole was there with her. Strong. Comforting.

And more loving than he seemed to know.

Chapter Seventeen

"I meant to tell you last night," Cole said as she was brushing her hair in front of the mirror the next morning, "Julie set up an interview." He paused, his gaze locking with hers in the mirror. "For us to talk about our marriage."

Anna had known something like this had to be coming, that Cole's fans would demand answers about his quickie marriage to a nobody. But that knowledge didn't make her any less nervous about it.

She was happy blending in, fading into the background. At least, she'd always thought so. It was only these past few days, in the hours she'd spent with Cole, that she'd begun to wonder at the truth of everything she believed about herself.

Still, finding a core of deep sensuality inside herself was a very different thing than wanting any part of the limelight.

"The writer is a friend of Julie's. You don't have to answer any questions you're not comfortable with."

Anna knew he was trying to reassure her. And though she was glad to hear the interview wasn't going to be televised, she needed to know something first. "Which paper?"

She watched him with rising alarm as he moved toward her, knowing it was his nature to instinctively try to protect her from things he thought would hurt her.

"*USA Today*."

The brush clattered from her fingers to the sink and he tried to smile reassuringly.

"They're probably just going to ask the same questions we've already answered for everyone else. Where we met. Why we kept our relationship a secret." His body was warm against hers, his chin too high to rest on the top of her head. "I'll field her questions, sweetheart."

How had their one little lie—no, their *huge* lie—for his grandmother spiraled off in so many directions?

"When is the interview?"

"Tonight. Six o'clock. At Max's."

Trying to act normally, she moved to pick her brush up, but Cole beat her to it.

"Let me."

Long strokes soothed her, had her unable to look away from the heat in his eyes.

She loved him. But he didn't love her.

It was one thing to try and hide the truth from family and friends, made easier in some ways by the fact that they'd see what they wanted to see. They wanted to believe she was the luckiest girl alive to have captured Cole's heart. They wanted to believe in love at first sight. They wanted to believe that an invisible girl like her could be a superstar's everything.

But strangers didn't care about her happiness. Some would be jealous, the ones who dreamed of men like Cole. Most wouldn't believe it. They'd all seen the kind of women he usually chose.

None of those women were short with slightly crooked bottom teeth. None of those women walked around with an extra five pounds on their hips. None of those women were first-grade teachers who usually liked talking with the kids way more than chatting with their parents.

And not one of those women wore a halo.

* * *

On the drive to her school, neither of them spoke about what had happened the previous night—or what she'd said to him—and Anna, for one, was glad for some time to try and wrap her head around the multitude of ways her life had changed in such a short time.

But it wasn't just her life that had changed.

She'd changed...shifting a little more each time Cole touched her.

She felt simultaneously uncomfortable and more in tune with her true self than ever before.

The discomfort came from her heightened sensitivity to everything. The sun was brighter. The sky more blue. She noticed every chirp the birds made. And her skin sizzled at Cole's slightest touch. Even when he wasn't touching her, just the heat in his eyes caused a flush to move across her chest, over her cheeks.

Before Cole, she'd been afraid to feel too much, had done everything she could to block sensation. From that first kiss, her husband had stripped away those layers, was still stripping them away one at a time, leaving her to look with surprise into the mirror each time she passed.

The woman staring back at her was similar to the one she'd seen for thirty years, only with an edge of sensual comprehension and pure emotion that she hadn't previously possessed.

He walked through the halls with her, his left hand never letting go of hers as he shook hands with what felt like every person in San Francisco. The ringing bell gave her license to drag him away to the relative safety of her classroom, where she all but slammed the door in the faces of her students' parents.

Not looking the least bit bothered or put out by any of the attention, Cole got down on his knees on the linoleum floor, surrounded by overexcited first graders. His laughter was contagious. He was a total natural with kids as well as adults. They didn't have to be a fan of his football skills to fall in love with him.

Anna put her hand to her heart at the sight of his gentleness, his laughter at the kids' antics, at his pure enjoyment of being with a bunch of six-year-olds.

He was going to be a wonderful father.

And as her hand moved from her heart to her stomach, Anna couldn't hide from the fact that her dreams and hopes for a family of her own—and a husband who loved her with all his heart—had already taken root.

She didn't just want Cole's love.

She wanted a family with him, too.

She wanted forever.

* * *

Later that night at Max's, all around them people in the popular city bar and restaurant were laughing, drinking, flirting. Some were playing with their cell phones. But all of them had one thing in common: They were all focused on Cole and Anna.

After years in the spotlight, he was used to being the center of attention in public. But Anna, his sweet Anna, wasn't. It was pure instinct to want to protect her from it. He was thirty seconds from dragging her out of the restaurant and locking her up in his bedroom until news of their marriage had blown over. Pissed that he'd let Julie talk him into this, he'd almost risked getting kicked off the team by tackling her husband in practice.

At one point the bastard golden boy had given Cole one of those shit-eating grins everyone so stupidly ate up. "Marriage kicking your ass, huh? I'd be happy to give you some advice on keeping your wife happy, if you need it."

Cole had almost jumped him right there. But he could see that was exactly what Ty wanted and he couldn't give the motherfucker the satisfaction of knowing just how twisted up in knots he was over his sweet, pretty wife.

"I've had gentle my whole life. Right now, I like it raw. Rough. I want everything you can give me. Show me how much you want me. I need to know how much you want me."

Jesus, just remembering what she'd said to him had his dick about to bust out of the zipper. He'd been surprised by her last night, and now, here she was surprising him again during their interview. He'd thought that Anna was going to be the nervous one, but she was amazingly relaxed. He was the one gritting his teeth, worrying about every fucking question. Pummeling the crap out of his teammates in practice hadn't taken the edge off a damn thing.

"So you grew up in the Bay Area?"

Anna nodded, smiling at the journalist in her open, friendly way. The same way she'd looked at him that first night in the club. With pure, shining innocence.

"My whole family is here."

"How did they react when you brought Cole home for the first time?"

He tensed at the question, but Anna's eyes sparkled. "They loved him, of course. Although one of my brothers-in-law almost had a coronary when he realized his biggest hero had just walked through the front door."

"What about your parents? How did they feel about their daughter dating a big, bad Outlaw? Were they worried he'd break your heart?"

Anna didn't answer right away. When she did, her words rang with honesty. "Of course they worried. What parent wouldn't?"

Cynthia raised an eyebrow in Cole's direction. "So then, how did you prove to them that they could trust their precious daughter's heart with you?"

His throat felt way too tight. For some reason, the man who had sweet-talked his way into more panties and out of more sticky situations than he could keep track of couldn't find any way out of this one.

Anna leaned her head against his shoulder. "The truth is, they never had a chance, not even my mom, who was worried about me at first. They love him as much as I do. How can they not?"

She tilted her face up to his, so beautiful that he had to touch her, couldn't stop himself from lightly brushing his thumb across her lower lip.

The photographer Cynthia had brought with her snapped a rapid flurry of shots, Anna's love for him a radiant, glowing presence at the table.

"Wow, it really seems like you two are the fairytale come true. The sweet schoolteacher who tamed the bad boy."

The journalist smiled and Cole thought it seemed genuine. Still, he'd been burned one too many times by the press to trust the woman any further than the next table over.

Anna's smiling eyes found his. "Did you hear that? She thinks I've tamed you."

Her laughter was infectious, even making his mouth move into a grin.

His wife shook her head, still laughing as she turned back to Cynthia. "Trust me, my husband is completely untamable." Her gaze flicked back to him, shot through with wild heat. "And the truth is, I wouldn't want him to be any other way. I wouldn't ever want him to be something that he's not or feel like he has to say or do the right thing to make me happy. He makes me happy just the way he is, just the way he's always been."

"I see why you fell for her." Cynthia broke the spell his wife was wrapping around his heart. "But since my readers aren't here with us to see the two of you together in person, I'd love it if you could tell me what drew you to Anna."

He didn't have to think about it, didn't have to pretend. "I've never met anyone so sweet. Or so beautiful that I can hardly believe my eyes every time I look at her."

"Cole."

Anna's whispered exclamation came with a deep flush in her

cheeks. Any other woman would have preened, but she was more embarrassed than anything.

"But what you can't see is how brave she is. She has more courage in her pinkie than a tailback running into a team of three-hundred-pound defensive linemen."

"Wow," Cynthia said as she scribbled in her notebook. "People are going to go crazy for you two."

But Cole didn't care about the interview anymore. He couldn't focus on anything but Anna.

"One more thing," Cynthia said. "When did you realize Anna was special, Cole? When did you realize you were going to marry her? When did you know you loved her and only her?"

Cole didn't look away from Anna, couldn't have torn his gaze from hers as he said, "The first time I saw her I knew I couldn't let her go. I asked her to marry me that night."

"Was it love at first sight for you, too, Anna?"

"I'd never done anything that crazy before," Anna said in a soft voice, "but being with Cole felt so right from the start."

"So, you're telling me that you asked her to marry you the night you met and you accepted right then and there?" She looked at Cole, then Anna, her eyebrows raised with surprise. "So then why wait months to finally do the deed? And why do it in secrecy?"

Anna response was quick, fluid, believable. "My sister was getting married. I didn't want to overshadow her wedding. And then, when she was heading off on her honeymoon, Cole showed up out of the blue. We just couldn't wait another second."

Cole's gut cramped at her easy lie. She could never have done that on Friday. He'd promised to teach her new things, but he'd never meant for one of those things to be twisting the truth.

How could he ever forgive himself for doing that to her?

Cynthia turned off her recorder. "Seriously, guys, my readers are going to love your story. It's so romantic. So perfect. Thanks so much for chatting with me. If I have follow-up questions, I'll be in touch. Look for the story in the weekend edition."

They said their goodbyes, walking the journalist out to a cab. They drove back to his house in silence. There were so many things he suddenly wanted to say to her. So many things he didn't know how to say.

Nothing in his life had prepared him for Anna.

For the love that she gave him so freely, no strings, no demands.

Just love. Pure and sweet.

Yes, he'd given her pleasure, but along the way he'd forced her to take on skills she should never have needed to know.

Lying.

Evading.

They walked into his house and Anna reached for his hand. "Are you okay?"

He wanted so badly to pull her against him, but he couldn't stand the thought of sullying her with his touch. "You don't deserve this mess. Not any of it."

Her hand slipped tighter through his, so warm, so soft. "You're not forcing me to do anything, Cole. Marrying you, staying with you, doing this interview—they were all my decisions, right or wrong. If I wanted to stop, I'd stop."

He didn't have the strength to keep his gaze off her beauty, the innocence that still clung to her, despite his bad influence. And then he saw it, the question in her eyes.

"What you said to Cynthia...did you mean it?"

Since that first moment he'd seen her, he'd been getting lost in her eyes. Lost again even as guilt bore down on him, he said, "I meant everything I said tonight."

She'd protected him from even one small lie, taking the weight of them all on her own shoulders. No one but his grandmother had ever protected him before. No one had ever cared enough to take a risk like that for him.

Her beautiful eyes swam with disbelief and confusion. "How could you possibly think I'm brave?"

It killed him that she didn't see it, that she didn't already know.

"Do you remember our first night together?"

She flushed, leaning her forehead into his chest. But he wouldn't let her hide from him, couldn't stand not to see the sweet heat in her eyes as she rewound back to their first time together.

"How could I ever forget?"

He grinned down at her. No one had ever made him feel this happy. This good. And not just in bed, where she kept blowing his mind. Just like this, talking, teasing.

"You could have told me to stop at any time." He brushed a

lock of hair away from her sweet lips. "You were so brave. Not just that night, but every time we've been together."

She shook her head, protesting, "That was just sex."

"I've had plenty of sex, sweet girl. Trust me, what we've got going isn't even close to 'just sex.' But if that's not enough for you, I saw you with your mom. In the kitchen at her house."

Her eyes widened in alarm. "How much did you hear?"

"Enough to be proud of the way you stood up for yourself."

And for him. She might not have been telling the complete truth about their relationship to everyone that night, but she'd told her mother a truth she'd held inside for far too long—about how lonely she'd felt in her own big family, surrounded by loving parents and siblings.

As lonely as he'd felt in his family of two.

"There hasn't been a single situation where you haven't held your own, no matter how strange it all is for you, like the VIP box or dealing with the paparazzi. By the way, Julie and Melissa already told me that if I ever screw up and you leave me, they've chosen you over me." He loved the small smile she gave him. "Hell, tonight during that interview, you were the calm one. The brave one protecting me." He tipped her chin up with a finger. "Do you believe me now?"

"It's just that no one has ever called me brave before."

"Then they're all wrong." He hadn't forgotten a word she'd said to him the previous night. And now, he was the one saying them all back to her. "They're all stupid. And blind. Crazy blind."

"Crazy," she echoed, the one word breathless with the same need that was killing him as they stood in the middle of his kitchen.

He needed to be closer to her, needed to know that she was right where she belonged...in his arms.

"I know I promised you crazy, sweetheart. I know you told me last night that you like it raw. Rough. And so do I. But right now all I want is to make love to my wife."

Her eyes widened at his choice of words. He'd never called it *making love* before, hadn't dared let himself go there.

"You make me a better man," he told her, his voice husky with need. And emotion.

"I love you, Cole."

He scooped her up in his arms, kissing her even as he walked across the room to the stairs, his heart pounding harder with every step.

Not just because of how much he wanted the beautiful woman in his arms.

But because for the very first time in his life, he was going to make love to a woman he actually cared about.

Chapter Eighteen

No one but Cole had ever looked at her with such powerful desire. But she'd seen that desire before.

This time it was the emotion in his dark eyes that captured what was left of her heart.

He hadn't said the three words she'd said, hadn't gotten down on his knees to declare undying anything to her. But she didn't need him to.

Because she could see it in his eyes, could feel it in the press of his lips in a kiss that had nothing to do with sex...and everything to do with love.

Love.

"Sweet Anna." He laid her in the middle of his big bed, staring down at her with such heat. With such need.

With so much love.

Love.

"My sweet Anna."

Aching to feel him take her over the edge, she said, "I need to love you, Cole." She reached out for him, desperate for his touch. For his love. "Please let me love you."

And then he was right there, his deliciously hard weight on top of her. She kissed him with ravenous desire, wound her limbs around his to pull him even closer, bucked her hips up into the hard press of his erection.

"Slowly, baby," he said against her lips when he finally pulled free. His tongue slid teasingly along the seam of both lips and she had to lick against him. "That's how we're going to go this time. Nice and easy. So slow. So good."

She didn't know who he was trying to convince, her or himself. But she knew how close she was to losing it already, with nothing more than his kiss—and his soft, sweet words whispering straight into her heart.

"Tomorrow," she said, begging, bargaining. "We'll go slow tomorrow." She reached for his shaft, pressed her hand hard over his erection, felt an answering twitch as he grew even harder, even thicker beneath her grasping fingers.

Pure lust filled his eyes, the lines of his face a picture of a man barely holding onto his control. "Tomorrow I'll fuck you rough. Raw. Tomorrow I'll take you so fast, be so deep inside you, make you come so many times that you won't know where one orgasm ends and the next begins. But right now—" He pulled her hands away from his belt. "—I'm going to love you right."

He nuzzled her neck, causing ripples of pleasure to move all across her sensitive skin.

"Promise you'll help me love you right."

"You've always loved me right," she gasped as his mouth found the swell of her breasts over the neckline of her dress. But then, instead of moving lower, instead of lowering his sinful lips over her aching, swollen nipples, he shifted his weight off her.

"No," she moaned, missing his heat, wanting him closer, not farther away.

"Shh, baby," he crooned. "I'm right here. Loving you. No bondage. No toys. Just me. And you. That's all we need."

Something inside her chest came undone at his soft words, a cold wall she'd built around her heart cracking in two. His fingers undid the top button on her dress. He stopped at the second.

"I can feel your heart beating, baby, so hard it's almost lifting my hands off you."

"I didn't know," she whispered, the adoration in his eyes making her braver than she'd ever thought she could be. "I didn't know I could ever love anyone this mu—"

He kissed her before she could finish her sentence, stealing not just her words, not just her breath, but her very soul. Her dress was open to her waist when he finally lifted his head.

"Let me look at you, baby. So beautiful." He reached out, his hand trembling as he brushed his knuckles over the swell of one breast and then the other. "So damn beautiful."

"You make me feel beautiful." No one ever had before, not until Cole.

"You make me lose my mind, my control." He tried to undo the clasp at the front of her bra. "My hands are shaking." He looked like he couldn't believe what he was seeing. "I've been having sex since I was fourteen, but I've never been nervous before. Not until you."

She covered his hands with hers, smiling as she helped him undo the clasp. But then her smile fell away as she arched her back to force her breasts closer to the heat of his mouth.

"I could just stop here," he said, between decadent slurps against the swelling flesh, the hard tips growing even tighter beneath his sultry tongue, "could just spend the rest of the night doing nothing but licking and sucking your tits."

Waves of pleasure shuddered through her pussy, her clit throbbing as if he was sucking there instead.

"I could just keep loving you like this until you come for me."

His sensual threat—or was it a promise?—sent another rush of arousal through her. His mouth burned hot across her breasts, laving her with his tongue, making her cry out with pleasure as his teeth scraped across her swollen flesh.

"That's it, sweet girl. That's how I want you to feel when I touch you. Now. Always."

His large hand flattened against her belly and she pressed her hips up into his fingers. He suckled her again, causing uncontrollable tremors to take over her muscles, her limbs. And then his hand was moving lower, beneath the lower part of her dress that was still covering her and she opened her thighs wide in a silent plea for him to touch her. Instead of sliding into her panties, he cupped her between her legs.

"I can feel how wet, how swollen you are for me even through the silk."

She was only just managing to take in his low words as he spoke against the curve of her breasts, when he nipped at her breast. Maybe it was the sweet flash of pain that cut the final thread that was holding her to reality. Or maybe it was the way he licked over the tiny abrasion so gently, so lovingly that had her crying out his name as the lowest part of her belly tightened, threatening to shatter. Or maybe it was looking down and seeing his dark head bent over her chest, that sent her orgasm slamming through her, from the apex of her thighs all the way down to her toes and fingertips and everywhere in between.

"Anna. Sweet Anna. I love hearing you come. Watching you come. Feeling you come."

Just the sound of his voice was enough to keep her orgasm

spiraling on and on, until she was fighting for breath, praying for oxygen to fill her empty lungs.

"I thought you were joking," she admitted when she was finally able to speak again. "I didn't know I could come like that."

"It will happen again. I can promise you that. Only next time we'll get there with just these." He pressed soft kisses to her breasts, first one and then the other, and her low moan sounded in the room. "Let's get this all the way off you."

His words were steady, his face focused, but his hands gave him away, the slight tremble that she'd never thought to see in the incredibly strong man she'd married.

It shouldn't make sense that having him undress her was such a big deal. Not when he'd had her naked so many times before, not when he'd had her tied up, not when he'd played with sex toys with her, not when she'd taken him down her throat and swallowed his come. But he'd never looked at her like this. Even when lust was tearing them both apart, there'd always been a barrier. Not just his, she realized with surprise, but hers, too.

Because even as she'd been falling in love with him, she'd been scared. Holding back if not her heart, then the last piece of her soul.

Tonight, he was claiming every part of her, inside and out.

"All of me," she whispered as he gazed down at her naked skin. "I want you to have all of me."

A sound—half growl, half groan—rumbled out of his chest and over her, but before she could reach out for him and demand the kiss she was so desperate for, his face was between her legs, her thighs spread open over his shoulders.

"I haven't spent enough time here, haven't tasted your sweetness nearly enough," he lamented as he gazed at her wet folds with something akin to rapt wonder. "My damn dick is just going to have to learn to share."

She shouldn't be able to feel such deep emotion, such powerful desire, and still laugh. None of those things had ever gone together before. But Cole tapped into every part of her: The part that wanted to laugh. The part that wanted to love. The part that wanted to fuck like a wild woman.

"You laughing at me, sweet girl?"

His tongue curled around the tight bud of her clit before pushing between her labia, and then his fingers joined his tongue, plying her open, sliding into her aching core.

She arched into his mouth, his fingers, opening wider, taking him deeper. And through it all, she was smiling, was so happy she thought she might burst.

"You make me smile."

And then Cole was saying, "You're right," and he was up and over her so quick she barely had time to mourn the loss of his tongue against her clit. How could she miss that when he was pressing the thick head of his erection between her slick folds?

"Tomorrow." Propping himself up on his elbows, he cupped her face in his hands. His mouth a breath from hers, he said, "I'll love you slow and easy tomorrow."

He thrust all the way into her at the exact same moment that their lips touched. It didn't matter that she'd detonated just minutes ago, that she should have been sated. In fact, her previous orgasm only seemed to make her more sensitive, more responsive. And when his tongue found hers and he kissed her like he'd never get enough of her, she came undone. Again.

Only this time, it wasn't just her pleasure that she was getting lost in. She was right there with Cole for every stroke, every thrust, every groan, feeling his climax as if it were her own. Just as her love for him meant that she would willingly take on his pain, she now realized she would always share his pleasure, too.

Chapter Nineteen

Cole was a master at holding focus. Even as a little kid, he'd been able to forget everything but the game. Didn't matter what else was going on in his life, as long as he was on the field, he was good.

He'd been off all goddamned day.

So far off that the guys were not just giving him confused looks, he could see a couple of the rookies, hungry for the chance to shine on the team, talking about him. Like hell if they were going to take his position anytime soon.

He ran faster. Tackled harder. Physical pain meant nothing as he worked to recapture the one thing that he'd always taken as a given.

But it remained just out of his grasp.

The linebacker coach had to pull him off the field. "Quitting time."

Cole looked up, saw that the field was almost empty. Only Ty was still out there, practicing hitting his targets.

"But if you want to run some more formation reads, Cole, I'm happy to stay a little longer."

Fuck. He didn't want to go in now. But Joe had a new baby at home and Cole knew he wanted to be there with his family. Not out on the field with some messed-in-the-head linebacker who didn't know which way was up.

"No, I'm good." He couldn't miss the relief in the other man's eyes.

Ty walked into the locker room just as Cole stepped into the hot spray of the shower. "You're not the only one, you know."

Cole slammed the nozzle shut. "Fuck off, Ty."

He'd spent some of his best nights with the guy, celebrating big wins with beautiful women, but that didn't mean he wanted to sit there in towels and share feelings.

"Planning on it tonight with my wife." Ty toweled off his hair, before twisting the towel around his waist. "Julie told me you met Anna in Vegas, but I told her you couldn't have found a nice girl like that in the middle of Sin City."

Cole turned to his ex-friend with murder in his eyes. "You won't be able to fuck your wife any time soon if you're not careful."

Not looking the least bit scared, Ty reached into his locker, actually turning his back on Cole. "Julie also said you were with Anna for months. Dating in secret." He turned back around, pinned Cole with a knowing look. "You're a lying sack of shit, aren't you? Your game was different this Sunday. Not worse, just different. Like football isn't the only thing that matters to you anymore."

Cole's fists tightened as he got ready to punch Ty's smug face, just hard enough to make him a little less pretty. Not that Julie would care. She'd still love the bastard anyway.

Just like Anna loved him. And last night, instead of keeping his feelings locked up like he should have, he'd given in.

And loved her right back.

What the fuck had he done?

He was a man with enough darkness in his soul to spill over onto her innocence. The thought of Anna waking up one day and wondering, "Why did I love him?" or realizing it was just great sex and the excitement of the situation that had her temporarily thinking she loved him, killed him.

Anna didn't care about his money, his fame. She cared about her family and her friends and her kids at school. Whereas, at his core, he knew he'd lived a totally selfish life—and enjoyed the hell out of it.

Odds were, one day he was going to wake up and feel trapped. And when he felt trapped, he acted stupid. He didn't want to promise her anything he couldn't deliver. Fidelity had never been his strong suit. Which was why he'd never limited himself to just one woman and had definitely never made love to one before. It was why he'd never, not once, let himself get involved with a good girl.

Not until Anna.

"Look, Cole, I know you were struggling out there today. Now you know love does that to you. Fucks you up for a little while. But then one day you realize you're actually better for it. So, how about you tell me the truth about where you found your wife? Just between you and me, Scout's honor."

Ty had never been a Scout. Neither of them had. And his friend's easy talk about love made Cole's insides go still. Cold.

He and Anna weren't real. Not the marriage. Not her feelings for him. He'd let the great sex confuse him just like it had clearly confused Anna.

"My grandmother needed to think I was settled. That I'd found true love. It was her last wish." Ty knew about Cole's grandmother and his eyes darkened with sympathy. "So I called 1-800-Good-Girl and they sent her over."

"Holy shit, are you saying that you married Anna only because of your grandmother?"

"I found Anna in a club Friday night, looking like a doe caught in the headlights. I convinced her to marry me, then presented her to my grandmother on a silver platter at the hospital Saturday morning."

Cole's gut twisted tighter with each sentence. He'd thought laying it out in black and white would help set him straight, that he and Ty would laugh at another play pulled off to perfection.

But Ty wasn't laughing.

And neither was Cole. Hell, he felt like a bigger shit than he ever had before.

"Are you telling me that the nice girl I met Sunday let you buy her?"

"No." Fuck no. She wasn't a whore—wouldn't even take money or jewelry for her cooperation. "She won't take anything from me. Says she doesn't want it."

"I think I hear what you're saying, but this isn't adding up. Especially since Julie said Anna clearly doesn't know the first thing about football. She's not a groupie. She doesn't want your money. Why would she actually go through with marrying you?"

"She's got a soft heart." Cole had seen Anna with his grandmother, with her family, with the children in her class. "I didn't play fair. I wouldn't let her leave me until she met my grandmother."

And he'd promised her pleasure, thinking it was a fair trade.

What a fucked-up asshole he was.

Ty's frown lifted suddenly. Too suddenly. He shook his head slowly, whistled between his teeth. "You do realize that she's doing it because she's in love with you, don't you?"

"She's not in love with me," Cole countered. "She just thinks she is."

"Right." Ty sounded less than convinced, but he dropped it. "So we shouldn't get too used to seeing her around, then?"

"We'll stay together as long as we need to." It went unspoken, but understood by both men, that everything would change once his grandmother passed away.

Ty zipped up his jeans. "Julie really liked Anna. Said she wasn't like the other girls you've brought around. She said Anna's soul hadn't been sucked out with a liposuction tube."

Maybe another time that would have been funny. But Cole didn't see a whole lot of laughing in his future. The time would come when Anna wasn't in his house, wasn't in his bed, wasn't in his life anymore. And it would suck.

"Look, I know I'm no expert in the whole relationship thing." Ty put his hands up and Cole recognized it as his usual tactic. Playing the nice guy before he went in for the kill.

"That's for damn sure," he bit out, fully aware of the way Ty had fucked things up with Julie, knew the fuckups had gone all the way back to high school. The last person who should be giving him advice was this prick.

Then again, Ty was happy now, wasn't he? With a wife any guy on the team would kill to be with.

Everyone but Cole.

Because he couldn't see past Anna to any other woman on the planet.

"I don't know much, but the thing is—" Ty stopped packing his duffel bag, looked Cole in the eye. "—I know one thing for sure. I couldn't live without Julie. Wouldn't want to do it, period. But I almost had to. Because I was an idiot. More than once. Truth is, I should have been down on my knees groveling, begging, praying for her to give me another chance and not screw it up years ago." Ty zipped up his bag, put it over his shoulder, and shrugged. "Anyway, see you at practice tomorrow."

Cole slammed his locker shut, the entire wall of metal shaking even after he walked away. Who the fuck did Ty think he was, giving him advice?

Cut and dried. The whole goddamned situation with Anna was cut and dried.

He'd needed a temporary wife. She'd agreed to a trade of great sex. Both of them were upholdingtheir sides of the original deal. Once they were divorced, once she wasn't coming around his dick every thirty minutes, she'd realize she wasn't actually in love with him.

And when she looked back, she'd see that loving him couldn't have been possible in the first place.

Working like hell to straighten himself out before he went home to Anna, he almost trampled a woman waiting in the hallway.

"Cynthia?"

What the hell was the journalist doing here?

She quickly shut the phone at her ear. "Cole. Your coach told me you were getting changed. I've got some follow-up questions about your career that I wanted to put in the article."

Cole worked to keep his expression clear as he walked with her and answered her questions.

Had the guard in the hall let Cynthia into the locker room while he and Ty were talking? He couldn't tell from looking at her, didn't think she was acting any differently now than she had the previous night.

What had she heard?

Shit. He couldn't just ask her, couldn't give her any ammo if she didn't already have it.

After she'd asked him her questions, he went down to his car. But instead of driving out of the underground lot, he sat and stared at the cement wall.

* * *

Cole walked into a scene out of every guy's fantasy. Dinner was on the table and Anna was sitting in her seat wearing nothing but one of his ties and spike heels, her legs kicked up on the table, ankles crossed.

"Welcome home, honey. How was your day at the office?"

His wife—his oh-so-beautiful wife—was smiling and sexy, but also shy and nervous.

And so sweet he couldn't believe she was his.

For now.

He moved across the room, dropped to his knees in front of her. Picking her legs up off the table, he put them on either side of his face.

"A whole hell of a lot better now."

He lowered his mouth down to her sweet pussy and her hands dropped from where they'd been covering her breasts—that combination of sinful and innocent that blew his head apart every time he looked at her.

Every time he loved her.

And when she cried out at just the barest touch of his tongue on her clit, so wet and ready for him, he had to pull her down onto the floor with him, had to be inside of her while she came.

Notorious among the football groupies for his staying power, Cole didn't have a prayer of lasting any longer than Anna had. And as he came deep inside the soft, sweet woman riding his lap, he knew himself for the fool he was after what he'd said to Ty.

Cole had found something special in Anna.

Now he just had to hope that one stupid, stubborn conversation didn't come to light...and pray that it didn't all go to hell.

Chapter Twenty

Anna had never felt so good. Or so happy. So incredibly happy that sometimes she was sure she must be dreaming, that she was going to wake up one of these days and realize Cole wasn't real, that she'd invented him to be her perfect man. Strong, dominant, sexy, and yet so caring, so warm, so wonderful.

Neither of them had to get up early on a Saturday morning and for the first time since coming home to San Francisco, they'd had a chance to have leisurely morning sex. Not, she thought with a smile as she burrowed deeper in the covers, that there had been anything particularly easygoing about it.

They were way too hot for each other to make it too long without combusting in each other's arms.

And the thing was, Anna had had enough easygoing sex before Cole. She loved the hot flash of attraction, loved how powerless she was to her desire.

Because that's what Cole was to her. A deliciously sensual drug that swamped her system. She craved his touch. His warmth. His words whispering over her skin. From the first moment that he'd kissed her, she'd been lost, with no desire to be found.

Time and time again, she'd forgotten to protect herself against pregnancy when they made love. But instead of being worried, instead of wondering how she could possibly have let herself get so carried away, she found herself noticing the tenderness in her breasts and wondering if maybe, just maybe, in nine months she'd be seeing Cole's eyes on a little girl or boy.

Everything she'd ever wanted was coming true, things she'd almost stopped dreaming about.

All because of the beautiful man walking into the bedroom holding two cups of coffee.

Her cell phone jumped on the dresser across from the bed. The ringer was off, but Cole eyeballed the screen. "It's your mother."

"I'll call her back later."

She took the mug from him, sipping from his lips first. She'd barely tasted her coffee before he took it from her and put both of their mugs down on the nightstand.

"You don't mind cold coffee, do you?"

She shivered in delicious anticipation at the wicked look in his eyes. "Isn't that why they invented microwaves?"

She went to her knees to reach for him and his arms immediately surrounded her, her mother's call and the coffee completely forgotten. But then, her phone jumped again—and this time she could hear his ringing, too, from the drawer in the closet where he put it at night.

Cole's hands stilled on her skin. He tilted back just far enough that she could see into his eyes. "Sweet Anna, you know how much you mean to me, don't you? You know how happy I was to find you in that club in Vegas, don't you?"

The only time she'd seen him look this serious was when he'd been talking to his grandmother's doctors. "I'm happy, too, Cole."

But the frown between his brows didn't ease, but only burrowed in deeper. "I should have told you how I feel a hundred times by now, baby. I should have been sending you cards and flowers to let you know what you mean to me."

Her heart all but stopped pounding. She had to force herself not to hold her breath, to keep breathing. She'd hoped, prayed, for this moment.

Both of their phones rang again and he seemed momentarily distracted. Now she was frowning, too.

"Tell me now, Cole. Whatever it is, I'm right here. Listening."

His gaze bored into hers and she swore her heart actually quaked behind her ribs.

"I love you, Anna. So much."

Dreams really could come true. Even the ones that seemed impossible.

"I love you, too."

"Promise me that you'll remember, sweetheart. No matter what happens. Promise you won't forget that I love you."

She opened her mouth to promise, to tell him there was no way she could ever forget that he loved her, but just then his doorbell rang in unison with both their phones.

"What's going on? Why is everyone trying to get a hold of us this morning?"

He didn't answer her, just cupped her face in his big hands and kissed her with the very love he'd just professed.

He moved away from the bed and put on his jeans, looking like he was going to face the executioner.

"What's going on, Cole?"

He closed his eyes, stood in the middle of his bedroom like a man who was just about to lose everything. "I fucked up, baby. Big time."

She was up out of the bed now. Her heart, which had been so full just moments before, was abruptly poised on the edge of a knife.

"How?"

"I said some things to Ty in the locker room. Stupid things. Because I was freaking out about everything." He ran a hand across his stubbled face. "The journalist came to the stadium to ask some follow-up questions. I think she overheard our conversation. I think that's what this is all about."

Everything froze for Anna in that moment. The very air went so still before her that she could see the dust motes stopping their dance in front of the window's morning light.

"What did you say to Ty?"

"I'm sorry, baby."

He was moving toward her, but when she held up a hand, he stopped immediately.

"What did you say?"

"Ty was pushing me, so I told him the truth about how we met. About why we got married." He ran a big hand through his hair so that it stood on end. "But the truth has nothing to do with how we met or why we got married. The only thing that's true is how much I love you."

The knife made its first cut into her heart.

"So, let me see if I understand you correctly. You told Ty our secret just because he asked you one little question, but I've lied to everyone I love again and again."

She couldn't believe her voice was so steady. But maybe it was because she was so cold. Frozen from the inside out. Tears couldn't possibly come from a block of ice. There had to be warmth for water to drip.

And there was no warmth anymore.

"I'd take it all back if I could," the man she'd loved so much swore. "I'd rewind back to Wednesday night and say different things. I'd go back to that moment and tell him I was in love with you. Hell, I'd go back to that night in the club and know without a doubt that I was going to fall in love with you."

"Wednesday night? You talked to Ty on Wednesday night about us?"

A quick reel played through her head of all the ways he'd touched her in the nearly three days since then, all the times she'd told him she loved him. She'd thought she was safe with Cole. She'd thought she'd found comfort in his arms.

Lies.

They'd all been lies.

"We don't know for sure that she heard what I said to him, that she printed it in the paper. Maybe everyone is calling to congratulate us."

"Don't lie to me anymore, Cole. At least respect me enough to admit that you know that's not why they're calling."

And the truth was, she didn't have to read the article to know that all of her dreams had come crashing down. Hadn't she known all along that this would happen if she were stupid enough—weak enough—to let herself fall for Cole?

She lifted her chin, standing there naked in front of him, her stupid body still wanting his despite the way he'd sliced through the center of her heart.

"We need to talk to your grandmother."

She saw the moment he realized the full ramifications of what he'd done, the way his face fell even further than it already had. "She doesn't deserve this."

"I agree. That's why I need to go apologize to her. In person." She paused, waited for her heart to start beating again, then realized it was going to take a hell of a lot longer than this. "And I want a divorce."

She couldn't look at him, couldn't bear to see his reaction as she picked up her phone and ignored the half-dozen messages blinking on it. She dialed the travel agent with whom she'd booked all of her siblings' wedding trips and honeymoons.

"I need to buy the very next ticket from San Francisco to Las

Vegas, please."

Cole took the phone from her before she could grip it tighter. "Make that two tickets. First class out of SFO. Yes, noon works."

Anna walked past him as he was reciting his credit card number from memory. She locked the bathroom door behind her, and as she stood beneath the spray of the shower she tried not to face the real reason her face was drenched.

She'd asked Cole for a divorce once before and it hadn't happened.

Looked like the second time was the charm.

* * *

"Hi, Mom."

Anna was sitting in the back of a taxi on the way to the airport, Cole tailgating them in his car. She hadn't said a word to him since getting out of the shower and though he'd barely taken his eyes off her until the taxi came, he hadn't pushed her.

She'd pulled up the article on her phone the minute she'd climbed into the taxi. Each word Cynthia had written—about how she and Cole had seemed like a fairytale come to life, only to realize that, unfortunately, their relationship really was too good to be true—had ripped another chunk out of Anna's heart. Now, as her mother poured sympathy over the wireless line, another wave of sorrow gripped her.

"I'm sorry," she said softly to her mother. "I should never have lied to you. Especially when you knew right from the start that everything wasn't okay." She'd purposefully avoided seeing or speaking with her parents and sisters during the week because she hadn't wanted to face the truth. She hadn't wanted to see that she was acting crazy.

Not good crazy, whatever she'd thought that was.

Bad crazy.

But now that she was forcing herself to be honest, completely, painfully honest, wasn't it also true that the way she felt as she sat in the back of the taxi wasn't entirely Cole's fault? He hadn't forced her to do anything, hadn't held a gun to her head and made her say the things she'd said to her family and friends and the journalist.

Just like she'd told him, everything she'd done, every lie she'd told, had ultimately been her choice. They were entirely on her own head. Weighing in her gut.

Creating the holes in her heart.

"No," she said to her mother, "don't blame Cole. He was doing what he thought was right for his sick grandmother. Marrying me was what he thought he had to do to make her happy."

The taxi driver turned his head slightly as if he was trying to hear her mother's reply. Frankly, Anna didn't care anymore. The whole world already knew what a fool she'd been.

The whole world already knew that she'd fallen in love with a man who didn't love her back.

"I'm not making excuses for him," she said. "What I'm finally doing is telling the truth."

It would be so easy to fall into her mother's comforting arms, to let her sisters rally around her, to let them all crucify the man she'd married. So easy.

And so false.

"I screwed up, Mom. And I'll survive."

Somehow, some way, she'd figure out how to pick up the pieces and move on with her life. One day people would stop feeling sorry for her. One day she'd find another man to date, to marry, to love. And one day she'd go to bed and realize she hadn't thought about Cole for minutes. Hours even.

But just then, just when she thought she was finally telling herself the truth, she made the mistake of looking in the rear-view mirror.

"Promise me that you'll remember, sweetheart. No matter what happens. Promise you won't forget that I love you."

Oh God, she hadn't forgotten. How could she, when his declarations of love were still ringing in her ears, when she could still feel the sweetness of his touch all over the surface of her body?

But accepting Cole's love wasn't about memories.

It was about trust.

And trust was something she was all out of.

* * *

Cole wanted to knock the teeth out of every single person who stared at them as he and Anna walked through the airport. After she'd insisted on taking a cab, rather than driving with him to the airport, he'd thought she was going to try to outrun him once they got inside. But when he caught up to her at the security checkpoint, she silently waited for him to put his shoes back on and they walked to the gate together.

She didn't look mad.

She didn't look like she was going to cry.

She just plain didn't look like she cared about anything either way.

That was the worst of all, Cole realized as he walked through the airport beside her: Her glow was gone.

And it was his fault.

He wanted to get down on his knees and beg her forgiveness. He wanted to hold her still in front of him until she agreed to listen to him. He wanted to kiss her until she believed that he loved her.

But they were onstage, so he couldn't do any of those things. All he could do was make it perfectly clear to each and every person watching that if they dared say even one word to either of them, or took a picture with a cell phone, they'd deeply regret it.

Shit. He couldn't stand this silence. Couldn't stand knowing how much Anna hated him.

Couldn't stand knowing how much he deserved it.

He got out his phone, typed in a text message.

He heard hers buzz in her purse and he thought for a minute that she was going to ignore it. But then she reached into her bag.

I LOVE YOU. PLEASE FORGIVE ME.

She ran her finger across the touch screen and deleted his message, then dropped the phone back into her bag, her expression not changing once.

What hurt the most was being so damn close to Anna, having a hundred things he wanted to say to her, and knowing that she wasn't going to hear any of them.

She was going to walk away from him before they got a chance to see what could have been.

And she would never believe that he loved her.

Chapter Twenty-One

"Mrs. Taylor, I stole your wish for your grandson and turned it into a horrible lie. I'm so, so sorry for what I've done."

Anna stood beside Eugenia's bed and waited for anger or tears or disappointment or all of the above from the woman she'd betrayed with a lie. Cole had wanted to come into the room with her, but she'd told him that this apology was something she needed to make alone.

Surprisingly, he'd respected that decision.

The other surprising thing was that his grandmother didn't look particularly upset about her confession. Anna couldn't understand it. According to the messages her sisters had been leaving her via voice and text and email, thousands of strangers were losing their minds on the Internet and TV over her fake marriage to Cole.

Shouldn't his grandmother be more upset than anyone?

"The truth is, honey," Eugenia said as she reached for Anna's hands and gently patted them, "love was never straightforward for me, either." She paused, held Anna's gaze. "And you do love Cole, don't you?"

"Yes," Anna admitted, unable to do anything but speak the truth now. "I love your grandson. But it doesn't matter. Not when I can't trust him."

"I know."

She couldn't believe his grandmother wasn't defending him. "What do you mean, you know?"

Eugenia sighed, shaking her head. "Just because I love my grandson doesn't mean I don't see his faults. He's bullheaded. Sometimes it's a good thing, like when he was chasing his dream to make a career out of football. But other times, he gets an idea in his head and follows it straight into a dead end." To Anna's surprise, the woman smiled. "Did he ever tell you about the first time I went to bail him out of juvie? He started talking back to me before we even got in the car, so I turned around and took him back inside. He didn't think I'd leave him there, but I did."

Anna shook her head. "He went to Juvenile Hall?"

"Oh yes. He spent a night in prison once, too."

Anna felt her eyes grow wide. "He was in jail?" She tried to tell herself she didn't care, that it didn't matter now that they weren't going to be husband and wife anymore, but she'd told herself enough lies already. "For what?"

"Nothing much. Drinking from open containers. Talking back to police officers. His father was just like that when he was young. Too much energy and nowhere to put it. That's when his father started flying, real fast planes that could take all he could give."

Anna could feel herself softening toward Cole. *No!* Just because his grandmother couldn't help but see the good in him, didn't mean Anna had to keep seeing it, too. She'd come here to apologize to Eugenia for her lies, not let the woman convince her to make the marriage real.

She needed to get their focus back on the apology. "I really am sorry about letting you believe my relationship with Cole was something it isn't. I hope you can find it in your heart to forgive me one day."

"Oh, honey." Eugenia patted her hands again. "I appreciate you coming all this way for me, but I don't think you really want me to forgive you for falling in love with my grandson. I think you should forgive yourself first."

"How can I?" Anna whispered. "I've lied to everyone. Not just you, but my family, my friends, my colleagues."

"Cole made his mistakes. And now you've made yours."

Anna shook her head, not willing, not able to believe it could all be that easy.

"I know you're hurting, honey, and I know my grandson is the reason for that. But I've never seen him look at anyone the way he looks at you. Like he's finally seen the sun, like he finally believes it can shine down on him."

Anna's heart almost stopped beating. "He needed to act like that so you would believe that he loved me."

"Oh no. My boy has never been able to get a lie past me. He loves you, honey. Funny thing about us Taylors—we're ornery about relationships. We do our best to act like we don't need anyone. But when we fall in love, that's it for us. Only once. But with every last piece of our hearts."

Anna didn't know what to say, not when the last thing she'd expected was for Cole's grandmother to sit here and talk to her about love. Blaming, yelling, hating—they were all easier than loving.

"If you could, would you take it all back? If I could clap my hands and send you back to Friday night and make sure that you never met my grandson, is that the path you would take?"

Anna opened her mouth to say yes, of course she would take back everything she'd done. But the words just wouldn't come.

"Or," his grandmother said with such kindness, such understanding, "would you have loved him anyway?"

* * *

"I'll never forgive myself for what I did to you, Grandma." A flash of pain shot through him. "And to Anna." Cole's grandmother held his hand, so gently, as if he were the one in the hospital bed. "I took her innocence and broke it in two."

"I'm angry with you, Cole. Anna's angry with you." His grandmother gestured to the stack of papers on her side table. "The entire world is angry with you. You've certainly got a lot of explaining and groveling to do. But anger fades."

"I don't care what the rest of the world thinks." And it was true, he never had. It was what had made him impenetrable. "I only care about you." His throat was almost too tight to say, "And Anna."

"I still love you, honey. And the last time I saw someone as full of love as Anna, I was looking into your grandfather's eyes. Your father loved your mother like that, too. All the way. Holding nothing back. No matter what."

"I made her lie for me."

"Cole." His name was a warning on his grandmother's lips. "Don't keep on with the lying. Don't keep getting yourself in trouble. Yes, you benefited from the lies. But so did she, otherwise she wouldn't have gone through with it."

But the fact that Anna had made her own choices didn't change the fact that he was ruining her life, that he'd gone and done it all in the span of one short week.

"I need to let her go she can have a normal life, marry a guy who's good enough for her." A guy he would dream of killing with his bare hands each and every night.

"I know you think you've broken her heart. But little cracks, that's all there are in it right now. You want to really see it break, you go ahead and let a better man have her. I thought you were smarter than this, Cole." His grandmother hadn't talked to him like this since bailing him out of jail his freshman year at college. "Do you really not see that your entire future is Anna? Are you really going to just up and throw it all away? You've fought before, honey. Fight again. Fight like hell to fix what you've done wrong. And when you get back on the straight and narrow, don't ever look back. Only forward."

Word for word, it was what she'd said to him when he was nineteen. How could he have forgotten?

Playing football had been important, had given him a purpose, a reason to feel good about himself in the morning. Football had been more than just his livelihood, it had been his everything.

But he could play a thousand more games, could keep getting up in the morning, keep depositing those big checks into his bank account, and it wouldn't matter.

Not without Anna.

Because *she* was his everything.

And he was going to get her back. Somehow, some way, he was going to convince her she needed to be with him.

When someone knocked, Cole looked up expecting to see Anna, and was surprised to see the doctor with her.

Please, God, no. Not this, too.

When his grandmother had been railing at him, trying to knock some sense into his thick head, he'd almost forgotten she was sick. She looked and sounded just like the woman of fifteen years ago who'd twisted his ear and told him, "Don't fuck up again."

"Mr. Taylor, I thought I'd bring your wife back inside so that I could give the whole family the news at the same time." Cole could barely process the hint of a smile in the doctor's eyes. "Eugenia, you are a remarkable woman."

His grandmother shot him a triumphant glance. "I've always told my grandson that."

"And I've always known it." Cole's insides were so fucked up by now that his words sounded like gravel scraping on the bottom of shoe.

"I'm sorry, this isn't fair of me to draw it out like this. It's just that it's so much fun, one of the highlights of my job, actually, to deliver such good news."

Cole almost shot up out of his seat to grab the doctor and shake the rest of it out of her, but a small sound from Anna distracted him, had him looking at her instead. She held one hand over her heart, the other wrapped tightly around his grandmother's hand.

"We'll have to do more blood work, but based on the tests we did last night, I think we're heading out of the woods. Hopefully for good."

Cole could have sworn the clouds parted outside the window, that sunlight streamed into the room just as his grandmother whooped like she used to in the casinos when they got a big winner at the slot machines, as happy for a stranger as she would have been if she'd taken home the jackpot.

The ray of light illuminated Anna and he was struck for the hundredth time by her beauty. Her innocence. The pure goodness the radiated from her core.

And as he met her eyes and smiled to celebrate his grandmother's victory, that was when his wife finally let herself cry.

Not because he'd just broken her heart.

But because a woman she'd only met a week ago might not die after all.

Chapter Twenty-Two

Cole had a game to play Sunday, but he wasn't the only one who hated the thought of leaving his grandmother again so soon, especially when there was such good news to celebrate. Anna barely knew his grandmother, but she was as happy about the news of her recovery as any one of Eugenia's close friends would have been.

For the first time, Cole was damn glad for the small hospital room. Because it meant Anna was close to him. It meant he could drink in her beauty. It meant he could listen to her sweet conversation with his grandmother. It meant he could soak in her laughter for a little while longer.

Still, the entire time the three of them were together there, Anna never once spoke to him. Or looked directly at him. She was wholly focused on Eugenia. He only left the hospital room once to make a quick side trip. The taxi waited outside the hotel with the package—a gift for Anna, one he hoped she'd love.

After booking them on the very last flight out of town, they got into the taxi. He could tell she wasn't going to say anything more to him on the trip home than she had on the way to Las Vegas.

"I, uh, picked up something for you."

Her expression became even colder. "I told you already, I don't want your bribes."

"I heard you, Anna. I swear I heard every word you said." He picked up the carrier bag that had been waiting on the floor of the taxi by his feet. "It's not jewelry."

She looked at the moving package on her lap in surprise. She shook her head. "Whatever it is, I can't take it. Not from you."

But he was already unzipping the bag, just enough that a wet nose and tongue licked across her hand. And then, just as he'd known she would, she was pulling the mutt out of his temporary home and hugging the fur ball to her. She didn't let go of the dog for the rest of the taxi ride, held the carrier bag close all through the airport, and constantly checked on the mutt under the seat in front of her during the ride home.

She loved the fifteen-pound ball of fur with everything she had from the moment it licked her.

That could have been me.

But he was an asshole who didn't deserve her. Even now, instead of finally letting her go to rebuild the life he'd torn apart, all Cole wanted was to hold her hostage in the limo and take her back to his house. All he could think about was finding some way to convince her that he really was sorry.

And that he really did love her.

But he remembered that first limo ride from the San Francisco airport, the way he hadn't asked her if she would come with him to his house. He'd demanded it, as if her opinion hadn't mattered.

He now knew that her opinion mattered more than anything.

"Where do you want James to take you?"

She looked at him in surprise, but the expression disappeared as quickly as it had come. "Home. My home."

Coming around to hold the door open for Anna, James looked at Cole like he was dogshit on the bottom of his shoe. His assistant waited until she was safely inside and the door was closed to say, "You're an idiot. A complete fucking idiot."

James didn't wait for a response, just went around to the front of the car and slid in behind the wheel.

With Cole's wife inside the car with him.

Possessiveness gripped him hard and he was just curling his fingers around the door handle to pull *his wife* out of the limo, to work like hell to convince her to come with him in his car, to try and get her to forgive him and give him another chance, when James hit the gas and the limo sped away from the curb so fast it almost took Cole's hand off.

"Fuck!"

Cole took off across the arrivals lanes at a full-on sprint, dodging each car as if he were on the field instead of a crowded airport, until he found his car. Jumping inside, he sped toward the exit with his car door still open, barely closing it in time to prevent it snapping off on a cement pillar. He threw a hundred-dollar bill at the ticket taker and almost crashed through the gate in his hurry to get to Anna.

He didn't know what he could possibly say, what he could possibly do, to get her to give him another chance. All he knew was that he couldn't give her up.

Not without a fight.

Not until he knew for sure that she didn't love him anymore.

* * *

He turned into her street just as James was walking down the steps back to the limo.

Double-parking his car, not giving a shit if it was towed or even totaled by another car, Cole jumped out. He barely heard James say, "Swear to God, you must be the biggest goddamned idiot I've ever met," barely saw the photographers clicking pictures outside as he ran past his assistant and up the stairs.

Praying she hadn't yet locked the front door, knowing that she was so trusting she often forgot, he pushed against it.

And it opened.

Anna looked up from the spot where she was kneeling on the floor picking up mail, the dog sleeping in his carrying bag by the hall table. In that moment, catching her completely off guard, Cole thought he caught something in her eyes that she'd been hiding from him all day.

Love.

"Anna, we need to talk."

She stood up, leaving her mail on the floor, her dark hair silky as it fell over her shoulders, her long lashes almost shielding her ocean eyes from him. She was so beautiful that simply looking at her made his chest hurt with every single breath he took.

"I don't want to talk."

She moved toward him and he expected her to slap him, to scream at him for ruining her life, to tell him to get the hell out of her house and her life.

Instead, her hands went to the hem of his T-shirt, pulling it up his body.

More confused than he'd ever been, Cole couldn't think fast enough to stop her from dragging it all the way up to his armpits. And with her fingernails raking across his chest, it was instinct to lift his arms above his head so that she could get it all the way off.

"Anna. Sweetheart." He wanted to pull her into him, wanted to force her to listen to him beg for forgiveness until she finally capitulated and forgave him for being the world's biggest asshole. "I didn't bring come here for this."

"I know."

She untied the bow at the front of her dress and a second later pulled it over her head and tossed it on the ground.

"Anna." He put his hands on her shoulders, stupid enough to risk touching her when she was standing there almost naked and so beautiful he couldn't believe his eyes, no matter how many times he looked at her. "You don't want to make love to me here. Now."

He hated the way she winced at the word *love*, hated it even more when she said, "You taught me too well, Cole, taught me not to fight what I really need." So matter-of-fact. "And I need you. Here. Now. Just like this."

Her hands went to his belt, unbuckling it, and he tried to still them with his own, but she was focused, one hundred percent intent on pulling his zipper down.

"Anna, baby," he said, dragging the words from his own throat, "listen to me. We need to stop before you do something you don't really want to do."

The pain in her eyes broke his heart as she said, "I thought that was true. All my life I'd told myself I didn't want this." She dragged his jeans down and the erection he couldn't contain jutted out at her through the thin fabric of his navy blue boxers. "I was lying to myself. You taught me all about lies."

She dropped to her knees and he tried again, tried to stop her from doing something she'd hate him for forever.

"Sweetheart, you don't have to do this."

She lifted her gaze to his, locked in tight. "I do." Her tongue slipped out in a wet caress across his bulging cock head and he couldn't stop his arousal from bursting onto her lips. "Even though you've broken my heart, I need this."

Her words tore at him. She wasn't saying she needed him. Just that she was addicted to exploring the deep sensuality that he'd helped her find.

She ran her hands up onto his stomach, his muscles tightening beneath her soft touch. "That first night in Las Vegas you unlocked the door to a part of me that I was denying."

She sucked his cock head inside, swirling her tongue around it. When she pulled back there was lust in her eyes—and so much bleak pain all Cole wanted to do was pick her up and tuck her against his chest and not let her go until it was gone.

"I can't help but crave touch now. Can't stop wanting that rush of release." The breath she took shook her body. "Crazy," she whispered. "I need crazy." Her voice, her expression was ravaged with painful knowledge. "I'll never be able to lock that door again. Even after you're gone. Even without you."

Jesus, she was outright telling him that she was going to replace him. That whether or not he was the man in her bed, she wasn't going to force herself to live in a sexual prison.

The thought of another man ever taking Anna—taking what was *his*—twisted up inside of Cole. His hands became fists in her soft hair.

"I'll kill anyone who touches you."

She answered his threat by cupping his balls and taking him deep into her throat.

Just like he'd taught her...that first night when he'd asked her to trust him.

Something inside his chest splintered apart even as his cock grew harder inside her sweet, sucking mouth.

He'd betrayed her trust again and again, from that first kiss, when he'd convinced her to come to the wedding chapel to say "I do," on that morning he asked her lie to his grandmother, when he'd sat beside her in her parents' house and let her lie to her own family.

He needed to stop this. Needed to stop himself from taking something he didn't deserve from her.

He'd never deserved her, not for one single second that she'd let him be a part of her life.

Her fingernails scratched along the skin behind his balls and he felt them tighten up into his body. She sucked him in deep while laving her tongue along his shaft. Using every last ounce of self-control he possessed, he dragged himself from between her sweet lips.

"No, baby. Not like this."

But her eyes were wild and that wildness made her stronger, stronger even than a man who tackled giants for a living. She gripped his hands, tugged him over her as they tumbled onto the floor.

Cole couldn't leave her, couldn't possibly walk away from her. He needed her too badly, needed to erase the storm in her ocean eyes—and even more, needed to find a way to smooth out the lines of sadness around her soft mouth.

He tried to thread his fingers through hers, but instead of letting him hold onto her, she put her hands on his face and leaned up to kiss him, biting, sucking, stealing his breath away.

A stronger man would have stopped her.

A good man would have known that kisses like this would only make things worse.

Fuck. He had no practice at being that man. Didn't know the first thing about taking care of anyone but himself—and his grandmother.

But even seeing the fallout right in front of him, even knowing he wouldn't be able to erase the guilt when they were done, he couldn't stop himself from pushing her thighs apart with his knee.

And then he saw the thin barrier of her panties.

Thank God.

He couldn't just take her. Couldn't do the one thing he knew he'd regret forever.

But just when he was on the verge of thinking clearly again, Anna dropped her hands from his face and yanked aside the crotch of the panties, revealing her sweet, silky pussy to him.

Even then he might have been able to fight himself back, might have had a prayer of getting off the floor and not pounding into her, if she hadn't said, "Take me, Cole. I can't stand it anymore. I need you inside of me. All day I've needed you. Even when I hated you, I still needed you. Still craved your touch. Your kisses. Your cock."

He'd loved to hear her beg, loved knowing he'd made her so crazy with need that she no longer had any way of fighting her arousal. But, God, he'd never wanted to hear her sound like this, like she was a woman who didn't have any other option but to beg a man who'd hurt her to fuck her. Like she was trying to screw away her pain, doing anything she could to trade it away for a moment's pleasure.

"Please." Her voice broke on the simple word.

And Cole's heart broke, too.

"I love you, sweetheart," he vowed. "I love you so damn much it's killing me."

Her eyes flashed with momentary hope before pain came crashing back down, so much pain that he'd never hated himself more even as he pushed into the warmest, wettest comfort he'd ever known.

"Anna." He had to drive all the way into her, watching her neck fall back as a whimper of deep pleasure left her throat. "My sweet Anna."

Her hands were where he'd taught her to keep them, up above her head, her nails scratching at the wood floor. But he'd taught her that when he'd stupidly thought that fucking her was just a game.

What an idiot he'd been. Because Anna had never been a game, not from that first second he'd seen her across a crowded room.

She'd always been perfection.

And pure love.

But he'd been scared of feeling so much, so fast. He'd thought he needed freedom, only to find out too late that freedom was the biggest lie of all. Freedom was nothing but missing her already, even while she was here in his arms. Freedom was nothing but wishing he'd had a fucking clue what he'd had when she was his.

He reached up for her hands again, couldn't stand not holding onto her, but when he placed his palms over hers, she flinched.

Cole bowed his head.

And grieved. For the woman he'd lost.

Because even though she was right there with him, the truth was that she was already gone.

And still, he couldn't let go, had to hold onto her as their bodies drove towards a completion that they simply couldn't fight.

A droplet of liquid fell from his face onto hers and she opened her eyes.

Cole didn't remember crying as a child at the loss of his parents. He hadn't cried when his grandmother had told him she was dying. He'd thought he was too strong to ever break.

How wrong he'd been.

"I love you, Anna. Forever."

At the same time as he made his vow to her with words, he made it with his body, driving up into the spot that was guaranteed to send them both over the edge.

But even as her ocean eyes swirled from green to a dark blue, even as she cried out against him, even as he made sure that she was connected to him in the most elemental of ways...Cole had never felt more separated from her.

She was giving him her body as openly as ever, but even as she'd let him kiss her, touch her, even as she'd cried out with pleasure beneath him, she was holding back the most important thing of all.

Not the love that he knew she still felt for him. No matter how well she thought she'd "learned" how to be sensual, it was love that made her respond to him.

But she didn't trust him anymore.

And losing the trust of the sweet, innocent woman he'd propositioned in a Las Vegas club was by far the hardest hit Cole had ever taken.

Big enough that he wasn't sure he'd ever be able to play the game again.

His grandmother's words came at him as if she were there in the room with them. *"Can't you see your entire future is Anna? Don't throw it all away. You've fought before. Fight again. Fight like hell to fix what you've done wrong."*

"Please, Anna," he said, their bodies still connected, "please give me another chance. I know you deserve a man who hasn't lied, cheated, and stolen. I know you deserve a man who doesn't break bones for a living. But Anna, can't you see that I'm the man who's in love with you? I'm the man who will do every single thing he can to make you happy for the rest of your life. I'm so damn sorry for every mistake I've ever made. But especially this mistake. Because hurting you is the worst thing I've ever done. The stupidest. Please give me the chance to prove to you that I can love you right this time. Please give me the chance to prove to you that I'm not going to blow it."

"Why should I?"

She was angry now and he could feel the tension thrumming through her, through muscle and bone and skin covered in sweat from both their bodies.

"I gave you the chance to love me. I gave you the chance to be a real husband to me. I trusted you, Cole. And you still hurt me. You still did the one thing you knew would tear us apart. You made sure it would happen. You taught me more than pleasure. You taught me how to close down my heart. How to protect myself from pain. You taught me how dangerous it is to trust."

Her breasts rasped across his chest as she finally let go of the anger she'd been holding inside, her hands fisted on him as if she wanted to beat him off her.

"You've already had every chance in the world to love me right. So why the hell do you think I would possibly give you another?"

Fight. He needed to keep fighting. For love.

For Anna.

"Because you're brave enough to trust me. Because you're brave enough to know the truth when you finally hear it."

She blinked and he could see droplets on her eyelashes. "Whatever you think you saw in me, it wasn't bravery. It was stupidity."

"No, baby, no more lies."

Still hard inside her despite his climax, he shifted her closer with his hands on her hips, and heard her gasp.

But she didn't pull away.

It wasn't much. It wasn't forgiveness or redemption, but it was something.

And he'd take any little bit of hope he could get.

"People have been running from me my whole life. I've got scary down to an art form. But you—you've never run." Her eyes widened with surprise. "You've never let me scare you away." He still held her close, their bodies still connected in the most intimate way possible. "Don't let me scare you, sweet girl. Not when telling Ty those things was just a stupid act, just me trying to pretend I was too tough to fall in love. Not when you're the bravest person I've ever met."

He could barely breathe, the blood rushing in his ears making it hard for him to hear himself say, "Be brave for me, sweetheart."

Chapter Twenty-Three

Anna's family crowded the VIP box, along with her friend Virginia. She'd asked them to come and even though she could see they didn't understand why she was here at Cole's game, they came.

She didn't understand it, either.

All she'd known was that she needed to do this, needed to prove to herself that she really was brave. Cole had said the words to her again and again, but believing it for herself was something else entirely.

Last night, after their crazy floor-sex, he'd gone back to his house. And she'd been so lonely she was surprised she'd survived the night.

Since graduating from college, she'd lived alone. She'd liked the silence, enjoyed reading or listening to whatever music she wanted. Sure, she'd sometimes longed for a partner to share her life with—more as the years went by—but she'd never once felt lonely.

Not until Cole had gone.

Cole had only been in her house twice, but she could feel him everywhere. She'd never look at the entry the same way again, or the kitchen where he'd picked her up and carried her the afternoon after their wedding. And her bedroom...well, she simply couldn't go in there. So she'd slept on the couch.

And wondered all night about Cole.

If he was sleeping.

Or if he was as tormented by loneliness, by desire, by regret as she was.

If he was barely able to keep himself from grabbing his car keys and coming back, just as she was.

If he dialed her number dozens of times, hanging up before the seventh digit each time, like she had.

If he missed her as much as she missed him.

Sunlight streamed into the box as Anna yawned. Even with her new dog—the name on his tag was Lucky, amazingly enough—she'd been so lonely, she'd woken up both herself and him from crying more than once during the night.

Frankly, the hardest thing of all at the moment was trying to act like her mother and father and sisters and brothers-in-law and her friend weren't all looking at her like she was going to break in two.

Julie walked in and came over to introduce herself. "Hi everyone. I'm Julie Calhoun. My husband is one of the guys down there."

Alan, one of Anna's brothers-in-law, all but leapt out of his seat to shake Julie's hand. "Wow, so nice to meet you. Ty is a legend. Congratulations."

If Julie was at all overwhelmed or amused by this greeting, she didn't show it. "I'll be sure to pass on your thoughts to him." She shook her head, laughing. "Although, frankly, that head of his doesn't need to get any bigger."

Knowing exactly how in love Julie and Ty were, Anna's heart squeezed with such longing she felt choked with it.

"Do you have a moment to chat?" Julie asked her quietly, after meeting the rest of her family.

"Sure." Anna forced a smile, knowing her family's eyes were on them as they moved out into the hall.

"How are you doing?" There was no pity in Julie's voice, and none in her eyes. Only natural concern.

"I'm here." Anna honestly didn't know how she was doing, just that she'd had to come to Cole's game.

She was surprised to see Julie smile. "I think they must put something in the Outlaws' water bottles to make sure they're irresistible." Her smile fell away. "Ty wanted to call you to say how sorry he was for his part in all of this. But I knew he'd only make things worse."

"None of this is Ty's fault." Anna shrugged, trying to act like she was more okay than she was, just as she'd been doing all morning. "It isn't even all Cole's fault. It's my fault, too."

Julie looked down. "You're still wearing his ring."

She knew she should have taken it off, that it should have been off since Saturday morning when the news broke about their fake marriage.

Julie looked like she was about to say something more, when

Melissa and Dominic came around the corner. If they were surprised to see her, they didn't show it.

Wanting to do anything but have another conversation about her personal debacle, she said to Dominic, "My father is a huge fan of yours. Would you mind coming in to say hello to him? It would absolutely make his year."

And as the great Dominic DiMarco charmed not only her father, but her entire family, Anna was able to step out of the spotlight for a little while. Only her mother continued to watch her with such deep concern that it broke her daughter's heart all over again.

* * *

During her breaks at school the previous week, when everything had been going so well with Cole, Anna had studied up on football. For her second-ever game, she was no longer in the dark, and couldn't help but be wrapped up in the action, especially with Cole out there.

And the truth was, knowing him so well lent an extra layer to the game. When he sacked the quarterback, she knew it was his testosterone coming into play. When he crushed a running back in the hole, she had to smile at his complete and utter confidence.

It had been a little over twenty-four hours since the article about them had hit. Twenty-four hours of being angry and feeling hurt and betrayed. And yet, she was here.

With the ring he'd put on her finger a week ago in Las Vegas still glittering on her left hand.

The field blurred before her eyes as she looked out on it and accepted the truth.

He'd hurt her feelings deeply and she didn't like him very much right now...but she still loved him. She would always love him.

He'd deserved to be punished by her for what he'd done—she valued herself enough to know that—but not being with him was punishing her, too.

A small half-smile curved her lips at the thought of taking him back—and finding other, far more pleasurable ways to make him pay. But then, gasps sounded in the room and half the people came out of their seats to press against the glass.

Anna looked around at everyone. "What happened?"

Her mother's face had gone completely white. "It's Cole. He was hit."

Anna jumped out of her seat and looked out the window, but she couldn't see Cole, only a dozen people making a circle around someone on the field.

Anna spun away, pushing blindly through the crowd in the VIP box for the door. She needed to be with him, needed to see for herself that he was okay.

"Anna." She realized there was a hand on her arm stopping her from running down the hall. Dominic turned her in the opposite direction. "The field is this way."

With that, he took off down the hallway, and she was so glad he wasn't waiting for her to catch up. As an ex-pro player, he was naturally fast, but love gave her strength and speed she shouldn't have possessed. By the time they got to the tunnel, she was running past Dominic, past all of the guards.

Heading straight for Cole, she didn't see the crowd on their feet, didn't notice the eerie silence. All she could see was her husband lying on the grass.

All she could feel was love.

Not anger. Not bitterness.

Only love.

She'd thought coming to his game was being brave. But as she pushed through the crowd of coaches and trainers, she finally realized what real bravery was.

It was loving someone so much that she would take his pain as her own.

And it was forgiving the little mistakes, the bad decisions, the sometimes hurtful words, because she knew that none of that really mattered when it came right down to it.

Her husband had told her she was brave, time and time again. She hadn't believed him, hadn't thought he was seeing the real her—when all along he'd known her better than anyone.

"Be brave for me, sweetheart," was what he'd said to her last night before she'd sent him home.

She hadn't been able to do it then.

But she would be brave for him now.

* * *

Jesus, his head hurt.

And he was tired. So damn tired. Cole wanted to stay asleep, knew that fading back to black would be a blessed relief from the pain shooting through him, head to toe.

But something stopped him from drifting away.

A soft hand in his, slender but strong fingers gripping his.

Anna.

No. She couldn't really be there, had no reason at all to be at his game. But the hand in his wasn't letting go. And he knew that touch. Would never, ever be able to forget her sweetly sinful caresses.

He had to open his eyes and even though it felt like he was trying to break through cement across his eyelids, he worked like hell to get the seal broken so that he could see his Anna.

Sweet Anna.

His reward was the most beautiful girl in the world smiling down at him. She wasn't crying. She didn't look scared.

She looked brave.

For him.

She was brave enough to declare her feelings for him in front of the entire stadium and the millions of people watching the game on TV.

He'd taken her love for granted once. He wouldn't ever do it again.

"I love you, Cole."

The words he hadn't heard her say since Saturday morning, words he'd been so desperate for, were like a shot of morphine, instantly taking away the pain.

"Ma'am, we need you to move away."

But instead of leaving him, she moved closer. She leaned down, the tips of her hair brushing against his face, her breath sweet on his earlobe.

"And I trust you."

Cole had been hit enough times over the years to know when to try to get up on his own and when to let the medics carry him off the field. But he hadn't had Anna at his side any of those times.

He hadn't had her trust, her love, to make him strong.

And now, there was something he needed to do, a reason he needed to get up that had nothing to do with playing football.

Pain came screaming back as he rolled to his side. Arms, hands tried to get him to lie flat, but when he growled at them to leave him the fuck alone, they backed off.

Only Anna remained, her hands giving him the strength he needed to roll to his knees.

Stars blinked in his vision and nausea roiled in his stomach as he pulled himself upright, still on his knees. Anna was right there with him, breathing with him. Apart from his grandmother, he'd never had anyone to lean on.

Until Anna.

She was the strong one, the woman who would be strong enough to give birth to their children, the woman who would be strong enough to forgive him for acting stupid sometimes, the woman who was strong enough to face down an entire stadium of people who probably thought she was crazy for still loving him.

And he would learn from her strength every single day.

She stood in front of him, both of his hands held firmly, lovingly, in hers, and he knew she'd wait patiently for as long as it took him to get to his feet.

But that wasn't where he was trying to go. Instead, he shifted again so that one of his knees was still on the ground, but his other foot was holding the rest of his weight.

Her eyes went wide as she realized what he was about to do. And then the woman who had been a ray of light for him from the first moment he'd met her threw her head back and laughed.

"Only you would stage something like this, Cole," she said when she looked back at him, even though they both knew he hadn't staged anything until now.

He knew what she was doing, knew that she was giving him back his strength, cell by cell, starting with his heart.

He looked up, saw the screens all around the stadium were holding tight on him and Anna, the crowd of medics and trainers and coaches moving away from them. Eighty thousand people held their collective breath.

"I love you, Anna." Each word cost him sweat as pain blistered through his ribs. "I've loved you from the first second I saw you. My sweet girl with the halo."

One tear fell down her cheek, and then another on the opposite side.

"Will you make me the happiest man alive, sweetheart, and

marry me all over again? For real this time."

He knew no one could hear them, although he suspected there was quite a bit of lip-reading going on. Just like everyone else, he held his breath waiting for her answer.

He didn't deserve a yes, but damn it, he wanted it anyway. And if—when—it came, he was going to grab hold of Anna's love and never, ever make the mistake of letting it go again.

Only, her lips didn't move into a yes. "No." She shook her head. "I won't marry you all over again."

He didn't know how he stayed upright, how he managed to remain conscious. But then she dropped to her knees in front of him.

"Our marriage was always real. Right from the start, right from that first kiss, I knew I loved you. And that I would spend the rest of my life with you."

She kissed him and eighty thousand people finally went wild.

But none as wild as the bad boy who never in a million years thought a good girl would be his downfall...and his entire salvation.

* * *

Three months later

It was one hell of a party, the kind an Outlaw threw when he wanted to share his joy with the world.

Sitting beside his grandmother, who was firmly in remission as of the previous month, Cole watched Anna dancing with her sisters, pride etched into every line on his face.

"Anna's going to be a wonderful mother."

Cole shot a surprised glance at his grandmother. He and Anna had found out she was pregnant several weeks ago, but they'd wanted to keep something for themselves this time. His wife wasn't quite showing yet, apart from the fact that her beautiful breasts had filled out a bit more, but they were planning to tell everyone the amazing news later today.

"And you're going to be a wonderful father, honey." Tears sprang into Eugenia's eyes as she gripped his hand. "Thank you for making my wish come true."

And when his wife turned and smiled her sweet smile at him from among the dancing, happy crowd, Cole simply squeezed his grandmother's hand in response.

Her wish wasn't the only one that had been granted.

~ THE END ~

Other titles by Bella Andre...

GAME FOR ANYTHING (Bad Boys of Football 1)

A wild pro-football star meets his match when his new image consultant turns out to be a lover from his past.

GAME FOR SEDUCTION (Bad Boys of Football 2)

The daughter of a powerful sports agent, Melissa McKnight has harbored lust-filled fantasies for Dominic DiMarco ever since she was an awkward teenager. Now Melissa's a beautiful, tenacious associate in her father's firm, and being around to-die-for hard-bodies is all in a day's work.

TAKE ME

Lily Ellis has curves--the kind of voluptuous body she fears Travis Carson, the man she's always loved from afar, would never crave. But Lily is about to be proven wrong. Her sensual adventure begins when, despite her inhibitions, the demure San Francisco interior decorator agrees to model a plus-size dress for her fashion designer sister. Watching this sensual beauty move down the runway with mesmerizing power, Travis can't believe it's the same Lily he's always known and always rejected. In a whirlwind of electric attraction, Lily is soon moaning Travis's name in his bed, not just in her wild fantasies. But Lily is all too aware that she's nothing like his past lovers . . . and now that she has him close at last, she's praying Travis likes what he sees *and* feels. Will she be burned by an ecstasy that's so all-consuming it has her seeing stars? Or will Travis open his heart to the sexy, exciting, and lasting love she has to offer?

LOVE ME

It's been five years since Lily Ellis and Travis Carson got married and fell in love in TAKE ME....now it's finally time for Janica Ellis and Luke Carson to get their very own happy ending. After a brutal night in the ER, Luke can't fight his desire for his wild sister-in-law another second. It's been a lifetime of doing the right thing. Tonight he's going to follow desire instead. But even after the man she always thought was such a good boy turns out to be sinfully bad between the sheets, Janica realizes she wants more than Luke's body. She wants his heart too.

CANDY STORE

On the verge of losing her candy store, Callie decides to blot out her troubles with a handsome stranger. Derek isn't about to turn down a cute, curvy woman who offers sizzling-hot sex at his best friend's wedding reception. The next day, they discover he's the consultant she has hired to save her store.

ECSTASY

Candace, a newcomer to erotica, is thrilled when an industry veteran agrees to be her mentor. But when Charlie's lessons on positions, toys and role playing spiral into hot, hands on education, her deception about the new erotic romance she's writing - where Charlie plays the starring role - threatens their one chance at true love.

SHOOTING STARS

Christina wishes her lovers could be more like the warriors of the past: strong, sexy and a little bit scary. In Scotland in the year 1320, convent-raised Christiania prays for a gentle man to save her from marrying a warrior. A wish upon a shooting star makes both women's wildest desires come true.

BOUND BY LOVE

After a lifetime of control, Elizabeth (Queen of Magonia) dreams of letting her walls fall down. When upsetting the Queen lands him in the dungeon, Gavin escapes into the castle to teach her a lesson. Could their battle for supremacy give way to a love that will bind them together forever?

AUTHOR BIOGRAPHY

Bella Andre has always been a writer. Songs came first, and then non-fiction books, but as soon as she started her first romance novel, she knew she'd found her perfect career. Since selling her first book in 2003, she's written fifteen "sensual, empowered stories enveloped in heady romance" (Publisher's Weekly) about sizzling alpha heroes and the strong women they'll love forever. If not behind her computer, you can find her reading, hiking, knitting, or lunching with her favorite romance writing ladies. http://www.BellaAndre.com
http://www.twitter.com/bellaandre
http://www.facebook.com/bellaandrebooks

Made in the USA
Lexington, KY
04 February 2011